# HOW WE PLAY THE GAME

Also by Alexis Nedd

*Don't Hate the Player*

# HOW WE PLAY THE GAME

ALEXIS NEDD

BLOOMSBURY
NEW YORK LONDON OXFORD NEW DELHI SYDNEY

BLOOMSBURY YA
Bloomsbury Publishing Inc., part of Bloomsbury Publishing Plc
1359 Broadway, New York, NY 10018
50 Bedford Square, London, WC1B 3DP, UK
Bloomsbury Publishing Ireland Limited, 29 Earlsfort Terrace, Dublin 2, D02 AY28, Ireland

BLOOMSBURY and the Diana logo are trademarks of Bloomsbury Publishing Plc

First published in the United States of America in November 2025 by Bloomsbury YA


For more information about Assemble Media, go to www.AssembleMedia.com



Library of Congress Cataloging-in-Publication Data
available upon request
ISBN 978-1-5476-0505-7 (hardcover) • ISBN 978-1-5476-0506-4 (e-book)

Book design by John Candell
Typesetting by Six Red Marbles India
Printed in the United States at Lakeside Book Company
2 4 6 8 10 9 7 5 3 1

For the Nedds of east and west:
Ashley, P-Bear, and Mom

# HOW WE PLAY THE GAME

# MEET IVAN

# CHAPTER ONE

IVAN HUNT WAS not going to play, until they promised no one remembered what happened last time. "Ancient history," they called it, which Ivan wanted to believe, but if there was one thing he knew to be true from his eighteen years of life, it was that "ancient history" and "the internet" were *not* compatible concepts. Still, the company insisted. "Consider it a second chance," the email read. And didn't everyone deserve a second chance?

So he showed up. And now he was here. The new year had just begun a few short hours ago, which Ivan imagined meant there'd be scores of leftover confetti swirling from the sky to herald his return to the Wizzard Theater, but that was not the case. By the time he emerged from the subway station at Forty-Second Street, all traces of the world's biggest party had been swept away and replaced with a bog-standard, cold afternoon in Times Square. Something about that gave Ivan hope for the day, even as he realized his trademark shearling leather jacket was nowhere near thick enough to keep him warm outside.

*At least I don't have to wait in line*, he thought. The line for convention security was so long it stretched the entire three blocks between the station and the theater, and some of the people waiting outside looked frantic, freezing, and miserable. A second thought clung to the end of Ivan's first, but it was unkind: *What a bunch of losers.* He shook his head, willing the thought to clear away like it was stuck in a cobweb of meanness and a good jiggle might get it out. It sounded like something his old team would say. That was a bad thing. This convention was his chance to leave them behind for good.

*What a bunch of . . . cold people*, he mentally amended, feeling a little proud of himself for making the change. Then he felt a self-conscious pang of guilt for feeling proud—if not calling a bunch of pre-pneumonic cosplayers "losers" meant he was clearing the bar of basic decency, then that bar wasn't a bar at all. It was a sewer pipe. In hell. *I'm sorry they're waiting out here*, he strove to think instead. *That looks difficult.*

The last thing Ivan needed today was a difficult crowd, and to make it worse, the fans were cordoned off on each side of the theater's grand double doors. The red carpet laid between them may as well have been a bed of hot coals for all Ivan wanted to step on it, but it was exactly that carpet he had come to walk along with the rest of today's VIP players.

Ivan let a wave of tourists shield him from view on the sidewalk while he assessed the people on the carpet. Some of them he didn't recognize. Those were his competition today, wannabe superstars who'd come to battle it out for one of the top two spots in today's *Guardians League Royale* match. Ivan wasn't too worried about them. He was more concerned about the ones he did recognize, the VIP selection of Wizzard Games' favorite influencers and players from their pro league. They were here to be seen, posed and ready to take advantage of the photo ops and exclusive drops the company doled out to appease famous faces at their competition events.

The sight of those people made Ivan's throat tighten up until he felt like he was breathing through a bent coffee straw. Some of the kids on the carpet had been his friends until last year, others he only knew from the predictably in-depth (and mostly wrong) videos they made online after he disappeared: "What REALLY Happened to TEAM FURY," "Is Ivan (VANE) BANNED FROM WIZZARD?" "My CRAZY THEORY about IVAN HUNT Was RIGHT????"

*I can go home*, Ivan told himself. *No one's seen me yet; I can turn around and just go home.* And he was going to, when—

"Wait, no way!" One fan's voice broke through the street noise. They pointed straight at Ivan. "Is that Ivan Hunt?"

*Dang it.*

Ivan expected to feel dread after hearing his name in that disbelieving tone, but he didn't. He felt the beginnings of an adrenaline rush, a bubbly, smiley feeling that used to make him feel so at home in front of an audience. That, or he was fully in fight-or-flight mode and his body was taking way too long to figure out which was less likely to result in serious injury or death.

When his body made the choice it was neither fight nor flight but freeze. This was what he signed up for, right? To be accountable? Whatever they were going to lob at him was probably rude, true, and nothing Ivan hadn't imagined hearing a million times before.

Would they start by calling him a cheat or get right to the part where he publicly betrayed the most respected player in Wizzard Games' pro league? Maybe they'd ask Ivan how he dared show his face, or assume he was jealous and here to ruin things for the better players, better *people* he'd hurt last year. Any way it came, he probably deserved it.

"We love you, Ivan!" Okay, not that; he did not think he deserved that.

"Hey, it's VANE! VANE is back!" Not that either.

By some miracle, more than half the crowd and nearly all of the VIPs seemed thrilled to see him, standing on their tiptoes to get a glimpse of Wizzard's prodigal son and waving stiffly with cold arms and hands. A smaller percentage stared at him with expressions that ranged from unreadably blank to the exact face a person would make in response to finding a spider in their pasta at a restaurant. They muttered disgustedly among themselves, and even from the short distance of the sidewalk, Ivan could pick out a few words. "*Last year's championship . . . huge tournament . . . girl who won . . . his old teammate . . . total traitor.*"

Ivan wasn't sure what to do with either reaction. The relief he felt when he realized he wasn't about to get heckled was immense, but clearly some people still remembered why he'd gone away in the first place.

"Can I get a selfie?" One of the girls in the fan crowd pushed her way to the front and pointed to her phone shyly.

"Sure?" Ivan nodded reflexively, then dodged a few fast walkers to lean over the rope barrier that separated the campers from morning foot traffic.

"Oh my god, thank you. I used to watch you play all the time!" The girl who'd asked for a selfie spoke incredibly loudly and was dressed like a character from *Guardians League Royale*. Her crop top, aviator helmet, and pink cargo pants were a streetwear spin on the *GLR* avatar's starter outfit. *Cool costume,* Ivan thought, *but isn't she cold?* He felt like asking her just to make conversation but stopped himself at the last moment. Was that weird to ask someone he didn't know? What was he even trying to say with that? *Hey, girl, your costume is great, but I've noticed there's not a lot of it, which doesn't seem weather appropriate, if you ask me, which you haven't.* What could he say instead that had a zero percent chance of being interpreted badly?

"You look sick," Ivan said.

"What?" the girl asked, blushing redder in the cold.

"Sick like cool!" Ivan corrected, hearing exactly where he went wrong. "Not like *sick* sick, I'm—oh my god, I— You look fine, healthy even, but I'm not privy to your private medical information, so obviously I can't really comment, which I shouldn't do in the first place. That's your business. Not mine. Or the state's, for that matter. Why are you looking at me like that?" He all but panicked. "Do you still want the picture? It's fine if you don't. I get it. I will scoot right on out of here, like, no problem."

"What?" the girl asked again, this time raising just the right side of her helmet to yank a wireless earbud out of her ear.

"I said nice costume," Ivan said. "Say cheese." He took her phone from her mittened hands and took a burst before showing her how to tap the screen and select the best one.

Another voice called out, this time from the VIP group. "Get this man to the front!" they said. A muted cheer rose up, and all of the players and influencers on the carpet parted to give him a clear route to the double doors. All of them, save one.

A girl Ivan did not recognize as a typical Wizzard VIP was arguing with the door guard. *Someone trying to talk their way in early,* he thought. *Probably got fed up waiting in the cold.* The energy of the crowd had reminded him of exactly who he was, which was Ivan freakin' Hunt, and he forgot what it felt like to be nervous about today. What was a closed door when Ivan Hunt had returned? His smile, his real smile, came back as he cooly walked to the front of the line. As he got closer, he heard more of the girl's argument.

"It's right there." The girl pointed past the security guards and through the glass doors at something on the floor in the theater's lobby. "I can physically see it; can you please just let me grab it?"

"Can't let you in without a lanyard," the guard said. "Move aside, please."

"You just let me in ten minutes ago. You saw my face. I had a lanyard then."

"Don't remember," the guard said dismissively.

"How about I *make* you remember?" she asked viciously. Ivan snorted. The girl earned points on ballsiness and lost some for having no idea what it really took to sneak into VIP areas. The snort caught her attention, and she glanced over her shoulder to see Ivan waiting, and for an unusually long moment their eyes met, locked, and perceived each other equally.

Everything from the girl's neck down was obscured by a long black puffer coat that gave the appearance of a lumpy, half-escaped cocoon with a pair of combat boots sticking out the bottom and one of those expensive furry microphones jammed on top. When she turned to look at Ivan, the tan fuzz of her hood framed her face like a cartoon lion and made her narrowed black eyes stand out against her dark brown skin. It also prevented Ivan from seeing if she had any hair, but she had the wide cheekbones and smooth skin of a girl whose face card had more than enough credit to pull off a buzz cut, had she wanted one. Her thick lips, one slightly pinker than the other, had the sticky, matte quality of medicated lip balm; as far as Ivan could tell she wore no makeup, not even the mascara his fellow streamers insisted was a requirement for their eyes to really "pop" on camera.

"I don't see the problem." The girl returned her attention to the guard. "You have my name on the list. It's Zora Lyon. L-Y-O-N."

*Weird name,* Ivan thought. It almost sounded familiar? *Cute girl.*

"Can I—" Ivan was about to say *get by, please,* since this Zora Lyon showed no signs of letting him step in front of her while she argued with the guard.

"Give me a second." Whatever the girl saw in Ivan while he was checking her out, she didn't seem impressed. She held her finger up to keep him beyond arm's length.

"Miss, you're holding up the line," the security guard intoned. *The same line that just let me skip to the front for no reason?* Ivan scoffed internally.

Zora jerked her thumb over her shoulder. "The line that just let that guy skip for no reason?" She echoed his exact thought, which was kind of wonderful.

Her mention of a guy made the guard look up from his clipboard and notice Ivan for the first time. Ivan pinpointed the second the guard clocked him; his posture became less rigid, and his face relaxed away from the scowl he'd kept up to intimidate Zora.

"Hey, look who's back!" the guard called out. Ivan didn't recognize him. Should he? "What's up, Ivan?"

"Hiya . . ." Ivan dipped his gaze to the man's chest and saw his name tag: *Hello, My Name Is Frank.* "Frank."

"Yeah, it's me, Frank!" Frank looked incredibly pleased that Ivan remembered his name.

"Of course! Good to see you again." Ivan chanced a glance at Zora and saw her gaze drift down to Frank's name tag. When she looked back up at Ivan, she rolled her eyes. *What? This is how you bullshit correctly,* Ivan thought. *Take notes.*

"Sorry about her." Frank gestured to the girl. "We've been dealing with player imposters all day."

"Imposters?" The word hit the girl like a physical blow. Her shoulders slumped, and her voice lost its punchiness in an instant. "All I did was drop my lanyard. I just wanted to get some air. I— You really don't recognize me?"

The incredulous, defeated tone reminded Ivan of someone he'd met before. Someone who was also told they didn't belong in the elite tiers of Wizzard's esports empire.

And just like that, Ivan knew how he was going to play this. He checked behind him. VIPs and fans alike held their phones directly in front of their faces, giving Ivan the dystopian feeling that everyone's bodies ended at the neck and their heads were nothing but shiny rectangular boxes that occasionally flashed white from one corner. *They could be posting this everywhere*, he thought, and for the record, they were. Now, to be the good guy.

It began with shifting closer to the girl and sharing a sneaky smile with the guard. "Hey, Frank?" he asked. "I feel bad; this is kind of my fault. I was supposed to get here before, uh, Zena here."

"Zora."

"Zora here," Ivan corrected. "She's with me, if you get what I mean."

"What?" Zora exclaimed and took a step away from Ivan, but he reached out and gently pulled her back so they were standing side by side. *Just go with it*, he willed her to read his mind. *I got this.*

"Aha." Frank nodded conspiratorially. "I see. Brought your own cheerleader for your big return, huh?"

"You know how it goes." Ivan finished the charade off with a wink. This time, Zora succeeded in pulling away from him, and the look on her face made it clear he shouldn't try again. Luckily, Frank didn't seem to notice.

"Well, that explains why your name is on the list but no lanyard," Frank said to Zora, while looking at Ivan. "Those are only for players, you know."

"Wait, are the *players' lanyards* only for players?" Zora asked sarcastically. Frank missed the tone and answered in earnest.

"Only for players. You two can go on in, though."

Zora shot Frank a look that could have boiled water and stomped through the doors without looking back. Ivan turned around one more time, waved at the crowd and the VIPs alike, and followed Zora in.

Front of house at the Wizzard Theater was a stylish, high-tech lobby with multicolored strips of LED lighting forming zigzag patterns on the dark black walls, and a smooth floor of seamless marble that must be absolutely lethal when it rained. Despite the sounds of setup coming through the open doors that led to the floor tier of seating and the occasional ding of the elevators in the back, there weren't a lot of people in the vestibule itself. The better to get to know this Zora person.

"Whew." Ivan grinned. "Can't believe that worked."

Zora wasn't grinning. Her hood had fallen down, and the boiling-water glare never wavered as she walked over to a discarded lump of ribbon and plastic on the floor near the doors. She picked it up, shook it out, and held it up like a show-and-tell presentation. It was a VIP player's lanyard, which she lifted above her head to work the fabric loop over the volume of her shoulder-length curly hair.

"It's bad enough I had to wake up at the crack to get here and that it's negative screw-you degrees outside," she said in a tone that suggested she was speaking to herself instead of Ivan, even though he was standing right there. "But yeah, no, sure. Let's throw in a washed-up eboy sneaking me in like an imperial concubine when I belonged here on my own."

"Washed-up eboy?" Ivan didn't love the sound of that. Also, who used phrases like "imperial concubine" in any situation, ever? "That's what I get for doing you a favor?"

"What favor?" Zora asked. Ivan got the feeling she meant it as a real question. Her face was calm. Passive. Uncharmed. Whatever Ivan had wasn't working on her. That made him nervous all over again.

"I thought you just wanted to get in early like a VIP," Ivan mumbled. "Figured I'd help you out."

"Why did you think I wasn't a VIP by myself?" Her tone was matter-of-fact enough to make Ivan see and more acutely feel where he'd gone wrong this time.

"I just assumed—"

"You assumed," the girl said, putting a premature period at the end of his thought.

Instead of berating himself and overthinking his words like he had in front of the theater, he dug his heels in. "Look, I've clearly touched a nerve here," he began. "But don't you think you're kind of overreacting?"

"Overreacting?" Zora's thin eyebrows leaped up toward her hairline. "You humiliated me in front of everyone! I fought my way through the preliminaries and earned my right to be here on my own, just like everyone else." Zora's hand went to the front of her neck to unzip her puffer coat, then appeared to think better of removing her protective outer shell, however fluffy. "And you told him I was your *cheerleader*?"

"*Almost* everyone else. And Frank said that, not me," Ivan responded defensively. This girl was a piece of work. Normally he wouldn't flex, but Zora seemed intent on seeing the worst in him regardless. "Do you know who Brian Juno is?"

"Of course I know who Brian Juno is," the girl hissed. "What kind of question is that? He literally cofounded Wizzard."

"Yeah, he personally invited me to play today," Ivan continued. "You had to play in preliminaries?" He clicked his tongue. "Yikes."

Zora took the bait, but not in the way Ivan expected her to. "You know that's not something to be proud of, right?"

"Why not?" Ivan shrugged. "Doesn't matter how I got here, as long as I make it into the top two in the battle royale. And I will."

That made Zora snort. "You sure about that?"

"I am," Ivan reassured her. *I have to be*, was the unspoken corollary. A top two placement today was the only thing that would get him back in the game, literally. He had to prove he wasn't the bad guy he looked like last time he left. That was what gave him his next brilliant idea.

"Hey," he began in the voice he used to adopt on stream when he needed to come off vulnerable and earnest. "I screwed up here, that's obvious. Is there a way I can make it up to you?"

"No," Zora said. Her tone was blunt, but not necessarily angry this time. Ivan hoped that was a good sign.

"How about this," he said. "I'm going to make it to the top two of the battle royale today."

"Yes, you mentioned that."

"I can make sure you're in the top two too. Wow. It's so weird when you have to say 'two' and 'too' like that. You ever notice how weird it sounds?" Ivan made one last-ditch effort to build any kind of rapport with this—honestly—super pretty girl with the personality of a scorpion.

"How would you make sure?" she asked, looking almost amused. The almost part made Ivan feel like he'd passed a high Charisma check in *Dungeons and Dragons*.

"Right. Yeah, so I know we're all against each other in *Guardians League Royale*, but there's nothing in the rules that says I can't watch your back in there."

"Excuse me?" Zora stepped back, her eyebrows once again high with disapproval.

"I just meant, like, if you need some help in there."

"Why would you do that? For me or anyo—"

"Because you remind me of someone," Ivan answered quickly. "Someone I should have protected. This girl . . . anyway, I'm different now. You can trust me." There really had to be a better way of putting that. And if there wasn't, Ivan was going to have to invent it.

It seemed to mark a change in the way Zora looked at him, though. "Trust you," she said under her breath. Then again. "Trust *you*." Then, as if the muscles in her face finally thawed, her expression softened.

"Normally you can't trust anyone in a battle royale," she said, "but, I don't know, it's my first competition, and maybe I could use a little help." One of her hands crept up toward the fuzzy curls that just brushed at her shoulders, where she twirled one around her finger. Ivan's eyes caught on the gesture and lingered there for a moment before he pulled his gaze away. *Don't be weird*, he told himself.

"If we have a secret ally in the field, we have a much better shot of making it. Together," Zora said matter-of-factly. "It would be nice to come out of today with a win *and*, you know"—Zora visibly fought the shy, borderline flirty smile that threatened to take over her stern face—"a friend."

Ivan was being weird. "My thoughts exactly. So . . . partners?"

"*Temporary* partners," Zora warned him playfully. "Just until we're both in the top two."

"Totally." Ivan nodded automatically. What would his naysayers say now, seeing him partner up with an unknown girl gamer to dominate a *GLR* match?

"Listen, I gotta go." Zora pointed over toward the auditorium doors. "If you're serious about doing this, I always start my matches on the ruined tower in the center of the map. My name in the game is ZORA." That unforgettable smile reached her eyes for the first time since their conversation started, and Ivan considered his victory secured.

"Of course, sure. Meet you there. I mean—mine's VANE. And I'm Ivan."

"Oh, I know who you are. Ivan." Zora lowered her gaze to the floor, trying to hide just how wide her smile had gotten since Ivan agreed to partner up. She'd be eating out of his hand by lunchtime. "See you in the battle, then. Partner."

"The battle, yeah." Ivan nodded, most of his attention focused on the way Zora was looking up at him through her dense, curling eyelashes. He tried to blink away the effect that sloe-eyed stare had on him. He—they—had a match to win. "See you in there."

Zora slipped through the theater doors and left Ivan to wrangle his thoughts in the vestibule. He was still wrangling them, barely believing his luck, when he headed up to the players' lounge, rubbed elbows with a few familiar faces who weren't as surprised to see him as he'd have thought, and walked out to take his place at one of the fifty PC stations laid out in rows on the Wizzard Theater's massive stage.

Ivan barely heard the countdown to the match through his noise-canceling headphones, but he felt beyond ready to take his rightful place in the top two when the starting horn blew. His character parachuted gracefully from the digital sky above the *Guardians League Royale* island arena and toward the familiar broken tower in the center of the map. He saw Zora's character already rummaging through an ammo chest on the parapet and maneuvered his parachute to land a few steps away from her.

It was a good place to start the match. High ground, good sight lines, plenty of cover—but before he could spin his camera around to send Zora an approving thumbs-up emote, he heard a laser shot reverberate through his headphones. *Pew—zap!*

His screen went red, then black, then scrolled the announcement no player wanted to read less than ten seconds into any game, ever.

GAME OVER. PLAYER VANE HAS BEEN ELIMINATED BY PLAYER ZORA.

You *really* couldn't trust anyone in a battle royale.

# ZORA

# CHAPTER TWO

EVERYONE KNOWS WHAT a battle royale is; they just don't know that they know. It's a fight where the only rules are survival of the fittest, everyone for themselves, eat or be eaten. They gave it a special name because *Battle Royale* is the English title of a Japanese book about a bunch of high schoolers trapped on a remote island and forced to hunt each other until one student remains. And, uh. Yeah. That pretty much sums up the genre.

Metaphors for capitalism's for-profit transmutation of youth into trauma aside, the concept of a battle royale is basically made to inspire video games, so it does, and it *whips*. Wizzard's *Guardians League Royale* is my favorite, and while there are many battle royale titles that are *like* GLR, none of them can touch it when it comes to player base and sheer originality. Some come close, but Wizzard Games is the industry's uncontested number one. This is the part where I toss my curls over my shoulder and say something arrogant like "Being number one? I can totally relate," so I will. Internally.

But seriously, I am so fricking good at *Guardians League Royale*. That is my mantra and I know for a fact it's all I need to survive this summer. As far as mantras go it's a little specific, but I've always had a hard time applying vague, universal language to myself. Like "I am a strong and powerful woman." Cool. That imparts zero information. Or "love and light." Anyone can say two nouns. My favorite unrelatable mantra is "I have the same number of hours in my day as Beyoncé," which, no. No, I do not. Beyoncé bends time, and anyone who doesn't believe that is delusional.

Focus, Zora. Get hype. Is it possible to do both? I need to calculate the precise emotional equilibrium between focus and hype that results in a positive outcome. In this case, a positive outcome means I roll up to today's orientation and unleash a can of digital whoop-ass on forty-nine other players who all want to do the exact same thing to me. As established, that's going to be the easy part. The hard part is everything else about today. New Year's Day was one thing, when the Wizzcon crowd made it easy to slip in and out of the theater without attracting attention.

Well, almost. There was that one . . . nope. Not thinking about him. That boy does not exist. I knocked him out of the running; I did it on purpose, and that means I never have to see or think about him again. Nothing—he, whatever. Never mind.

I reflexively yank my phone out of my jean shorts pocket and check my texts to see if anything has changed. Nothing new, just the last three messages from "Your Nemesis," aka Cassius Sharpe, the other winner of the January battle that day at Wizzcon. In the parlance of the summer academy, we were both considered "top two winners," so I don't like to admit that Cassius beat me, not the other way around. I'll only agree to admit it because Cass is kind of the best thing ever.

I'm not the most gracious loser, in fact I would rather lick the sidewalk and die, so my second-place finish must have activated my Resting Murder Face. I didn't have high hopes when the winner that day, a tall, skinny boy wearing the classic T-shirt and cargo shorts fit in January approached me after the match. I thought he was going to say something condescending at best or embrace the toxic gamer stereotype and be a legit Nazi at worst (both options are subtle variations on the ways people communicate the extent to which girls, especially Black girls, don't belong in games). I was loading several ways to say "kick rocks" into the chamber and getting ready to shoot, but Cassius stayed my trigger finger by offering me a rematch. Not onstage, obviously, but later and online, just for fun.

So we kept in touch. We got in the habit of voice chatting while we kicked everyone's butts, and those hours added up. Cass is an apex predator of the East Coast server and the best friend to have if you're really frickin' good at *Guardians League Royale* and have trouble reading social cues.

*From: Your Nemesis*

*running late*

Attached is a GIF of a guy running away from a dragon. Cute.

*From: Your Nemesis*

*theres big red stairs here im gonna wait here*

*From: Your Nemesis*

*just saw a naked guy with a cowboy hat n a guitar is that normal for summer camp?*

I resist the urge to correct him on the use of the term "camp." Band geeks go to camp. Hot people telling ghost stories around a bonfire unaware that they're about to get murdered by a lake-dwelling maniac go to camp. Wizzard's top players go to an *academy*. The Wizzard Games Summer Academy Royale, to be specific. A two-month summit where, starting today, we'll sleep in dorms but basically live at the Wizzard Theater—fifty of the best *GLR* players in the country duking it out in battle royales (battles royale?) for the top two spots on the end-of-summer leaderboard. And those top two players?

They only get to face off in a live, streaming debut of the new *GLR* mode everyone's been begging Wizzard to add to the game since it launched: *Guardians League Royale: 1v1*.

And while I will say I'm not as enthused about playing a game mode where you only get to hunt down and snipe *one* player, I am enthused about the part where we get to try new maps and modes before they launch. When Wizzard announced the competition, they said it was an opportunity for the studio to get top players' feedback on new content and the upcoming season of *GLR*. That means talking to studio heads, developers, artists, and writers—and that access is priceless. Especially if working for Wizzard Games has been your dream since you were eight years old, when your cousin sat you in front of an Xbox to shut you up while she babysat and you took her brother's high score on *Guardians League III* by the time someone came to pick you up. Good times.

*I've come so far*, I think, even though it feels like one of those cliché mantras. I really have. This homeschooled, touch-averse nerd from New Jersey is heading to the big city to basically make a video game with her favorite studio!

And by "heading to the big city," I mean I'm already here. The moment I emerge from Penn Station, New York City announces its presence with a moist blast of hot street air slapping me in the face. It takes me a moment to tap around my hairline until I find my sunglasses and yank them down over my eyes like protective goggles. A group of neck muscles I swear I didn't know existed unclenches in relief. I love wearing sunglasses. There's something about hiding my eyes that makes existing in public so much easier. I don't have to worry about giving strangers an involuntary stink eye (my face just looks like this, honest), no one can tell when I'm staring at them in a totally normal, academic, people-watching way, and I think the glasses make me look like a big weird bug, which I love for some reason and refuse to interrogate why.

Now I am armored and on time. You'd think a Wizzard diehard like me would jump at the chance to be the academy's most obvious teacher's pet and show up early with a batch of cookies for the program leads and a big ole "love me" smile, but that's not in my strategy. I need to be smart about this summer, and that means not wasting time making small talk with my competition. I did not come here to play.

Okay, technically, *literally* I came here to play, but what I mean is I didn't come here to make new friends. That's what Cass is for, and that is why instead of heading straight through the double doors at the Wizzard Theater, I will meet him on the big red stairs next to the naked guy with a guitar and a cowboy hat.

*How to make a good first impression on the cofounder of a game studio*, I tap deliberately into the search engine on my phone as I turn north toward Times Square. The top results are unhelpful. *Have a firm handshake*, some corporate-pilled lunatic with a blog suggests. *Use people's first names and make lots of eye contact!* Yeesh, pass. How about searching *talking to people in real life vs. online*, return with a handful of judgy articles about online friendships that, if I read between the lines here, add up to "touch grass, dork"? Let me try a new tack: *What does Brian Juno look for in a mentee*—I hover my thumbs over the screen while I think this one through—*and is it a 17-year-old Black girl*—I add to the query—*low-key on the spectrum*—seems relevant—*who's followed his work forever and wants to basically be him when she grows up*. Hit Search.

No results. Not like I expected any. It only takes a few more minutes for me to make it to the part of Times Square that leads up to the Wizzard Theater, where costumed characters from the *Guardians League* series post up alongside the legion of Captains America and Elmos who winkle tips out of tourists for a picture. The multiversal effect is jarring. Some studios rely on famous character cameos and franchise partnerships to get people interested in their games, but because of Brian Juno, Wizzard has always been about generating their hype in-house. The result is a game series where the players are the true stars of every match. We create our characters, embody them, dress them up in limited edition avatar fashion drops and hard-earned 3D bling to indicate our win count and tier status. No Deadpools required.

Some of those players extrapolate that stardom into real life, making names for themselves in Wizzard's esports league or streaming on WiTch, Wizzard's all-*Guardians* livestreaming platform. And it's fine that they do that, really. A hustle is a hustle, and if someone can leverage their natural ability to get strangers invested in their fake life while they play video games in a pair of kitty cat headphones, then more power to them. It's just that I, personally, would rather bite the head off a living pigeon than be perceived on that level. My talents begin when I boot up *Guardians League Royale* on my gaming PC and end when I log out.

That middle period where I'm completely absorbed in the game, laser focused on my opponents while hunting them down one by one like a shadow in the night . . . that's the good stuff. It's where I get my ideas on how to make *GLR* better, or for new games and challenges that would make a killer spinoff title, or a plot arc that could make the upcoming season the most downloaded version of the game yet. So I don't have time to follow the online drama between *GLR* streamers or catch up on who's trading whom around the competitive circuit. Look at me, using "whom" right and everything. If that's not an underutilized skill in my generation, I don't know what is. I'll stand out this summer to Brian Juno. I have to.

The red stairs Cassius mentioned have a perfect view of the Wizzard Theater's entrance: its famous double doors are works of art, made of special black glass that reveals glowing neon circuitry running in randomly generated patterns all day long. The building used to be an old-school theater, so there's a real marquee, but instead of those rearrangeable black letters that inevitably fall off and leave typos like "WELCOME HO," there's a high-tech LED "Summer Academy Royale" chyron spelling out a welcome that's significantly more difficult to vandalize.

It doesn't take long to find Cass. I scan the crowd on the steps and spot his Muppet-y mess of blond curls before I see the telltale black Wizzard Games Summer Academy Royale T-shirt we're all wearing today. I also notice with very little surprise that he's zoned out and staring into the middle distance while I approach. "Space cadet" is one of my many nicknames for Cass for a reason. Head always up in the air, while I'm firmly planted on the ground. If we played one of the *Guardians League* games that requires a team, we'd probably tear each other apart, so it's a good thing neither of us wants to.

For an elite gamer, his peripheral vision is awful. I'm halfway up the stairs and he's still in la-la land. I sit next to him and he automatically scoots over to give me more space but doesn't look at me. I even take a Red Bull out of my jacket, crack it open, and still he has no interest in turning his head and looking to his left. It's a waste, really. If we had a match today he could totally channel that focus into *GLR*, but the first two days of the academy are just for orientation. And we're almost late for it, and it's disgustingly hot out, so let's move this along, bud.

"Hey." I finally tap Cass on the shoulder. He springs to life like a haunted animatronic, his blue eyes blinking as if he's suddenly been teleported from his bed in Delaware to the bleachers in the middle of Times Square and has no idea how he got there. "You're finally awake."

He looks up to see me sweating like a half-sipped iced coffee left out in the sun. Ten bucks says I look gorgeous. Twenty says I look like what would happen if Chewbacca lost a fight with a curling iron.

"Zora!" Cass's hand flies up into his hair in a bold, if futile, attempt to make his messy bangs behave.

"Hi!" I give him a little wave. "I'm looking for my nemesis?"

"Nemesis? I think you mean your rival," Cass goads me.

"Rival?" I reply. "That's a crazy way to pronounce 'piñata.'"

"Yep." Cassius nods. "You're definitely Zora."

I manage to hold on to the seriousness for a few more seconds before I crack. "Dude, I can't even believe it's really you again, here, in front of me right now, alive!" I'm basically squealing, but I don't even care. "I mean awake!"

Cass laughs. It's a happy, snorty sound I've heard a hundred times before, but until now it's been modulated through the crackle of our headsets as we blast each other to pieces in *Guardians League Royale*.

"Yeah, man, we made it! Summer Academy Royale, let's go!" Cass leans toward me like he's going for a hug, but I hold my fist out for a bump instead. He happily knocks his fist against mine.

"We can totally go; I've just been waiting for you." Cass stands up and—*whew*—that is a long boy. He must have hit another spurt in the six months since then, he's got to be six feet by now. "Unless you don't want to go in yet? Where's all your stuff?"

"Right here." I twist around to show Cass that I have my backpack.

"Is that all you brought?" Cass asks and stands up on the stairs. His bag is a lot bigger than mine; it's a proper camping duffel with a waist strap and everything. My backpack mostly contains my toothbrush, some underwear, and just enough clothing to get by. My standard fit of a T-shirt and shorts will serve me well this summer, with minimal laundry breaks and no worrying about what I look like. Just pure, uncut competition and a chance to show everyone at Wizzard Games that I belong not only *on* their radar, but also behind the radar, alongside them, interpreting the blips and dots that come together to make extraordinary games at an extraordinary company.

"It's all I need," I answer and get to my feet too. I slam the last dregs of the Red Bull, slide the empty can into a mesh socket on the side of my backpack, and yank a new can out from the front pocket. It's going to be a two-can type of day, I can just tell. Now that we're both standing, I see that I'm not as tall as Cass, even if I'm tall for my age and for a girl. My hair adds a few inches too, especially on days like today, when my twist-out curls attract every stray molecule of water in the air and grow accordingly, like the ever-expanding roller ball in a *Katamari* game. "Come on. We're off to see the Wizzard."

Cassius groans but joins me as I pick my way down the stairs and cross the plaza toward the theater. The theater's aura is very different now that it's mostly empty. There is no crowd waiting outside, no bonehead security guards keeping people out. Dozens of people are passing it by without looking. Don't they know that this is the first all-esports theater in New York? Don't they know Brian Juno is in there somewhere right now? As we get closer to the theater, I think for a moment that those big dark doors look like a perfectly rectangular black hole eating away at the front of the building from the inside.

Ooh, that's a good one. I pull out my phone again and tap "black hole doors on a bright summer sidewalk. Pulls people in but no one notices. Building is hungry?" into the digital scratch pad I use for errant *GLR* ideas. You never know what might be a good foundation for a story.

"So," Cass says as we approach. "How did you get your uncle to sign the permission slip for the academy? Last I checked he wasn't too keen on you going away for the summer."

"Oh, that," I reply. "I lied to him."

"Lied to him *how*?" Cass asks cautiously. He also holds the door to the theater open for me, which is amazing because it proves the doors are indeed corporeal objects, and the action bathes us both in a waft of air-conditioning. There's not much in the lobby except a pile of bags on the far side next to a sign for luggage drop-off. Wait, they'll bring our bags to our rooms for us? Fancy.

"Lied to him as in he thinks this is an all-girls coding camp for aspiring game developers," I say.

"Zora!"

"What?" We both walk over to ditch our bags with the rest. Where is everybody? They must be in the theater already, but I have a plan for how Cass and I will sneak up unannounced. "It's going to have the same result anyway." I crack open the second energy drink and take a sip. "Brian Juno gets, like, a zillion applications a year for his mentorship program, and I need something to make me stand out from the rest. Anyone can code, but the winner of his Summer Academy Royale? That's a bingo."

"Why don't you just tell Clive that?" Cass sets his bag down and pauses, waiting to follow my lead for our next move.

"Because it's not the way he thinks."

Everybody knows of Clive Lyon. They just don't know that they know. He's a cautionary tale more than anything else, the top draft pick college football star who tore his meniscus days before his NFL debut and never played another game again. The boogeyman coaches invoke when they tell their guys to stretch before and after each game. The unspoken worry in the back of every player's mind when something twinges wrong on the field.

I point toward the elevator in the back and wave Cass over to follow me. "He's fine with me working in games, but he wants me to do it by the book. I don't know if he thinks I'm going to engineering school or what, but he doesn't believe in shortcuts."

"In his defense, he is Clive Lyon," Cass adds. "I get why he'd maybe have a thing against shortcuts." The elevator doors slide closed, and he presses the button for the upper floor, level with the top and last row of the amphitheater.

"He also doesn't want me anywhere near boys until I'm forty."

That changes Cass's tune. "Clive, my guy," he says, shaking his head. "Ya gotta let Zora be Zora, am I right?"

Clive and I are not that far apart in age. Clive was twenty-two when our grandma died and left him the responsibility of raising a ten-year-old me, but that twelve-year age gap made him enough of an adult to give him authority. The older I get, though, the slimmer that margin starts to feel.

"Exactly, which is why I laid the groundwork for this being an all-girls thing early. I didn't even tell him about the Iv—about that guy from Wizzcon."

"Dang it." Cassius snaps his fingers. "I should have set a timer. I thought we'd at least get through orientation before you brought him up, but nope. It's been, like, ten minutes."

"It's relevant to the conversation!" I argue. It's possible I may have brought up Ivan Hunt a few times since I ran into him at Wizzcon in January. But it's not every day you meet someone with such a legendary capacity for being a dick. And that's not just my opinion. There's a reason Ivan Hunt disappeared for a year before showing up to compete in *Guardians League Royale*. He couldn't show his face after his old team fumbled Wizzard's *Guardians League Online* championship by kicking their only female player—who was Ivan's own in-game damage partner, no less—off their team before the final match. They kicked her to the curb, sat by while she was harassed and doxxed, and did absolutely nothing to help her.

And yeah, he publicly broke off from his team in the weeks after they lost the championship and did everyone a favor by going away afterward, but our encounter at Wizzcon proves to me that he hasn't changed. People like Ivan don't think people like me belong in their walled-off boys' club of elite gamers. For that, he got a laser to the face. Some people don't deserve a second chance.

That's what I would think about Ivan Hunt, if I thought about him at all, which I don't.

"Uh-huh," Cass continues. "Are we allowed to say his name or are you worried we'll say it three times and summon him like Beetlejuice?"

"We can say his name," I say. "It's fine. Ivan Hunt. Bleh. See, I said it."

"*One*," Cass says with faux foreboding. Then he drops the act and sounds much happier. "But it's nice to hear I don't have to be jealous."

"Why would you be jealous?" I respond. What a weird thing for Cass to say. "If there's one crystal clear theme of my past interaction with Ivan Hunt, it's that I absolutely, one-hundred-percent loathe him and all he stands for, from the top of his perfectly coiffed head to the bottom of whatever gamer boy nightmare hell he crawled out of. He treated me like a prop."

"I know," Cass says. "Also, that's two."

"And he thought he could charm me into partnering up with him like I don't know who he is and what happened to the last girl he called his partner in a game. Like that's not a whole ticker tape parade of red flags."

"I *know*." Cass looks at me sideways, like I'm the one who's missing something.

"He wouldn't have fit in here anyway," I assure Cassius. "The academy is for the best players, not wannabe teen heart-throbs who think they can smile their way through life and get everything they want. This academy is about skill." I punch a fist into my open palm for emphasis. "And . . . and merit. And ruthlessness. That's how I made sure I'd never have to see Ivan Hunt again, and that's what—"

The elevator dings. I step out and motion for Cass to be quiet. There's no need to announce ourselves to the rest of the class when we can just slip in the back. I carefully open the theater doors an inch at a time to make sure Cass and I don't make any noise when we step in. It could not have mattered less.

The first few rows of the theater are packed with a teem-ing mass of students in matching black summer academy T-shirts, and they are extremely distracted. Cass and I could have busted through the wall like a wrecking ball and no one would have noticed. Their focus is on one person who looks like they're holding court at the edge of the stage.

My eyes are sharp, any serious *GLR* player's must be, but it's impossible to see who's standing at the center of the crowd from this angle. Whoever it is, they're causing a legitimate sensation. There had been hints that Wizzard would bring out some of their Guardians League players for a few sessions, but this mystery superstar, from what I can tell, is wearing the same student tee as everyone else.

BOOM! The noise is loud and far too close, and I feel the whoosh of wind from a slamming door on my back. I whip around and see Cassius wincing, his palm held out an inch away from catching the slamming door. So much for a stealth approach. Below us, the conversational tone of the room flatlines as every single person in the theater stops talking, swivels their heads on their creepy little necks, and stares up at Cass and me.

And yet, when I look back, I only see one face among the crowd. On a boy about my height. Straight brown hair, strong brows, and teeth so white I half imagine a pinprick sparkle on his canine when he smiles all the way up at me.

"Zora!" Ivan Hunt exclaims from below. "You made it."

*Three*, I think, entirely too late. Looks like I summoned Beetlejuice after all.

# CHAPTER THREE

I KNEW IT. I knew it. I mean, I didn't know it; no one could have known it. But I knew something like this was going to happen. From the second I met Ivan at Wizzcon, I had a horrible, tickly feeling that it wasn't the last time I'd see his smug face, and this is when that premonition comes true.

So why am I surprised? Like, stomach-flipping, breath-caught-in-my-throat, what-do-I-do-with-my-mouth surprised.

"You made it," he said. *Of course I made it*, I think. *It's you who wasn't supposed to make it.* I have no idea how the fiftieth-place finish I made sure Ivan got in the Wizzcon battle earned him a spot in the summer academy, but that is a mystery I'll have to solve later.

Ivan looks pleased to be in his element, in the Wizzard Theater and at the center of attention. It's weird seeing him again, but only in the way it's weird when you go to a farm to pick pumpkins and see a peacock hanging out in the pen with the goats. It's jarring at first, but after a few seconds you remember what a farm is, and that animals live there, and it's not the peacock that's incongruous; it's you.

I'm going to ignore Ivan entirely and plop down in the first seat by the theater doors. I hope that if I stay up here deliberately enough, my peers' sudden, uncomfortable interest in me will wane—and it does. Some conversations resume, but my interruption came just late enough for people to start wondering if now would be a good idea to sit down.

Ivan is exactly as I remember. His coffee-brown hair looks freshly cut, short on the sides and long on the top with piecey strands that bounce against his cheeks when he moves his head to survey his domain. His essence hasn't changed either, and those green, green eyes are the same as I've been seeing in my sleep. I could sniff him out in the dark, recognize his core Ivan-ness if I were spun around and blindfolded. He's just that awful.

"Zora . . . ," Cass begins a warning tone.

"I'm fine," I cut him off. "Let's just sit up here." I'd prefer to have an ocean between Ivan and myself, or maybe a planet just to be safe, but I'll settle for a majority of the seats in Wizzard's indoor amphitheater.

"Just." He sighs. "Don't let him ruin your summer."

"I won't," I promise. "Unless he does something stupid. Then I'm going to ruin his."

"*Welcome to the Wizzard Games Summer Academy Royale*," a disembodied yet familiar voice intones through the theater's million-dollar sound system. Cass and I have a millisecond to exchange a glance and sit up in our seats before every light in the theater goes out. A few players squeal in surprise, and down below a handful of them wind up looking unintentionally spooky as the glow from their phone screens suddenly backlights their heads with a ghostly halo of white light. One by one those lights go out too, extinguished in a chorus of digital clicks that echo around the room.

It's finally starting, and the excitement I feel rising up in my chest reminds me that Cass is right. I can't let Ivan being here ruin my summer. What's about to happen here is bigger than both of us.

*"Please welcome to the stage . . . summer academy president and cofounder of Wizzard Games, Brian Juno!"* A single light flashes back on, and standing center stage with two hands on a mic stand is indeed *the* Brian Juno. His purple three-piece suit makes him look like he just stepped off the page of one of the many, many magazines who have profiled his genius, but I know he's not dressed up just for us. A flawless bespoke suit has been Brian Juno's everyday uniform for as long as he's worked for Wizzard. It's not always purple, not always three-piece, but I've never seen him wearing anything casual. I don't think anyone has. He probably sleeps with a pocket square. The look, combined with a slick haircut and a camera-friendly face, sets him apart from the stereotypical game studio grunt who shows up to work in a hoodie and jeans. The difference is intentional; it's the costume of a ringmaster, the showman who knows it takes more than a good idea to sell a game. It's genius, really, when you think about it. Instant brand recognition in the form of a popular industry figure who looks like a movie star, in an old guy kind of way. But Brian Juno is definitely a genius.

Brian may not have created the *Guardians* series, but he was the one who believed in what it could become. He transformed a suite of pretty good games into a ubiquitous name and used the money from those sales to make even better games, pushing the boundaries of what multiplayer and competition could look like when you build a dedicated audience of a million hyper-focused, obsessive weirdos like me. He is a kingmaker, and in light of that I can ignore the fact that he's decided to punctuate his entrance with one of those Kendrick Lamar songs you *really* should think twice about using if you're a white person.

"Thank you! All right! Yeah! Hello, New York!" Brian waves at us, graciously accepting the applause that peters out only when the music fades completely.

"Before we start, here's something you need to know." His voice drops solemnly, with the unsubtle touch of a French Canadian accent echoing alongside his words. "You. Are all. Rock stars!"

I know he's addressing the room, but Brian's face is too earnest and his aura is too wholesome not to feel like he's talking directly to me. I have never once identified myself as a rock star, but if Brian Juno says I am, then it is so. It's impossible to take my eyes off him. He has that same gravitational, eye-dragging magnetism that makes people want to stare at Ivan. Who is not what I'm supposed to be thinking about right now. Wait—*about whom* I am not supposed to think.

"When I suggested that *Guardians League Royale* should kick off its one-versus-one mode with the biggest battle royale competition in company history, what do you think they said?"

Brian trails off, as if waiting for someone to respond, but no one says anything. The moment drags on, past the point of my personal comfort. I mean, he asked a question, right? It's only polite to respond.

"They said yes?" I pipe up.

Brian points up to the last row, right at me, and snaps his fingers. "Exactly! They said *yes*."

I feel like I just gained a permanent buff to my intelligence stats. Too bad he couldn't see it was me up here being right. *Hi, Brian! Teach me how to be you, please.*

"And from that one yes, our journey together began. You all battled online preliminaries for a chance to compete in one of twenty-five regional competitions with fifty players each." Hell yeah, bro, do that math! "From those twenty-five competitions the top two players from each battle emerged, and here you are now. Champions in your own right." An explosion of applause makes Brian break the stride of his speech to give us credit. He sweeps his hands up, welcoming us to clap louder. "That's right! Give yourselves a hand; you earned this!"

Not all of us did, though. At Wizzcon, Ivan said he didn't play in any preliminaries and that Brian Juno himself had asked him to compete. Is that how Ivan got another chance? How did he do that? Can I do that too?

"Players like you are the future of Wizzard. You know our games inside and out, you know what it takes to win, and you know what you love about *Guardians League Royale*. I can't think of a better focus group to help us make *GLR: 1v1* the best game mode we've ever added, or a better pool of people in which to find the two players most worthy of revealing *1v1* to the masses in our first event ever streamed worldwide, live from the Wizzard Theater!"

Brian leans forward and grips the microphone like he's about to burst into an Adele cover. He lowers his voice again, a repeat of the trick that forces us to lean forward in our seats and pay attention.

"But how will we find our final contenders? A true top two, but this time only one can win eternal glory."

Cass leans over in his seat and suggestively bumps me with his shoulder.

"*Piñata*," I whisper back at him, but turn my head so he can see I'm smiling.

"I will tell you," Brian continues with a flourish. Flourishes are also one of Brian's *things*. Whenever he speaks, even if it's just a video call interview, he moves like he's conducting an invisible orchestra. He shrugs and nods and bops around like every moment in his world has a kick-ass backing track that only he can hear. One day I'll hear the music too.

"But first, who better to herald the first steps of a new class of champions than Wizzard Games' first-ever champions?"

First-ever champions? Wait. No way. There's no way *they* are here today too. Brian's white spotlight suddenly expands to cover all of downstage, making it bright enough for Cass and me to see each other's faces, but our hype is beyond words or expressions. Instead, we smack each other on the knees a few times in the universal gesture for *Are you hearing this shit?*

"Please welcome Team Unity!"

Okay, okay, wow. So. Unity is a *Guardians League Online* team composed entirely of GOATs. And not the peacock farm kind, the actual greatest players to ever play a Wizzard title. *Guardians League Online* is a team game, which means I'll never play it on purpose if I can help it, but everyone who's even remotely interested in Wizzard knows Team Unity.

It's a huge deal when a game company decides to launch their own esports division. It's a huger deal when they launch the league with a championship tournament that ends with an underdog win. The deal assumes another level of hugeness when that team has not one, not two, but three girls on their roster, which gives Wizzard an incentive to build a diverse (if moderately feral) fandom that has no time for gatekeepers in esports.

The Big Three members of Team Unity playfully jog onstage to join Brian at the center, looking clean-cut and dominant in brand-new blue jerseys emblazoned with the Guardians League crest.

"We have Bob Quince, team captain! Kiki Kim, damage-dealer extraordinaire. Penelope Howard on heals!"

Even the most sleep-deprived student in the theater is wide awake now. We know what comes after the Big Three.

"And of course, the ones you've been waiting for, the healer and the dealer, it's Emilia. And. Jake!"

Team Unity's deal goes beyond huge when you throw in the Emilia and Jake factor. It blows up; it cannot be contained. The deal has its own gravity and a moon and potable water in underground springs. They have something Wizzard couldn't manufacture if they tried: crossover appeal.

Onstage, at just the right moment, Emilia and Jake emerge from the wings holding hands. Emilia's big, Disney-princess eyes brighten her tan face and her long brown curls almost reach her waist, which is nuts because I don't think she's wearing extensions. Hot girl magic, I guess. Jake has the wisdom to look primarily at Emilia as they cross the stage with laser focus; his thick glasses and sweet face scream both "sex nerd" and "babygirl."

They're gorgeous, they're dating, and their timing is unimpeachable. Emilia and Jake revealed their relationship live onstage right after Unity won the championship, and with one kiss they gave everyone something even more fun to root for than checkmates and team kills: true love. Now Brian has them at every single Wizzard event like photogenic human mascots, and they basically keep WiTch afloat with the popularity of their co-streams. You can't even say one of their names without the other; it would be like saying Salt without Pepa or calling Chappell Roan "Kayleigh." It's Emilia and Jake, Jake and Emilia, and—oh. OH. There's one more thing I forgot.

This is more delicious than I thought. It's extraordinary. Better than I could have imagined to the point where I almost want to laugh out loud. Ask me why. Okay, fine, I'll say it. Only because it's funny.

*Emilia is the girl Ivan's team tried to bury.* She was Ivan's playing partner before his team, Team Fury, kicked her out! Emilia came back for the finale as a member of their rival Team Unity, and they beat every one of those boys, Ivan included, with the digital, barbed-wire baseball bat of karma. He must be miserable right now. Kind of hard to swing for a second chance when the reason you screwed up your first one is basically Queen Wizzard. Talk about rubbing his failure in his face.

I happened, very accidentally and not because I was looking, to see where Ivan sat down before the lights went out, so

I glance down to see if he's there. Nope, he's gone from his seat. *Great time for a bathroom break,* I think. *Coward.*

"Hey, every— Hold on." Emilia tries to speak through the same microphone Brian was using but isn't anywhere near tall enough to use it. She looks over her shoulder and doesn't have to say anything for her own personal Jake to step forward with a shy smile and start adjusting the height of the stand. Someone in the first few rows of the audience whistles at him. The blush crawling up his cheeks is so red I can spot it from all the way up here, and he promptly drops the microphone with an earsplitting squeal of feedback.

"Ouch!" I can't help but scream when the speaker next to my seat starts to screech. Now I know what a million dollars feels like when it's trying to drill a hole in my eardrum. Someone in the small crowd below has the audacity to laugh at my very real pain. Good, another jerk in the building. Ivan will have a friend.

"Sorry!" Jake yells from the stage. "Sorry about that, person in the back. Sorry."

I am begging the gods of whichever crossover pantheon governs both video games and live theater to end this moment before people start looking at me again. Luckily, Emilia isn't the type to miss a beat. She picks up the microphone and holds it like a normal person, without the mic stand getting in her way.

"Kiss!" someone shouts from the crowd. Emilia rolls her eyes and looks over at Jake, who allows the briefest flicker of annoyance to cross his face.

"Yeah, no, we're not doing that," she says dryly before readjusting her smile. "But we do want to tell you guys that we know how it feels to be where you are right now. It's okay to be nervous. You're gonna do fine. You are here because you're amazing players, and all you have to do this summer is remember that and be yourselves. Except for you." She points in the direction of the heckler. "You might want to consider being someone else if that's how you beha—"

Jake coughs loudly behind her. Somewhere in the rough noise it almost sounds like he's saying, "Em!" She hears him, glances very quickly at Brian, and skillfully backtracks to continue her spiel about how being ourselves is very important this summer.

Which is fine; I just can't figure out why she's telling us this. I don't understand why a battle royale competition needs me to "be myself" to succeed.

By the time I start paying attention again, Team Unity is leaving the stage. Talk about a quick appearance; that was barely a drive-by.

"Are you guys ready to find out the rules for the Summer Academy Royale?" Brian sets the microphone back in the stand, yoinks it back up to his full height, and resumes his part of the program. "Are you ready to find out what you're up against?"

Behind Brian, the huge LED screen at the back of the stage turns on with a sudden flash of light that illuminates the whole theater. At the top, Wizzard Games Summer Academy Royale. The rest of the space on the screen is taken up by some kind of list.

I lean forward to get a better look at the list and spot my name somewhere in the middle. I also see Cassius and Ivan on there too. It doesn't take a genius to assume that the other forty-seven names on there are our fellow competitors.

"This summer you will be competing in weekly *Guardians League Royale* matches with your fellow players, but the real field of play is right up here on this screen," Brian says. "You begin your journey here, unranked." He gestures up to the screen. "But that's not how the summer will end."

It's not a list, I realize. It's a leaderboard. But how is Wizzard going to rank fifty players from a handful of *GLR* matches? That math doesn't math.

"Your score will be determined by"—he pauses dramatically—"the Wizz-Algorithm!"

The Wizz-Algorithm? Sounds like a chatbot that tells people when to use the bathroom. This is why I need to work for Wizzard. I could fall asleep on a keyboard and my forehead would come up with a better name than that.

"Part of it is determined by your in-game performance. Personal kills count toward the score, as will average match longevity and wins."

That makes more sense. Only one of us can win each match, so we'll have to score based on the thousands of other mini victories we can achieve in the battle royale format.

"The other part," Brian says, in a tone that makes me think he says "other" when he means "greater," "will be determined not by in-game statistics and numbers, but by a group of people all of you know very, very well." He leaves us quietly guessing for another long moment. I wonder if anyone here has any idea what he's talking about, or if it's just me who's out of the loop. "Your fans."

Whose fans? I don't have fans. Were we supposed to come here with fans? I'm not the only person confused. There's a low murmur spreading around the theater as people whisper to one another.

"And by your fans, I mean the ones you'll earn this summer while you go through the program. To make things fair, all of you will get a new WiTch account to stream, post, and interact with viewers. From there, the Wizz-Algorithm is designed to track your successes, generate an audience score, and factor it into your end-of-week ranking."

I genuinely cannot tell if I'm hearing this right, so I ask Cassius.

"Yo, am I hearing this right?"

"You are."

That conversation was shorter than I expected, but okay. I'm not losing my grip on reality. Brian Juno did just say that being really frickin' good at *Guardians League Royale* is barely half of what it's going to take to win.

"New positions will be calculated after each match, and the top two players at the end of the summer will play for the *GLR: 1v1* reveal event."

I think back to what I said to Cassius earlier. About how this academy is about skill and merit and nerds, so people like Ivan don't belong. That was uncharacteristically naïve of me. Peacocks like Ivan will always belong, and I'm the one who might not have what it takes to win.

# CHAPTER FOUR

THERE ARE FIFTY rolling desks set up on the stage of the Wizzard Theater. Each time Brian calls a name, a player stands up, walks over, and claims a desk as their own. Center stage fills out quickly, but after those are gone the choices seem more personal, and therefore unpredictable. If there was a pattern, I'd have figured it out by now, but even if I did, it wouldn't help me. We are called alphabetically by first name, so any Zoras in the program are doomed to pick last. Fitting.

At least I have Cass fighting for me down there. He went down before me and grabbed a spot in the second row and has been defending the seat next to him like a FIFA goalie. If he can keep it open, that's my choice made for me and one less thing to think about in what has quickly become a very eventful morning.

We're almost at the end of the list when I hear the telltale click of a door bar pushed in slowly. Someone is trying to sneak in like Cass and I tried to earlier, through the door at the top of the amphitheater's aisle. I don't need to look;

I know who it is. He wasn't in his seat when his name was called because he was still avoiding Emilia, but the queen has left the building and it's once again safe for Ivan to show his face. The door clicks closed—see, he managed to shut it quietly—and now Ivan is standing in the aisle next to me.

I don't want to lose this game. What game? No idea. But I know if I look at him I'll lose. I keep my eyes trained on the stage and ignore him, searching instead for the pattern of desk choice that does not emerge.

"And finally, Zora Lyon!" Thank god. I don't know what my parents were thinking when they named me. They were either extremely well versed in the history of Black women in academic anthropology or really into *The Legend of Zelda*, and I've never had the opportunity to ask them which it was. My mom is a splash of ink on a birth certificate. My dad lives in some flyover state with the family he made years after I was born. And Clive, my uncle and guardian for as long as I can remember, has no idea where "Zora" came from. All I know is it's at the end of the alphabet and gift shops never have premade items with my name on them. Think of all the key chains I could have collected, the commemorative mugs I could have used three times and ignored for years!

Still, my name is my name, and it's my turn to grab my desk. I stand up and shuffle sideways toward the aisle, where I know Ivan is standing. I'm smart enough to ignore the scent of soap that washes over me when I shuffle closer. I'm above noticing how the soap smell blends in with a faint whiff of boy sweat just smothered by deodorant. I'm so good at ignoring Ivan Hunt that I think I'll just go the entire summer without talking to him.

“Surprise,” Ivan whispers as I slide past him with great elegance and condescension. “Bet you thought you’d seen the last of me.”

“You know, I actually did,” I snap back reflexively. “Mostly because I shot you.” Dang it. I’m going to never talk to him again starting *now*. I start to descend the precarious steps toward the stage and feel my shoulders slump when I hear the sound of Ivan’s footsteps following me down.

“You know it’s just a game, right?” Ivan leans down a bit to whisper. “Just because you betray someone and leave them to die on the little computer screen doesn’t mean they die in real life.”

“Not yet.” Oh my god, Zora, stop talking. “But gaming technology makes new and exciting strides every day.”

Ivan laughs. That wasn’t supposed to be funny. It was supposed to be a threat.

“Besides,” I continue. If I’m going to talk to him, I may as well make it hurt a little. “You would know all about betraying someone and leaving them to die, right?”

“I—” He doesn’t know what to say to that. Point to Zora! If I give him credit for somehow getting me talking, the score is 1–1, and I can work with that.

We’ve reached the bottom of the steps. Ivan shoots a glare at me and wordlessly breaks his stride to head center stage, where Brian Juno himself greets him with a high five. I cannot ignore the stab of jealousy that shoots through my chest, but I’ll unpack that later. Here is when I get my first good look at the full roster of the academy.

Is it mostly white and Asian boys? Yes, but that’s to be expected. The next biggest demo is white girls. Also expected, girl gamers for the win, love it. The smallest group is my group: Other. Nonwhite people of all persuasions and three Black guys I spot chopping it up in the back. Honestly, it's more diverse than I thought it was going to be. My brain attributes this to Brian being awesome, but then I remember everyone had to win to get here.

Then I double remember that's not exactly the case. How much of this crowd did Brian engineer? How many were hand-picked instead of competitors? Come on, Zora. Enough. I sound like a conspiracy theorist. Ivan must have been a special case; there is no way Brian Juno manipulated the results for every match because that is deep, deep weirdo behavior.

"Over here!" The girl sitting a seat away from Cass waves to me. An Other, like me. She is cross-legged on the rolling chair set up at her desk. When I get closer, I can see her long black hair is tucked under her butt and she has the most perfect brown-skin contour I've ever seen on someone who wasn't waltzing to a string quartet cover of a pop hit on *Bridgerton*.

"Hi! I'm Kavi, she/her," the girl says. I manage a wave while fighting the urge to turn around and see if Ivan is still talking to Brian. Isn't it kind of unprofessional for Brian to single out a player like that on the first day? Most people who play favorites have the decency to hide it. But wait—instead of resenting Ivan, I should find out what he did to get in Brian's good graces. If there's room for one favorite, there's room for another. I file this plan away in an accessible corner of my mind palace to visit later.

"I'm Zora," I say. "Uh, she/her."

"I'm Trieu," the boy sitting next to Kavi offers. "He/him/they/whatever. You have very pretty eyes."

I don't know what to do with that, or any other compliment, really. Especially coming from Trieu. He is beautiful in the way the pictures people use to advertise video filters are beautiful; he is meticulous, decorated—a gold hoop through his lower lip, a barbell piercing his eyebrow, with masterful monolid eyeliner and blended streaks of starry highlighter accentuating his cheekbones. Basically he looks like he belongs in the character roster in *Genshin Impact*. I can't stop looking at him. I get the feeling he knows that I can't stop looking and is the opposite of bothered.

"And I'm Cassius," Cass says and sarcastically holds his hand out for a shake. "Super great to meet you, and I think we should be best friends." This time when I leave him hanging, it's on purpose.

"Very cute, Cass," I say, then clarify for Kavi and Trieu, "We know each other from Wizzcon."

"That's nice!" Kavi smiles and looks from me to Cass and back to me. "Wizzcon friends taking on the academy together. That's a great angle!"

"Agree." Trieu nods. "A solid hook to follow straight out the gate; I'm jelly."

"What?" I look to Cass, who shrugs, and Kavi, who tilts her head at me like I'm a particularly challenging piece of modern art. "Who's following what hook?"

"A hook," Kavi reiterates. "To get people to watch you. Gotta get a gimmick."

My blank face is all it takes to tell Kavi and Trieu they're going to need to give me a little more detail than that.

"Like, I do makeup tutorials," Trieu breaks through my confusion. "I do them based on the characters from *GLR* or whenever new skins come out. I'll do the look live, play as that character for the rest of the stream, and edit the tutorial into a short that I'll post everywhere linking back to my channel. It's going pretty good, though it sucks we have to start on new WiTch profiles. I'm gonna have to post so much to get my followers to migrate to the new handle."

"Uh-huh." I don't know what else there is to say. I mean, that explains why Trieu's makeup is on point, but also, what? He's here because of makeup? Where's the love of the game? The spirit of domination over one's enemies?

"What about you?" Cass asks Kavi. "What's your hook thing?"

Kavi looks thrilled to have been asked. She sits up straighter in her chair, her small body framed entirely by the broad back of what I now recognize as one of the most expensive gaming chairs on the market. There are buttons on the armrest, lights embedded around the edges . . . It has as much technology in its design as the computers themselves.

"I mostly do reviews, sometimes streaming, sometimes not. I do headsets, keyboards, mice, monitors, focus pills, smart bulbs, custom skincare, teeth-whitening blue lights, skin-firming red lights, hair and nail gummies, apps, aimbots, online therapy, alternative console controllers, and period underwear. As long as the company isn't literally using slave labor or has one of those CEOs who gets weird about genocide on social media."

"Or makes people hate themselves," Trieu interjects.

"Or makes people hate themselves," Kavi agrees.

"As far as standards go." Cassius illustrates his thoughts with a firm thumbs-up while he spins slowly and smoothly in his chair. "Ten out of ten."

"I can't tell if you're kidding or not," I admit. It's true and I can't.

"Oh, I am." Kavi nods solemnly. "All the money is actually from bank fraud, and I'm wanted in the state of Michigan."

My unexpected seal bark of a laugh echoes off the walls just as everyone onstage decided on now to stop talking. I clap my hand over my mouth and instinctively hunch over, like squeezing my shoulders down a few inches is going to hide my lanky self from the dozens of people who are all pretending not to look at me. All except one.

Ivan is dead-eyeing me from halfway across the stage, peering just over Brian's right shoulder. When the conversations pick back up again, I notice the staring; he doesn't look away or even seem embarrassed that I caught him. He actually looks delighted, and something about his smirk unlocks my terrible inner second grader. So I stick my tongue out at him.

Now it's Ivan's turn to bark out a laugh. He doesn't mind when it echoes off everything, and the sound simply lands as a brief high note before melting into the rest of the noise without notice. After a beat he breaks eye contact with me and nods along with whatever Brian is saying, as if he's been paying attention the whole time. Something Brian says makes him smile, and when he flashes that bone-white grin, he catches the tip of his tongue between his teeth for the fastest of seconds.

It's for me, or at least I think it is. And now my ears are burning hot with what I can 100 percent correctly identify as pure, unadulterated loathing.

"Cool hooks," Cassius says, looking as impressed as he gets (not very, but we're both the "conceal, don't feel" type). "But, uh, I don't think I have one."

"Me either," I add, happy to break Ivan's eye contact and return to the present. "I just like *GLR*."

"We all like *GLR*, babe," Trieu says, not unkindly. "But what else do you do?"

That's the worst question I've ever been asked. Cue internal crisis, cue five-alarm fire in my head right now. Somehow I have accidentally wandered into a place I've never been before and never even considered could exist: an entire roomful of *GLR* players who have one up on me.

"Can't my hook just be being really frickin' good at battle royale!" I splutter out.

"Apparently not," Trieu says.

"I mean, hey," Kavi says. "We all thought this was just going to be, like, a focus group combined with battle royale camp."

"Academy," I correct her quietly.

"But it kind of seems like Brian is looking for people to be the face of *Guardians League Royale: 1v1*. Well, two faces. Who doesn't want that?"

"Me!" I respond. "Kavi, I barely want to be the face of myself."

"It's true," Cass adds. "She doesn't."

"If I wanted an online fanbase," I continue, "why would I have put all my skill points into being good at video games? Nothing on this earth is more invisible than a Black girl with a Steam account. Nothing."

"Not anymore," Trieu says. "Team Unity saw to that. It's anyone's game now, and I, for one, am grateful. Growing up,

I never felt like I fit in with other gamers because I'm gorgeous and charismatic."

"Don't forget 'humble,'" Kavi adds dryly.

"And now there's a place for hot gamers of color right at the heart of Wizzard's strategy," Trieu continues, ignoring her. I have a feeling the two of them knew each other long before this orientation. Their rapport reminds me of me and Cassius, but considerably perkier. "As long as we kick ass, don't age, and work a jillion times harder to get half the recognition white boys get just by showing up. No offense," he directs at Cassius.

"A little bit taken," he responds. "But we're cool."

"And hey," Kavi says with incredible kindness, "we already figured out something you guys can do to carve your niche. IRL besties fighting side by side . . ."

Trieu picks up where Kavi trails off. "Maybe there's a little spark between you, get things going with a will they, won't they . . ."

"I'm in a nightmare," I think out loud. "I'm sleeping right now, or I'm in hell, or it's both and I'm literally having a nightmare while taking a hell nap."

"Come on." Kavi yanks her sentence back like a star quarterback plucking a ball from the air. "It'll be fun, we can help you."

"How would you feel about a makeover?" Trieu asks.

"Terrible," I say, too quickly to be polite. I should try that again. My gaze sweeps over Kavi's and Trieu's objectively lovely faces. They're both the kind of cool that could easily add up to "you can't sit with us" energy, but instead of gatekeeping they've patiently opened my eyes to what exactly I've gotten myself into. They didn't have to do that. "But I don't think I'd hate hanging out with y'all, like, normally."

"That means she loves you," jokes Cassius. "You kind of have to think of her like fostering a cat."

"You sure you want to antagonize someone who knows all of your embarrassing stories?" I ask as I try to gracefully take my seat in the rolling chair beside the last empty computer. I fail, and the chair rolls a few inches behind me. I grab it in time before I sit, but these pro gaming chairs are way slipperier than I'm used to. "Shit—" The backslide of my chair misses hitting someone standing behind me by a hair.

"Watch it!" a hatefully familiar voice calls out. "Caught ya."

I turn around and see Ivan again. "Oh my god," I say as I stomp a foot down to stop my chair from moving any farther. It's bad enough that Ivan's close enough that I can smell his spicy-clean body wash and the slightest waft of citrusy conditioner again, but to have him this close while I almost slide butt-first off this chair would be too much for me for one day. I would have to go back to sleep right now and start again tomorrow, and that would throw off my whole first week in the academy.

"What? What is it? Why are you here? What do you want?" I ask, rapid-fire. "Are you lost? Can I help you? What's the deal, Ivan? Can you tell me now so we can end this conversation a little faster?"

It's not very civilized of me, I know. But a girl has her limits, and he busted through the last of mine long ago. I don't know how much more unpleasant I have to be before Ivan takes a hint, and I'm running out of ways to escalate. And the worst part, the part that really grinds my gears, is that none of it seems to have worked at all. Most people, if I don't want them around I can crack them like a nut and keep it moving. Ivan . . . I can't even tell what kind of nut he is. It's vibranium or something. Adamantium walnut–ass man. Something has to get under his skin, and I will go to the ends of the earth trying to find it. Later.

"I have to tell you something, I was just about to tell you, I'm here to tell you, I very much want to tell you, no, like you care, can you wait for, like, five seconds? and I'm trying," Ivan spits back, smooth as if he's reciting the stats from his favorite in-game weapon. Even I have to think back to what I said exactly to realize that, yeah, he answered every question, in order. Color me impres— NO.

"What's, uh, what's going on there, friends?" Hearing Trieu's voice after concentrating so hard on Ivan's brings me back to reality with a jolt. Ivan and I both look to the side and see Cassius, Kavi, and Trieu staring at us with differing expressions of comprehension. In their defense, we are, like, four feet away from them. And have both been too busy fighting to remember that.

"She"—Cassius points to me—"don't like him." He points to Ivan.

"He doesn't seem too thrilled with her either," Trieu observes.

"Correct," I say.

"Correct," Ivan says too.

I'm not sure which of us is more upset that we've said the same thing at the same time, but I'll admit my own bias and still choose me.

"Uh-huh," Kavi says slowly, eyeing the both of us like we're newly dressed mannequins in the window of her favorite boutique. "So what did you want to tell her?"

With one final glare in my direction, Ivan rolls his shoulders back, closes his eyes, looks up at the ceiling, and then back down at the three of us—with completely different energy. Gone is the tension in his neck and smart-ass smirk he wore when talking to me. He smiles, and it actually reaches his eyes, his posture straightens, and he looks . . . friendlier. More open. It's remarkable, actually. I thought I'd have to live a lot longer before I met the One True King of Social Bullshit, but here I am, not even eighteen, refusing to be humbled by His Majesty.

"It's actually something I have to tell him." He gestures to Cass. "But Zora was the person to crash her chair into me and ask a bunch of mean questions, so I addressed her first."

I keep my face perfectly still. I am a statue. Statues do not respond to provocation. But they remember.

"Well, now I'm intrigued," Trieu says slyly. I see the way his eyes flick up and down Ivan's admittedly buff-ish body and make a mental note to warn him that Ivan may look pretty, but he's also the woooorst.

"You." Ivan points to Cassius. Cass makes a silent "who, me?" face and points to himself. "Yeah, you. Your seat is over there." Ivan points to the other end of the stage, at the other empty seat left over from the roll call.

"What?" Cass asks Ivan, but looks at me.

"There's only a handful of lefty desks, and you're sitting at one," Ivan clarifies. "Are you a lefty?"

Cassius glances down at his desk and sees that, yes, the whole keyboard setup is indeed configured for a left-handed player. He shakes his head in answer.

"No," comes out of my mouth before I mean it to. "I don't believe you. Say something else."

"Do I look the most thrilled about it either?" Ivan asks.

"Little bit," Kavi mutters. She's sitting closest to me, so only I hear her. I give her a questioning look, to which she does not respond.

"Okay," Cassius says stiffly. He stands up and pats his pockets to see if anything fell out when he was sitting down. "Bye. I guess."

"Cass." I grab on to his arm. "You're not really moving over there; he's just messing with us. I bet he's not even left-handed."

"Actually, I am," Ivan adds. "And you might want to move a little faster."

"Why?" I ask.

"Because the show's about to start," Ivan replies distractedly. He looks over his shoulder at Brian, who is stepping back up to his microphone for the next part of the program.

"The desk you chose today is your desk for the rest of the competition," Brian's voice booms from the speakers again as he swivels in place to address the full academy seated upstage. What about those of us who didn't choose, Brian?

At that moment, without any of our input, all of the monitors switch on simultaneously and Cassius is jolted into action, crossing the stage without so much as a look back. Ivan calmly takes the chair that Cassius just vacated and rolls himself over to his computer in one smooth, almost balletic motion.

"You know what comes next!" Brian says with another wild smile. I thought I did, but apparently I don't. There are more people on the stage now, men with steady cameras mounted to their waists and technicians rushing between the rigs to make sure the webcams at the top of our monitors are turned on. I am so not ready to stream right now. Maybe I can ask for an accommodation?

I reach down to adjust my chair and accidentally send myself plummeting to the floor butt-first. Ivan laughs. I pretend I can't hear him through all the steam coming out of my ears.

"Battlers, get ready!" I swear the little chair-lever thing that controls the height of my seat has straight-up disappeared. I'm feeling (okay, wildly slapping) down there to see if I can grab on to anything when Ivan leans over and holds a small button on my armrest. The seat rises. God damn it. I refuse to look at him, or think about his finger manipulating my chair while my butt slowly ascends to an optimal gaming height.

"You're welcome," he says.

"I didn't need—" Ivan cuts me off by sliding the provided headphones over his ears and turning his attention to the screen, where the ten-second countdown to our *GLR* match is already down to five. I trade in my annoyance for practicality and slip my headphones on as well. The noise cancellation kicks in and trades the chaos of the stage for a thick, pressurized silence that immediately primes my brain for competition. The countdown hits zero, and the match begins on-screen.

# CHAPTER FIVE

EVERY ROUND OF *Guardians League Royale* starts the same way. Your character and everyone else's are crowded onto a flying barge that makes a slow circuit above the map. You have a minute to jump off and parachute to your preferred starting area, and the moment your feet touch the ground, there's a target on your back. Anyone can kill anyone, which means everyone is the enemy. Only one player comes out alive.

The barge for this game is packed with impressive player characters. There are talking lizards outfitted with custom fits that cost hundreds of Wizzcoins, alien bipeds with trophy crowns that denote a hundred, five hundred, even a thousand individual wins, and people like me who personalized their character to look like them. Avatar ZORA has dark skin, afro puffs tied high on her head, and a tactical black jumpsuit that is tighter than anything I'd wear in real life but not as obviously porny as some of the other skins Wizzard offers in the online store.

*Boing!* I hear a comically overproduced bouncing noise, and ZORA tumbles off the barge and into the open air. Did somebody actually use a bump hammer to push me off? I spin my camera around in my few seconds of free fall and see one character holding a pink, fuzzy spring-loaded hammer while they spam the hi emote. Floating above their head is the name VANE.

"Son of a—" I can't finish my sentence; fuming at Ivan has left me with a scant few seconds left to pull my parachute before I take fall damage. I slam on the button and feel genuine relief when ZORA lands, hard but not damage hard, on the roof of a squat cylindrical tower.

Damn it, I'm exposed and I need to move, now. I don't hear or see anyone else, but that doesn't mean they're not there. Let me just crouch down and see if I can get my head around where the hell I am and if there's any loot before I jump.

Spinning my camera around gives me a better look at my surroundings. At first glance the map layout looked totally new, but now that I have a second to breathe, I can see that's not the case. It's a version of the classic *GLR* map they first put out at launch, which hardly anyone plays on anymore because all the decent players memorized the field. This version is strange and run-down, and I'm sure there's some lore reason why a giant crater is visibly smoking in the northeast quadrant. Whatever next chapter of *GLR* this map is supposed to introduce must move the story into seriously apocalyptic territory, and I feel a flutter in my chest when I realize that we are the first players to try this map, ever. It would be an honor if I wasn't low-key panicking right now.

I'm not far from where I'd have chosen to land if I had any control over this situation. That's some good luck, I guess.

There's also a glittering obsidian chest at the dead center of the rooftop here with no one else gunning for it, which is as good a reason as any to start moving in that direction. That's the first thing you learn when you want to get good at *Guardians League Royale*—always be on the move. Even if it's just jumping in place or moving in a zigzag line from cover to cover. Staying still makes you a sitting target for anyone who might have you in their sights. Which in my case might be any of the best players in the country and a bunch of scene-chewing streamers who'd love a quick kill. Yeah, I'm getting out of here.

However, my ears pick up on something that absolutely has to be an error. My noise-canceling headphones are supposed to isolate my game's sound so I can concentrate on my playing, but I hear an almost imperceptible clicking noise and the low, expectant hum of an open voice chat line. That's impossible. No one's allowed to talk to anyone in *GLR*. It negates the entire point of the game.

I'll figure this out later; I need to raid this chest and escape to some cover, but when I turn I see the man of my nightmares standing on the other side of the roof. VANE looks as much like Ivan as ZORA looks like me. His Guardians store haircut mimics his real floppy 'do; a Diamond-tier exclusive bandanna is tied around the bottom half of his face, exposing only his avatar's acid-green eyes, which are brighter than his real eyes but somehow less striking . . . None of this matters. Ivan has to go.

VANE spots both me and the chest. Instead of making the smart move and trying to take me out, he charges for the treasure instead. Come on, the least he can do is make this hard.

I only have the standard-issue laser pistol everyone starts out with at the beginning of a match, but that's more than enough to put a hole in this dork. I don't have time to aim as I race him to the payload but I don't need time; at this range getting a kill is basically reflexive. Tap. *Bang.*

Nothing. He shielded at the last second.

"Yeah," Ivan's voice crackles on the other end of my headphones' open communication. "That's not going to work twice."

"What the hell? Go down. You're done. Die!" I say out loud, punctuating each phrase with another shot at Ivan's character. He dodges like Neo in *The Matrix,* but doesn't return fire. Somehow, that makes this even more infuriating.

"Do you know what the definition of insanity is?" Ivan asks. I can hear his smirk over the microphone, and my imagination helpfully projects it onto his character's pseudo-Ivan face, just hidden by the bandanna. "Doing the same thing over and over again and expecting a different result."

I'm going to get a different result. I dash around his character and kick the chest open, which sends a collection of power-ups, weapons, maps, and special attack indicators scattering across our segment of the roof. Nothing too bad, though I'd really like to get lucky and snag the one rocket launcher Wizzard always hides on the map somewhere. I snatch up a decent bow-and-arrow set, one explosive arrow, and a belt of antigravity grenades before lasering a circle in the tower roof below me and dropping through the perfect hole I've created like a cartoon character. That's all, folks.

Shit, no, it isn't. I hear Ivan drop from the hole behind me and ignore him to crack open a new loot crate on the top floor. This time I'm not grabbing anything. I take a few huge steps back and send an arrow straight through Ivan's back when he dives for the cache. *Twang. Snap*. The arrow cracks in half when it meets Ivan's extremely basic armor.

"You know, this whole time I assumed you were having a bad day back at Wizzcon," Ivan says with an audible laugh hiding in the back of his throat. "Thought maybe we just got off on the wrong foot."

"This is a bug," I whisper to myself.

"Now I don't feel so bad." Another hit, another wasted arrow. "Because you don't have a right foot."

I'm assuming Ivan can hear me too. "We have to tell them the match is bugged. It's illegal to force me to hear you talk."

"It's not bugged, Zora." Ivan's character rifles through the loot and grabs a second-tier rifle. "It's proximity chat."

I look at my heads-up display and shrink back in my seat like a wilted houseplant. Sure enough, the minimap in the top right corner of my screen shows a halo around the little green dot that is my character. Chat mode is auto-toggled for this match. I've never, ever played with it on before, because why would I want to talk to my prey before I shoot it?

"This sucks." It's all I can think to say.

"So true, bestie," Ivan responds sarcastically. "But you won't be playing long. This is for Wizzco—"

Like I'm gonna fall for that. I drop an antigravity bomb that glues Ivan's dramatic ass to the ceiling and sends me bouncing back up through the hole in the roof I made before. I think about using my explosive arrow to take him out, but I don't have the time to draw it and still escape. I perform a quick aim check before I leap to the next roof and see a player enter my crosshairs. I use a regular laser arrow this time. *Twang.* Jackpot.

FIRST BLOOD: PLAYER ZORA HAS ELIMINATED PLAYER LEAR.

That's what I do! Now, to escape. I leap to the next half-ruined building and land right beside someone hiding inside. Throw grav bomb. Aim at the ceiling. Shoot. Done. Two kills down. Now I just have to—

"You're player ZORA, right?" The voice is friendly, conversational. And not in-game.

In an instant, the fantasy of *Guardians League Royale* dissipates in my mind. There is a man, a real, three-dimensional man with a camera in my face and a boom microphone dangling above my head. He has asked me a question.

"I . . . uh . . . what?" I turn my gaze back to the screen and see a stun grenade come flying through a window into my hiding spot. I roll away from its area of effect and leap out that same window, taking out the dummy crouched right outside. Three kills.

"Zora?"

"Yes, I'm Zora!" I snap back. I don't care if I sound rude; who interrupts someone in the middle of a battle royale? "Can I help you?"

I take a hit on-screen. Damn it. This wouldn't have happened if this camera wasn't in my face and getting closer by the second.

"First blood in the first match of the summer academy—how does it feel?" the man asks and bends the microphone down. Too close. Way too close. I push it away with my palm—an unforgivable waste of my hands right now—and get back to playing. I reload my lasers and quiver before booking it to the next zone, trying to regain the focus I lost.

"Zora," the man says again, less patiently.

"Feels great, I don't know!" I flick my eyes up toward my live webcam and scowl. A camera on my computer. A camera in my face. Forty-odd players left to go. This is starting to feel bad to me, inside. "Can we do this after?" I notice my hands are shaking. Not enough to throw me off the rest of the game, but that's not normal.

"After defeats the point of an introduction. The audience wants to meet you!"

"Well, I don't really want to meet them, so." I know it's the wrong answer, but he's standing so close to me I can almost feel a dull pain under my skin.

"Anything else you want to say to the fans?" the man asks skeptically.

More players have come into my proximity zone, and with them comes their chatter.

"So, what do you think? Should I build up a fort or—"

"—outfit only costs like 5k Wizzcoins, but the backpack is from the—"

"Zora!"

"Please go away," I say quietly. The microphone picks me up or doesn't.

A handful of shots ring out from around a nearby dumpster, and I toss a gravity bomb in that direction. The two players hiding behind are thrown up into the air and suspended for the shortest of seconds. My shaking hands make me miss the dual shot that could have taken them both out.

"—what you get for messing with RUDY!"

"—hopefully next time I'll be able to see chat so I can—"

"—been to New York, but I'll be doing GRWM vids starting—"

"Zora," the camera man begins again.

"I said FUCK OFF!" I all but shout. The mic definitely picked that one up. I glance up to see if anyone noticed. The players haven't, we all have headphones on, but I do catch a glimpse of Brian Juno staring right at me. Frowning. That can't be great.

Camera Man yanks the mic away from me and steps back like I've shocked him through the lens and hurries not toward the next player in the row, but toward Brian. It's then I notice that there are multiple camera guys onstage, at least ten, each one currently engaging in pleasant back-and-forths with other players. No one is bothered by their presence except for me, and probably Cassius, if I could see him.

I may be failing at meeting my audience, but I have the highest kill count of anyone in the match. That has to be enough to make up for any popularity points I lost by skipping my inconvenient intro.

A loud horn blast interrupts the match, signaling that we're down to the top twenty surviving players. To make sure we run into each other, the play area shrinks and those of us outside the safe zone have less than a minute to make it in before we are automatically disqualified for the rest of the match. I cast around for something that can help me move faster and see two important things.

First, I see a unicorn. A scaly, leathery space unicorn. In *Guardians League Royale*, unicorns can fly, which would be very useful to have right now. Second, I see VANE again, gunning for the same god damn horse.

"No!" I yell out.

"Yes," Ivan's voice says sweetly. He mounts the unicorn and soars up above me, cackling over chat.

If there's one thing I have to give Ivan credit for, it's his uncanny ability to find the right person to put him in the wrong situation. I've been sniping up all match, so it only takes a second for me to look up, aim, calculate the trajectory of his flight, and shoot not at him, but at the unicorn's hindquarters.

*Zip. Neigh!* The unicorn's legs flail in the open air, and I hear a faint whickering noise before it pops out of existence. VANE has nowhere to go but down. His character falls quickly, too quickly for him to pop his parachute, and his avatar crashes to the ground before blipping away just like his noble steed. Big RIP, you absolute fool.

So that's taken care of. I could have really used the transport, though. Without it, I have to leap from rooftop to rooftop, with each bound exposing me to fire from unseen enemies. I check the player count—we're down to seven, and when I land in the plaza, I do so on top of someone else, smooshing them with my superhero-landing stomp.

Immediately, I take a laser blast in the shoulder and see my health dip down a few notches. Damn it, it's over. They have the high ground. I don't have any defense glyphs to protect myself from another shot, so I'm going to have to avoid dying the hard way. I dash toward cover, use the water spouting from the plaza's central fountain to send myself shooting up into the air, and use my laser gun's special attack to shear the health away from whoever is bad enough to have his head poking up from behind his cover. Three players left now. One more kill will put me in the top two, but this isn't Wizzcon and a top two doesn't mean anything until the end of the summer.

Some tussle across the plaza takes out number three. Now it's me and the chunky silhouette of a special edition player avatar. I don't need more detail to identify CASS—he plays as a dinosaur in a chicken costume. A quick speed boost sends me rocketing across the plaza toward the last place he dove, my lasers ready to take him down with a forehead shot when I hear the *crack* of player-generated lightning. I backflip out of the way of Cass's spell cast, thinking briefly of Ivan's quick evade from earlier, and load the explosive arrow into my bow.

The arrow, thicker and easier to follow than the thin laser types the bow usually fires, arcs gracefully across the sky and lands directly behind Cass's cover. The *boom* is satisfying. The message **BATTLE WIN: ZORA** is even more satisfying. If there's one thing that might make up for my reaction to the cameras, it's a first place win. *How's that for a rematch, bro?*

When I wrench my headphones off, I shudder with relief when the individualized attention gives way to the relative anonymity of being one in forty-nine players onstage. Somehow the racket of people emerging from the game in real life is less overwhelming than having their conversations float in and out of my ears against my will.

"That was brutal." Hearing Ivan's voice next to me as opposed to projected directly into my ear confuses my brain, and it takes a moment for me to orient myself toward the actual source of his voice.

"For real," Kavi adds, beads of sweat visible around her hairline. "What a match."

"Not the match," Ivan says. "*Zora* was brutal."

Excuse me, sir. This isn't *Guardians League Tea and Crumpets*. It's *Guardians League Royale*, battle implied. Brutal is the name of the game, literally. Metaphorically. I'm not sure which one I mean, to be honest.

"Does anyone know what happens now?" Trieu asks. "I thought there'd be some kind of, I dunno, confetti cannon? Champagne? Something to mark the end of our first match?"

"I don't think we're that bougie," I offer. But Trieu has a point. The other players onstage are all out of the game now, headphones already hung around their necks or on their desks, but there's radio silence from the theater's front row of seats, which is where Brian retreated once the game began. And now he's not alone.

The camera guys are crowded around him, each one holding their device down as they appear to be scrubbing back and forth to find a specific moment. Before I can ask myself what they're all looking for, I hear it.

"I said FUCK OFF!" plays from one tinny camera speaker.

That gets my attention. And Ivan's. And everyone else who's close enough to the front row to hear it.

From another camera, fainter but still audible in the background of their footage, "—said FUCK OFF!"

"OFF!"

"I said—"

"FUCK—"

So, it's possible I didn't "all but shout" that particular phrase. I may have truly, loudly, and with astonishing powers of vocal projection screamed that particular phrase at a volume high enough for everyone's microphones to pick up my voice.

Kavi looks at me, a hint of panic in her eyes.

"Zora, you didn't."

For the first time since emerging from the game, I peer over at Ivan. He looks relaxed as ever, slouching low in his chair with that smirk on his face.

"Oh, yes she did."

Come on, it was one curse word. One of the stronger ones, but still.

"Grow up," I snap at Ivan. "I shot a unicorn in the butt and landed so hard on a guy he exploded, but the f-word is a bridge too far?"

"Unironically, yes," Trieu says.

"But why?" I ask. It doesn't take long to find my answer. Every eye follows Brian as he rises from his seat and glides toward my desk, the long lines of his purple suit accentuating each click of his heeled black boots against the stage. This is how I meet my hero.

"You are Zora Lyon?" Brian asks with a glance down at the tablet in his hand. He pronounces my last name like the city in France, which I hoped one day he'd do just so I could correct him with a joke about actual lions, which would make him laugh, which would make him remember me forever and support my dreams like a Canadian fairy godfather. This does not happen.

"I am," I say instead. Up close Brian looks, and it may just be the circumstances, more intimidating than his wholesome image might betray. He has blue eyes, unusually bright against his tanned face, and right now they are staring at me so incisively I half expect him to start communicating telepathically. I thought he'd look younger, and I suddenly realize my error: the version of Brian Juno in my head is actually a combination of the many Brians I've watched in Wizzard Games creative interviews going back almost two decades.

I've seen what he looked like ten years ago followed by what he looked like in his twenties, clicking through to the well-lit, cheery face he wore to accept Wizzard's trophy at last year's Game Awards, and on and on with each video I cued up. All out of order. But time doesn't work like that. It just goes forward, and the twenty-year-old Brian I've imagined as my bestie only exists as a memory inside the fortysomething-year-old man directing a deeply furrowed *Max Payne* squint at the seventeen-year-old me sitting in front of him.

From the videos I know Brian has this habit of pausing when he's asked a question, both in English and in French, and I always thought it made him sound thoughtful, but now he is looking at me and the wordless scrutiny of that pause makes an awful don't-cry pressure build up behind my eyes. I will my cheeks to freeze and my teeth to clamp shut tight to slam a lid on my emotions.

I wanted to be him. I still do, but I'm scared. I'm scared that my reaction to being crowded, overwhelmed, surprised, annoyed, and "brutal" according to Ivan has gotten me in trouble with Brian before I even got to tell him what his work means to me. Let alone convince him that I should be working with him.

Maybe I can get ahead of this.

"I'm so sorry, Mr. Juno. And to you, Mr. . . ." I don't know the camera guy's name. He's standing off to the side like a low-HP minion backing up the boss in the first phase of a fight. "I know I reacted kind of poorly back there, but I'm, uh." How do I put it? I wasn't going to let anyone know about me being on the autism spectrum because in my experience, all it does is make people treat me like a toddler holding a pair of scissors the wrong way.

I'm not going to do it. I'm not telling Brian why I'm like this. I won't give him a reason to pity me.

"I, um," I say again. "I don't always react to things the way I wish I did."

"The way you wish you did," Brian parrots back, his eyes searching over my face like he's trying to find something hidden under my skin. It's hard for me to decide where to look. His eyes are too scary, his lips are too thin when he's pulling this face. I settle on the patch of skin between his eyebrows, which I've learned gives the impression that I'm making eye contact to people who value that sort of thing.

It's only after I look there, faking contact, that Brian speaks again.

"I understand," he says softly. And, oh, I feel relief. Of course Brian Juno understands. I knew he would. I'm glad he does. I let out a breath I was definitely, 100 percent aware that I've been holding.

This appears to be the end of our interaction. Brian turns away from me, swiveling on the heel of his boot to address the rest of the players onstage. Here, his voice carries just fine without a microphone.

"Does anyone know the first rule of streaming a *Guardians* game on WiTch?" This question is not rhetorical, but I don't know the answer this time. I feel like I'm about to find out.

"Um," Trieu says quietly, a note of apology in his voice. I don't check to see if he's looking at me when he says it. "Rule one is maintaining a PG-13 or below content rating for language, behavior, and character simulation activities."

"Very good." Brian nods at Trieu. "And does anyone know what happens to videos that violate Rule One?"

Another student answers this time, from somewhere across the stage. "Auto-removal of content and a three-day ban."

"Auto-removal of content," Brian agrees. "And a three-day ban." He really likes repeating the last thing people say for emphasis. It's the kind of thing that can make people feel stupid or seen, depending on the context.

"Due to an audible language violation during today's match," he continues, "the audio for several videos will be automatically flagged for removal and their accounts will be unable to post. To be fair to everyone, we will apply the same treatment to all fifty academy player accounts."

That gets a reaction. It's more than an outcry, but less than a riot. I'm guessing a lot of people had plans to start getting their followers over to their new accounts as soon as possible, and I've just ruined the opening salvo of the competition for them.

Brian sighs and pinches the bridge of his nose. "Quiet."

We deliver quiet.

"We are on a tight schedule this summer, so to salvage something out of this"—his eyes flick down to look at me one last time, as if mentally taking my head's measurements for an imaginary dunce cap labeled "THIS"—"we will calculate our starting rankings solely using the data from your in-game performance today."

Wait, that's opposite of a punishment for me. It's what I've wanted all along. To have my *Guardians League Royale* skills speak for themselves in this stupid ranking system, and since I won, I should start out in first place!

"With the exception of our . . ." He pauses. "Loudest player. Who will have her scores disqualified."

Disqualified. I'm disqualified? Just for the one game, though, right. Right?

Brian fiddles around on his phone, taps something, and the new rankings pop up on-screen behind us all. We roll around in unison to watch our names shuffle up and down the rankings until the words lie still.

"Congratulations to our first number one winner," Brian says, some of his previous enthusiasm seeping back into his voice. He straightens his tie and rolls his shoulders in the same way I noticed Ivan rolling them earlier. It's a behavioral reset, a magical gesture to call forth the character within. The ringmaster has returned, and the circus must go on. "Mr. Cassius Sharpe!"

I don't think anyone knows if we should applaud Cass's victory or not, but I feel grateful to the people who try. I can't catch Cass's eye from here, but I wonder what he thinks of where I've ended up. Up on the screen, after everyone else, there's my name dead last in the rankings. I am the Wizzard Games Summer Academy Royale's player number fifty, but by the scathing looks every other player is sending in my direction right now, I'm also public enemy number one.

# CHAPTER SIX

"WELL, THE GOOD news is they didn't kick you out," Cass says, clacking his chopsticks together like a hungry crab with skinny wooden claws. His hand hovers over the few pieces left in the take-out sushi container and selects the tempura roll I mentally marked for him before we started eating. It's the one with the tail, and while I'm no vegetarian, I still think it's a little messed up that they give you food with its butt out.

"I know," I say and slide the clear plastic lid we've been using as a shared soy sauce reservoir across the floor. "But they might as well have. I'm last place in a popularity contest, and every other contestant hates my guts. Who knows what those rankings could have looked like if Brian factored in their social performance metrics or whatever. Ugh. I hate this. I hate it here. I wish I never won that stupid battle at Wizzcon."

"No, you don't," Cassius says around a huge mouthful of shrimp. Gross. I think he senses my disapproval, since he swallows before he speaks again. "Or else you wouldn't have met me."

"You're right," I admit. "Even if you're totally not supposed to be here right now." Cassius gives me a quizzical look. "I mean in my dorm room, alone, with me. No boys in the girls' dorm rooms?"

"Oh." Cass shrugs. "Well that's stupid. Why are they all up in everyone's business deciding who's a girl?"

"Good point," I say and pick up a piece of avocado roll. "And it's like, people are gay sometimes, Brian."

"Not me, though," Cass says quickly. "Just putting that out there."

"And, like, people have all kinds of friends," I continue.

"Friends, yeah," Cass echoes.

"I mean"—my train of thought is picking up steam—"I don't have friends, plural. I have you. And everyone else thinks I'm the academy's resident Benedict Arnold."

"Listen, I'm not sure that tracks, but either way we're going to have to work on you making more up-to-date references."

"Fine." Cass knows I had a *Hamilton* phase that included going extra hard on the homeschool curriculum for the Revolutionary War. "A more game-adjacent example of someone who ruins everything for everyone." I rack my brain. "Ganondorf? I don't want to be Ganondorf."

"You are not Ganondorf," Cass assures me. "Though if you take Kavi and Trieu up on that makeover, you could totally cosplay a Gerudo. They're basically an entire town of autistic black hotties."

I'm so caught up in thinking about betrayal that I almost—almost consider cosplaying my way out of this. No, that's ridiculous. And likely expensive.

"Anyway," Cass continues, "if they really wanted to stop us from boning, they'd put an RA on our floor. Or, like, cameras."

"Ugh." I shudder. "Please, don't give them any ideas on how to make this even more of a reality show." I point my chopsticks at the tray to make a claim on the last spicy tuna roll, and Cassius hums the wordless note that means he's fine if I take it. Don't mind if I do. Who knew the Food Emporium had such edible sushi?

"We'd be a scandalous early season plotline." Cass makes a full meal out of that word, "scandalous." It's a rare display of his latent sense of drama. "Illicit yellowtail in the middle of the night, oh my."

"Middle" is a strong word for the part of the New York summer night we're avoiding by staying indoors. It's just after eight on Sixty-Second Street; the sun is still out and burning copper in the reflected windows of the midtown skyscrapers I can see from the dorm window. It's a southern exposure, with a floor-to-ceiling view way higher up than anywhere I've lived before.

"Yeah, we should have gotten way more food," I say. "We could have eaten it all on live stream like a mukbang and rake in the tips."

"Then we could use the money to buy more sushi," Cassius adds thoughtfully. "Unlimited sushi hack: Unlocked?"

"Capitalism. The word you're looking for is 'capitalism.'"

There's a knock at my dorm room door, which I have propped open with the lock as a gesture of goodwill toward anyone who might find me definitely hiding in here with a boy.

"Zora?" It's Kavi. We all have single rooms, which is excellent, but hers is right next to mine. The top floor of this building is girls only, the boys take up two floors below us, but from the amount of activity I've been hearing outside in the hallway, I think there's plenty of socializing happening regardless of where everyone keeps their stuff at night.

"Hide," I whisper to Cassius. We scramble to our feet to hide both him and the sushi before Kavi comes in and are remarkably unsuccessful. When Kavi presses on the open door, Cass has half a leg inside the wardrobe and my pose near the bed makes it look like I'm trying to tuck an armful of supermarket sushi trays under my pillow for a midnight snack. It's about a billion times more suspicious than if she'd found us eating dinner on the floor like humans.

Luckily, she doesn't bat an extended eyelash. "I just wanted to see if you were okay after what happened. I was gonna say we should all get some dinner after the match, but you just, like, nyoomed right up Broadway once they let us out." I watch her spot the sushi trays, to which she apparently declines to react.

"I'm fine," I say, dumping the containers in the trash. "Thanks for asking."

"For the record," Kavi continues, "the general vibe is that it was pretty crummy for Brian to surprise everyone like that. No one blames you for being confused."

"No, they do," I respond. It's nice of her to try and minimize the damage, but they do. Today's match was supposed to be a celebration, a chance for every student in the academy to reintroduce themselves to the world and start their journeys. Instead, today ended with a fart noise, a confiscation of everyone's video files, and a ranking based on the boring reality of how well everyone played the game.

"Well, they shouldn't," Kavi amends her statement. "You're not the only one who didn't react well to being on camera."

"I also low-key flipped out." Cassius backs out of the wardrobe and brings the doors together gently. "Told the guy to get out of my face, same as you. I just didn't say, you know."

"You can say it in real life, Cass," I say sarcastically. It reminds me of something Ivan said earlier, about things in games not translating to reality. That was about me shooting a guy, though. This is just language.

"Personally, I think you did everyone a favor," Kavi says. "You gave us a dress rehearsal for when we actually start competing on Wednesday, and that's not the worst thing ever."

"Does anyone else see it like that?" I ask.

"Not now they don't."

For all her blinding good looks and popular girl aura, Kavi is really nice. And funny. Ah, hell, am I forming a bond? A real-life, non-*GLR* alliance? A coalition, but casual? What would that even be?

Friend. The word *I'm* looking for is friends.

"But they might," Kavi continues, "if you show your face at the party that's forming in the lounge on our floor. Let people meet you, so your whole aura is less . . ."

"Elphaba in the first half of *Wicked*?" I try to finish her sentence.

"Abstract," Kavi corrects. "No one knows who you are yet, so it's easy to villainize you."

Normally I would object to compulsory socializing, but she's got a point. If I'm going to belong in this competition, I need to be someone other than who I was this morning. More importantly, I need to show people that I'm not who they think I am. Can't do that eating floor sushi with Cass.

"Sure, I'm in. I'll be out in a bit."

Kavi claps her hands excitedly. "Yay! You're totally welcome too, by the way," she tells Cassius.

"Oh gosh, thank you!" Cassius's smile is genuine. "But I woke up at, like, two this morning, so I'm going to bed." Cass does look tired.

"Some other time, then," Kavi responds, unfazed. "Come out whenever, Zora. We'll be just outside at the end of the hall." She waves her pinky finger at Cass before backing out the door and leaving us alone.

"That 'we' she keeps talking about"—Cassius says, oblivious to Kavi's finger-flirting—"do you think that includes Ivan?"

"I mean," I begin, "I think she means the other players, which technically includes Ivan. I highly doubt he's out there advocating for my inclusion."

"Do you really think he still has a problem with you?"

"Why does it matter? I have a problem with him. 'I hate you' is a complete sentence. Gandhi said that, I think."

"Hey, I get it." Cassius puts his hands up guiltily. "You know I'd never try to nudge you off a grudge."

It's true, he wouldn't. Cassius accepts me exactly as I am: awkwardness, introversion, near-permanent rage, and all. The academy is a program designed to make me change who I am to succeed. I don't want to let that happen, but what choice do I have? Speaking of changing, I should probably put on a shirt I didn't walk twenty blocks in eighty-degree heat in. I walk over to the wardrobe and pull it back open. I know exactly what I have in here. Six T-shirts for game days, four sleeveless tops for when I want to show these guns off, my jean jacket with all my Wizzard pins, two pairs of jeans, exactly one summer dress because Clive thought I should pack it for "girls' nights," and a thrift store jean skirt I'm not sure fits but looks very 2002. I am very good at packing a lot of stuff into one bag, but if I knew I was going to be auditioning for the gaming equivalent of a K-pop competition show, I would have brought something a little more camera-friendly. Skirt'll have to do.

"If it was just the Wizzcon stuff with Ivan, I'd be over it by now," I say and pull a purple tank top off its hanger. Cass makes a noise of disbelief.

"What, I would! But he's clearly not over it, so I can't be over it. Turn around." I could change in my en suite bathroom, but these dorm doors are pretty much solid wood rectangles and I'd prefer not to have to shout to be heard on this particular topic.

"Why not?" Cass asks, walks over toward my bed, and turns around to face the window. "Wouldn't that make you the bigger person?"

"Yes," I answer flatly. "But I don't want to be the bigger person. I want to be small. Microscopic."

"Quantum?" Cass offers.

"Quantum." I like the sound of that. "Quantum-level petty."

"God, you're cool. Can I turn around now?"

"Yep, done."

Cass turns around and leans back against my bed, elbows back, while he sweeps his eyes up and down my outfit. "Oh, you're wearing a skirt," he says with the tiniest hitch in his voice. Maybe he has a little bit of sushi stuck in his throat. "You look—"

"Focus," I interrupt.

"Focusing. But also I should go."

"I know." I smile. "Thanks for the sushi."

"No problem."

"And don't forget I'm coming for you, Number One."

"I know. And that"—Cass grabs the belt bag he tossed on my bed when we walked in and slings it over his arm—"is exactly how I like you."

"Yeah, you like me now."

"I'm always going to like you."

Something in the way he says that, quieter than before and finally looking me in the eye, makes me think he's talking about more than my ruthlessness.

"Cass, I—"

"Never change, Zora." Cass slips out the door, letting in a three-second audio sample of almost-college party clamor before leaving me alone to process that. "And text your uncle."

Was that weird? I'm not sure why it would be weird. Not the uncle thing; that's my own business. But what he said before that. Of course Cass likes me; I'm his best friend. His best friend who would never make herself worse to make him look good, which he respects in a "comrades on the field of battle"–type way. That's all. He's my friend and— Oh, wow, I just caught a glimpse in the mirror, and this skirt makes my butt look like a whole nectarine. Move over, shrimp tempura. It's a new vibe for me, but so is becoming an overnight super-villain, so I guess I'll switch it up.

Deep breaths, in and out. My hair has doubled in size since the morning's humidity, but I've already made it clear to this group that neither my looks nor my personality got me here, and it definitely wasn't my propensity for accidental '70s Diana Ross hair moments.

When Cass and I first rolled up to the dorms Wizzard rented for the academy players, I literally thought the building was a part of Lincoln Center—all wavy glass and modern white concrete out front. The rooms themselves are small but new, with a shared common room and kitchen at the far end of the hall. All of the rooms on my side of the building have a floor-to-ceiling window facing south into downtown. Now that it's a little darker, I can see a hazy white glow hanging in the air twenty blocks south around Times Square, making it an even brighter spot in a city that doesn't really do dark in the first place. Which reminds me. Open messages, tap Uncle Clive's smiling portrait in my most-texted list . . .

*Made it to code camp! Huge day, I'm super tired. Call soon.* Send text. There. I shove my phone down the front of my shirt since the pockets on this jean skirt couldn't hold a grape.

When I open my bedroom door there's already around two dozen people milling around in the common area at the end of the floor, with more just arriving as a few of the players I recognize from this morning come through a propped-open stairwell door. One of them kicks at whatever was used as a doorstop, which on closer inspection is a scaled-down

Companion Cube toy from *Portal*. I wonder how everyone would react if I tossed it in the oven. How's that for a supervillain move?

When gamers party, we take our fun in a different direction. Someone's already rigged up the common room's old TV with a vintage Nintendo 64 and has a *Super Smash Bros.* tournament getting rowdy on a ragged-looking couch. A few others have Wizzard trading cards out on the kitchen table and are sitting there expectantly like a pack of grizzled travelers from *The Witcher III* jonesing for a game of Gwent.

I'm trying to look for Kavi or even Trieu to get my party bearings, but what I get instead is Ivan, who steps in front of me the moment I emerge from my room. How is one person so consistently inconvenient?

"Oop, sorry!" he says. "I was coming over to knock. Can we prop your door open so people can use the bathroom in here? Your room is closest to the stairwell."

"Hell no," I reply. I just moved in and this place is spotless. I don't want a legion of gamers pounding Monster and peeing neon all over the seat. "Prop your own door open. No boys allowed in here anyway."

"Is that why I saw your friend sneak out earlier?"

"No," I say sweetly. "Cass was just helping me out with a little postgame nunya."

"I'm not falling for that," Ivan deadpans.

"'Nunya business," I finish dejectedly, disappointed but not surprised he didn't let me have that one.

"Whatever." Ivan takes a dramatic step out of my way and half bows as if to usher me into a royal ball. "Enjoy the party, Maleficent."

I'm sure if I concentrated I'd be able to come up with some variation of "I'll put you to sleep forever," but Ivan isn't worth any more of my time tonight. I have bigger problems.

Like the fact that the aura in the hallway noticeably cooled when I opened my dorm door, and the common area isn't much better. Maybe I can think of this like a video game. Like *The Sims,* but without all the aliens and vampires and drowning in the pool because someone (me) took out the ladder. If this were *The Sims,* I could raise my popularity just by greeting other people and starting a group discussion about the nearest lamp.

"Cool shirt!" I wave to a pale, short boy with broccoli-cut hair and a Megadeth tee. His lip curls like a dog spotting the mailman through the living room window. A failed interaction. Let me try again.

Here's a girl, and a Black girl at that. She might have some compassion for me.

"Hey, girl!" I smile at her.

"Nah," she replies and turns her back to talk to someone else. Honestly, fair.

I'm almost at the end of the hall, where an open archway leads to the common area. One group of players standing just outside looks me up and down as I pause near them. They all look like they belong in a spinoff of *Euphoria*. Not the drugs part, the "being really hot and the blond one is stacked" part.

"S-slay?" I attempt. The blond silently takes out her phone and takes a picture of me before going back to ignoring my presence entirely. What does that mean? And why does it hurt so much?

This is why I don't play *The Sims* without cheat codes. I cross the archway and pray to find Kavi there, or Trieu, or both preferably. These leper vibes are starting to get to me.

It strikes me that I had the huge benefit of a blank slate coming into this academy, a chance to define myself for myself, but Brian scratched out my entry in the dictionary before I even knew there was anything to write. I am not in control over how people see me, and since I'm apparently here to be seen, that lack of control extends to everything else in this program. That's the most annoying part of all of this.

Actually, wait. No. Ivan's the most annoying part. But the surrendering of my personal narrative sucks too.

"Zora! Over here!" Kavi waves me over to where she's standing with Trieu, near enough to the archway to greet people as they walk in but far enough to keep an eye on everyone else. I feel a few sets of eyes following me when I cross over to them, but now that someone who's not them has given me a place to stand, the bulk of their attention returns to themselves.

"One twenty-block walk and you already got a little bit of a tan," Trieu says appreciatively when I shuffle over to only two people at this party who don't want to kick me down a well. "Girl, you are glowing."

"I believe that," I say. "If only because people around here seem to think I'm radioactive."

Kavi laughs. "Radioactive isn't so bad. I mean, everybody loves *Fallout*."

"'War never changes,'" I quote with a half smile. "And neither will I, I guess. Pigeonholed on day one."

Trieu looks over my shoulder at our so-called guests. “Maybe,” he says. “But ‘pretty girl outcast’ is something we can work with. If you still want our help in standing out.”

“Thanks, but no thanks,” I say, hoping that my newfound tan hides the blush I feel creeping up into my cheeks.

“I think trying to manipulate this situation will only make it worse. I’m not really built for all of this.” I gesture at the growing crowd of shiny gaming influencers and feel even more out of place, if possible. “But I still don’t want to stay in last place? I don’t know. It’s been a day.”

“Wait, so do you want us to help or no?” Kavi asks.

“I don’t want you to get radiation poisoning,” I reply.

“Did someone call a row-two team meeting?” Ivan saunters up to us, having finished his circuit of the room. I caught him out of the corner of my eye a few times, glad-handing his ass off and kissing metaphorical babies like the self-appointed mayor of Wizzardland. I took my eyes off him for a few seconds, though, and now he’s here. Again. I should have known better.

“Shoo, you,” Trieu says, more flirty than demanding, “this is girl talk.”

“All right.” Ivan holds his hands up and smiles at Trieu. Really turning on the charm for that one. “Let me know if you want to boy talk later . . .” He trails off and walks toward another group of people. His path takes him all the way to the other side of the common area, past more than one cluster of players. I see a girl stop talking when he passes by and hope for a second that he’s more of an outcast here than I assumed before, but there’s no reproach in her eyes. Just naked, obvious attraction.

“Might wanna back off that one,” I say, loud enough for her to hear me. Ah, there’s the reproach I was looking for. They were saving it for me.

“Seriously, what is your deal with Ivan?” I’m a little shocked at the sudden vehemence coming from Trieu.

“What isn’t my deal with Ivan?” I reply. It’s not my best comeback. Might actually be one of my worst, but it was a reflexive response. It sucks being the one human alive who doesn’t think Ivan Hunt walks on water. “Am I the only one who remembers what he did to—”

A commotion rises up from farther down the floor, closer to the stairwell and my bedroom door. For a moment I think it’s more people freaking out about Saint Ivan walking among them, but it’s something more exciting than that. My height lets me see over everyone’s heads and spot the source of the commotion before Kavi or Trieu gets a good look.

“—her!” I finish my sentence with a new note of triumph. I feel like Lex Luthor getting his hands on a giant chunk of kryptonite. There is one thing—two things, really—that I know will throw Ivan off his game.

Emilia and Jake are in the building.

# CHAPTER SEVEN

THE HALLWAY CROWD parts around them like a school of fish around a pair of sexy-ass sharks. Up close they're even more perfect than I could tell from the cheap seats in the theater earlier. Jake's shy smile is genuine, more charming, so is the way Emilia chats people up like a princess going down a line of well-wishers at a royal wedding. They are fantastically compatible, and it shows.

All it takes is two seconds of watching Jake put his hand on Emilia's lower back to move her out of someone's way, or Emilia tossing her curls to look up at Jake's cute face to see they are madly and charismatically in love with each other. It's simply coincidence that their love sells tickets. And merch. And gets Wizzard some clutch partnerships from companies that wouldn't have touched esports with a ten-foot pole if there wasn't a legit streaming teen romance holding the league together at its core. That kind of power is intoxicating to witness. All I want right now is to find out how I can generate some of that on my own.

If being memorable is what it takes to succeed this summer, I don't want to be remembered as a screwup. I don't know exactly what I do want to be remembered for, but I want it to look more like the way Jake and Emilia move through the world. Confident, admired. A true dynamic duo. Except without having to worry about relying on anyone else, because that's stupid. I need to be one of one, a dynamic uno.

"Oh my god, hi!" Trieu confidently waves the two superstars over as if they were old friends. Which, to be fair, they might be. I haven't asked. It's entirely possible everyone in the Wizzard esports community knows each other except for me and Cass.

"Sorry we're late," Jake says.

"You're really not," Trieu responds.

"That's just how he says hello," Emilia clarifies. "We can't stay for long, though."

"All good. How's Bob?" Trieu asks.

"Still in love with you," Emilia blurts out before Jake gently nudges her in the ribs. "What? He totally is."

For the first time since I met him, Trieu looks a little bit bashful. I can't tell if his blush is genuine or excellently blended makeup, which I think he would appreciate if I told him.

"Well, you know how it goes with these kind of things . . . ," Trieu begins, then seemingly finds himself at a loss regarding how to end that thought.

"Can we meet your friends?" Jake asks, successfully pivoting away from a potential awkward silence.

"Oh, right. Duh." Trieu turns around and gestures to Kavi and myself.

“I’m Kavi Khurana.” Kavi’s smile is so wide it looks about to split her face in half. “Super great to meet you; we should talk about collabing sometime.”

“And this—” Trieu grabs my elbow to drag me a little closer into the group.

“Is Zora,” Emilia finishes for him. “The mystery knight. I’m Emilia. You guys mind if we talk to Zora for a second?”

That was directed to Kavi and Trieu, who bow out of the conversation without so much as a “catch ya later.” I’m so shocked that Emilia and Jake want to talk to me alone that I forget to hate Ivan for a second and peek over to check if he sees this is happening too. Except I can’t, because he’s gone. Totally vanished even though he was only a few yards away a moment ago.

“Hi?” I reply. “I mean—yeah, I’m Zora, and I know who you are, of course. Both of you, I mean; you’re legendary. It’s an honor to meet you.” Is that too familiar? Too groveling?

Emilia rolls her eyes, but I get the sense that she’s not doing it because of me. “You single-handedly got fifty live streams taken down by Brian Juno’s own content filter and forced him to temporarily rewrite the rules of the academy on your first day. It’s an honor to meet *you*.”

“Seriously, good job,” Jake adds. It feels like I’m missing something here.

“Wait, I’m confused,” I say. “You think it’s a good thing that Brian hates me?”

Emilia and Jake laugh in tandem.

“Trust me,” Emilia says. “Brian does not hate you.”

“The only things he hates are the ESRB and bad investments,” Jake adds.

"You got his attention," Emilia continues. Hearing them talk feels like talking to one person spread across two very different bodies. "That's all that matters."

"To think," I say sarcastically, "coming in today I thought being a good player was all that matters."

A shadow passes over Emilia's face, just a hint of discomfort that I don't think most people would pick up on. It's the shadow that comes when someone says something rude and true, and you don't want anyone to know about the true part. I often see that look on other people's faces when I talk.

"Yeah," Emilia replies. "A lot of people think that."

"I just didn't think I signed up for all of this." I gesture to the whole room. "I'm completely out of my depth." It feels weird to admit that to someone I just met, but something tells me Emilia knows she has that effect on people. I think it's why she wanted to talk to me in the first place.

"Looks like it, yeah," Jake agrees. His bluntness surprises me. Is he trying to make me feel better or not? Another commotion rises from the sitting area across the lounge, where a crowd of people are gathered around the TV. One of the *Smash Bros.* players has apparently ceded his controller to someone whose skills have a handful of the most prominent gamers in the country completely enraptured. It must be down to the wire, because someone immediately shushes the crowd to allow the players sitting all the way forward on the couch to focus harder on their combos.

"You wouldn't happen to have any advice, would you?" I ask Emilia and Jake. "On how to recover from this whole 'enemy of the people' vibe? Almost everyone in this room acts like screwing up is contagious."

"Let me think about that for a second," Emilia says. Another cheer floats over from the *Smash* match, and a player stands up to take a victorious bow. When the crowd parts briefly, I see what I should have already guessed. It's Ivan, of course it is, with his toothpaste-white smile and floppy hair intermittently illuminated by camera flashes and the glow of recording screens. Even without the extra light, there's something shiny about him when he's playing to a crowd. He looks taller, more relaxed, and friendly in the same way that Emilia and Jake look when the spotlight is on them. It's an obvious front, but an effective one. Regardless of who I know he really is, Ivan Hunt has the look of a hero.

"Got it," Emilia says suddenly, shaking me out of a reverie I never consciously consented to experiencing.

"Got what?" I ask.

"Advice," Jake clarifies for her.

"Right!" I did ask for advice. Less than ten seconds ago. I remember doing that, before Ivan . . . Never mind Ivan. I pointedly drag my eyes away from his victory celebration and try very hard to concentrate back on the literal celebrity wasting her valuable time on me right now.

"Why are you here?" Emilia asks me.

"I— What? That's a question, not advice."

"It's relevant," Jake replies. He's looking at Emilia lovingly, probably reading her mind again. What is it about a guy in love with a woman who could kick his ass that makes me trust him implicitly?

"I . . . uh." I look around the room again. Everyone within earshot is pretending not to listen, but they are. "I want to make games. Write games, Wizzard games. And I have ideas for *Guardians League Royale*. Like, good ideas, or at least I think so. I'm here to make sure everyone at Wizzard knows who I am so I can work there in a few years. I want the Juno mentorship. I don't know, it's stupid."

"Don't say it's stupid," Jake says.

"It's actually perfect," Emilia adds. "You want to tell stories?"

"Yeah," I say. Then, with more of the confidence I'm borrowing from her presence, "Yes, I do."

"Then tell a different one," Emilia says. "Like, yeah, the end result of today was kind of bad for you, but it's not the ending. Do something totally different tomorrow, be unpredictable, don't be defined by one event."

"Become ungovernable, fight the mailman, run with scissors," Jake adds.

That's a thought. "Okay, but what about everyone else here? I'm in last place in half of a popularity contest, and no one will even talk to me."

"But they're talking *about* you," Emilia points out. "Again, the hard part is done. Keep their attention, just for something else. Take it from me." Emilia gives me a knowing stare. "People around here have very short memories."

I know where she's about to look before she does it. Emilia narrows her eyes at the corner of the common room where Ivan is sitting. For a second, I have an overwhelming desire to ask for her side of the story on the Ivan thing—I'm sure she has all kinds of tea on him and how much he sucks.

That, however, is one of those topics that only appears as a conversational option when Sims are Good Friends. I'm not there yet with anyone at this party, let alone Emilia and Jake of "Emilia and Jake" fame.

A blue-eyed boy with a jawline I'd describe as "intense" half steps between Emilia and me, holding his phone up like he's trying to sell it.

"Hey, I'm Chaz. Can I get a picture?" he asks Emilia, ignoring the surprised "um" noise I make when he almost steps on me. I decide in that moment that if I have a choice between being disliked or being invisible, I might actually choose disliked.

"No." Emilia holds her hand up. "I'm talking to my friend here."

Friend? I peek quizzically at Jake, who winks at me behind his thick-framed glasses.

"You know Zora, right?" Emilia asks. She makes it sound like the most obvious thing in the world, that this random boy should know me. Chaz steps back, as if Emilia's acknowledgment of my existence made me magically appear in his peripheral vision.

"Hi." I give Chaz a little wave. "We haven't met."

"We were just talking about how messed up it was that Brian just, like, shoved cameras in everyone's faces without any warning," Jake lies. He makes it sound like that read on the situation is the obvious, universal reaction everyone had to the events of this afternoon.

"Oh, for sure, for sure, super messed up, yeah," says Chaz, nodding furiously. I knew being popular was probably fun, but I didn't know it conveyed the power of rewriting reality! It's giving *Alan Wake*, and I love it. How exciting. I wonder what they'll say next.

Nothing. Emilia and Jake say nothing next. Oh! Am I supposed to talk here? It's my turn, okay. Write a new story. Say something unexpected.

"Yeah, like . . ." I peer wildly around the room until my eyes fall on Kavi. She told me earlier I did everyone a favor by getting the footage flagged. I gave them a dress rehearsal. That's not a bad angle. "I'm just kind of big on boundaries, you know? And I don't know about you, but I was not camera ready when they surprised us like that."

"For sure, for sure," Chaz says again. I get the distinct impression that pulling on the cord in this guy's back results in his speaking one of two totally boring phrases. "Do I know you, from streaming or something? What's your channel name?"

The only WiTch account I have is the one Wizzard made for me this morning and somehow hooked up to my desk setup—how did they do that, by the way? Is it possible that Wizzard has a back door into our accounts and can remotely port everyone's characters? How did I miss that before? Something to consider for later.

"I, um. I don't . . . have one," I admit sheepishly.

"Oh," Chaz says, his interest waning more with every word I say. "Cool. I gotta go do . . ." He trails off. Now that he knows I'm not actually popular, it seems he's over getting to know me, which is rude. What kind of nickname is Chaz anyway? Your mother named you Charles, stop fronting.

"Well," Jake sighs. "It's a start."

"Yeah." It's time for me to cut these cool kids loose before I almost put a dent in their shine. "Thanks for the advice. I got it from here, though."

I pretend not to hear Emilia stifle a laugh, because I know it was involuntary and she means it in the nicest way possible. Also she's right. It is laughable that I can convince anyone, let alone Brian Juno, forty-six teenagers, and an entire niche internet micro-celeb fandom ecosystem that I belong here.

"Sorry, that laugh wasn't at you," Emilia clarifies. Oh. Never mind, I'm fine. "I just looked over your shoulder and saw Ivan, like, sprint down the hallway and run into someone's room."

All the questions I had about Ivan before come rushing to the front of my mind, but they're just as rude now as they were before. I want to ask Emilia how exactly Ivan's team screwed her over at the championships. I want to know if she knew what happened to him when he disappeared. I'd ask her if she thinks he's run into someone's room to avoid her specifically, how she makes him do that, and if it's a skill anyone can learn.

Wait. Ivan ran away and went into someone's room. On the girls' floor. Without a key. And my door is still unlocked from when Cassius was in there.

That motherf— He's in my room!

"Excuse me," I say to both Emilia and Jake. "Thank you both so much for talking to me and the advice and . . ." I peek down the hall. No sign of Ivan coming out of my room. He's still in there.

"No problem," Jake says.

"And for telling that guy you knew me, even if he didn't totally believe you, but I have to . . . I gotta—"

"Go," Emilia says with a smile. "And forget that guy. Who actively chooses the nickname Chaz, anyway?"

“I know, right? Thank you!” I enthusiastically agree, then give them both an awkward military-adjacent salute before I peel off from the party and jog back down the hall with my heart racing. Maybe I was wrong before. Someone else could have left their door open. Ivan could be in their room, not mine.

# CHAPTER EIGHT

I WAS RIGHT about one thing. My door is still propped open with the locking bar sticking out when I slow my jog at my end of the hall. I smack the door open, half expecting Ivan to jump out at me like a poltergeist. Nothing. The room is empty.

In the handful of minutes I've spent in the lounge, the sun has set, casting my bedroom in a bluish darkness split only by a streak of bright fluorescent light coming from the cracked-open bathroom door. I didn't turn that light on. Even if I did, the motion sensor inside should have turned it off by now—which reminds me: I need to remove that sensor. I'm eco-friendly in a lot of ways, but I take long showers. With hair like mine, I kind of have to. That, and showers are the one activity during which no one outside of Norman Bates is likely to interrupt me and I can actually think. *Note to self: Disable that sensor.*

That's a tomorrow problem, though. I can hear more of today's problem rustling around in my en suite, accompanied by the tinny clink of glass bottles and—there! A toilet flush.

I grab the bathroom doorknob and fling it open, realizing a second too late that if Ivan really is in there using my toilet without my permission, it's possible I've just walked in on him with his literal pants down. I quickly see that's not the case, but it could have been. He still jumps with surprise and drops an empty plastic jug on the tile floor, where it bounces and rolls away until it's stopped by a shopping bag with a huge hole ripped in the bottom.

"Shit, shit shit shit." Ivan bends over to pick up the handle and drops another plastic bottle in the process.

"Ivan," I say calmly, but not without menace.

Ivan looks up at me, visibly exhausted, upset, and desperate. Neat.

"Look, Zora," he says, setting his bottles back upright. "Whatever Emilia told you about me—"

"What?" I interrupt. "Emilia didn't say anything about you. We weren't even talking about you."

"Oh." He looks puzzled for a moment. "Then, uh. Mind helping me out?" Ivan steps aside to reveal the collection of bottles he has clustered around the foot of my toilet bowl. All of them are some kind of alcohol. Cheap stuff, less useful as fuel for bad teen decisions and more for disinfecting an action movie protagonist's bullet wounds when going to the hospital isn't an option for plot reasons.

"You brought booze into my room?" My mouth drops open in sheer disbelief.

"To get rid of it!" Ivan says. "I was taking it downstairs, but the bag broke, so I panicked and ran in here to flush everything. Now help me trash these bottles or everyone is screwed."

"No." I shake my head. "This is a you problem. Get out. Now."

"It's an everyone problem," Ivan argues. "And I can't. I need to get them out of the building, but there are too many people."

He has a point. The very nature of this academy means people will do anything to get ahead, and a blurry background image of a competitor holding alcohol is a guaranteed way to get them kicked out. Which makes it even more messed up that he's brought these bottles to my literal doorstep.

Let me take a moment and pause the game here. Ivan looks genuinely terrified, and he's right that getting rid of contraband booze means doing everyone at this party a favor. There aren't a ton of bottles, maybe just enough to fit inside a tote bag, but we can't recycle them in the bins on our floor. We will have to dump them somewhere outside.

Hold up—who is we? I am not in on this. Ivan can do whatever the hell he wants, but the first step of whatever he does has to be getting this out of my room. He may be doing the right thing, but I am not the one to help him do it. You'd think he'd have learned that by now.

"Lock the door," I hear myself saying. "I don't want anyone walking in. Anyone else, I mean." Wait. Did I not just say I wouldn't help him? I don't know who's in control right now, but it's not the Zora I know.

"Got it." Ivan steps around me and leaves the bathroom. I hear him reset the door lock and pull the door closed with a click; then he makes as if to turn my main dorm light on. I stop him.

"Don't!" I say quickly. I haven't turned that light on since I arrived for a reason. "The, uh. The light will show under the door. I don't want it to look like anyone's in here," I say. It's only half a lie. The truth is I hate big ceiling lights. Always have. They're harsh, too white, and they hurt my eyes. I'd do everything after 8 p.m. by lamplight if I could, and for the most part I do.

"Okay." Ivan doesn't argue. Without the smart retorts, his statements feel somehow unfinished to my ears.

"I have a backpack in the wardrobe." I gesture toward that side of the room. "It fits more than you'd think. You grab that and I"—there's a coarse roll of single-ply paper towels sitting on my bathroom counter; I grab that, as well as two of the bottles—"will use this to muffle the sound of the glass."

"Thank you," Ivan says with audible relief. "Here, I'll start wrapping them."

His calm irks me. I should be furious right now, but instead I'm handing him secret bottles like we're 1920s bootleggers running a joint operation.

"I just have one question," I say as Ivan yanks my empty backpack out of the wardrobe. "Were you born entitled, or did you wait until you got internet famous to walk all over everyone's boundaries?"

He cringes. "So, Emilia did tell you about me."

"For the last time, no." Much as I would have liked her to.

"Wait, so why do you think I'm entitled?"

I could start listing the reasons tonight and still be talking when the sun explodes, but I'll keep it succinct for now. "You are literally in disbelief that two women *weren't* just talking about you."

"Touché." Ivan winds the paper towels around a bottle one, two, three, four times before ripping the sheet away from the roll. I go to the bathroom to grab him more bottles. The adrenaline of the situation makes my hands shake, and the bottles clink around when I come back out to hand them over.

"Jeez." Ivan looks up at me with faux concern. "Is there anything in the universe that chills you out or are you just up here"—he holds his hand a few inches above his head—"like . . . all the time?"

"I am chill," I lie for the sake of argument. "I'm so chill it's nuts."

"I could maybe believe that," Ivan says with a scoff. "You were pretty chilly back in January. The phrase 'ice queen' comes to mind."

I think he thinks that's an insult. I don't take it that way.

"I'd rather be an ice queen than some kind of . . . bottle-juggling party clown. Did you perform enough tricks out there? Got enough attention to sustain you until your next feed? Give me that." Ivan's wrapping these bottles at the speed of snail, so I grab the roll and start pre-ripping lengths of paper for him.

"Considering 'ice queen' is what made you go from total unknown to bonkers unlikeable in one day, I think I'd rather be the clown," Ivan says. "People like clowns. Name one time a clown was the bad guy."

"*It*, both chapters," I reply, too distracted by the obvious to be anything but 100 percent reactive right now. "*American Horror Story*. Literally John Wayne Gacy. *Killer Klowns from Outer Space*. That one really uncomfortable episode of *CSI* when the dad—"

"Okay, fine!" Ivan chucks a wrapped bottle into my back-pack. For a moment I'm afraid it will break; then I see he deliberately picked a plastic one. "That was a bad example. When's the last time an ice queen got to be the good guy?"

"*Frozen*."

"That was *one* time."

". . . *Frozen 2*."

"Oh my god." Ivan throws his hands up. I'm frustrating him. Good. "Captain Pick-A-Fight. Stand down."

"I don't want to fight." How is this fight my fault when he's the one who started all of this? From Wizzcon to this afternoon to right now in my dorm room with these contraband bottles. Everything has been his fault.

"All you do is pick fights! We could have been friends at Wizzcon, but *no*. You had to ruin my chance for no reason."

Okay, never mind. Imma fight.

"Oh, I'm *so sorry* about that." I coat every syllable with sarcasm. "Was I supposed to throw away my strategy in the most important game of my life because some puffed-up eboy batted his eyelashes at me?"

"I did not bat—" Ivan slips the last bottle into my backpack and gives it an experimental shake. No clinking, no clanking. Now what?

"You batted." He absolutely batted. "Does that usually work for you, by the way? I've been racking my brain for where you might get the audacity ever since we met."

"So, you've been thinking about me." Ivan slides one of the backpack straps over his shoulder, stands up, and tries to get me to meet his eyes. Not a chance—shit, I did it. Even in the dark, those eyes drink up the multicolored shine of nighttime city lights and reflect it all back green. On someone else they'd be almost pretty.

"Not . . . not like that, no."

"It's okay," he continues, smug as hell. "I thought about you too."

"Well, don't!" Ugh, he got me to raise my voice a bit too loud. I lower my tone to a whisper and look through the peephole of my door. Bad news. The party has outgrown the lounge, and now there are players hanging out in the hall, some leaning against the walls and others sitting in groups on the carpet (gross). Ivan is going to have a lot of eyes on him when he leaves, but if he times his exit he has a straight shot from here to the elevator. There are already some people waiting for said elevator to arrive.

"You can't, like . . . charm me," I continue quietly. "I am famously uncharmable."

"Is that a medical condition?" Ivan whispers back. "Doctor said you're rizz intolerant?"

"I'm bullshit intolerant. And at Wizzcon, I could smell you a mile away."

"You were smelling me too? Was that before or after you lied to my face and turned on me when I tried to help you?"

I'm reaching my limit. I want this conversation to be over. BUT.

"It was a competition, Ivan! It's not my fault you have the self-preservation instincts of a grilled cheese sandwich."

"A grilled cheese—" Ivan parrots incredulously. "You know what? I've got this from here." He dramatically hoists my backpack up higher on his shoulder and makes for the door. "I'll bring the bag back, but after that, could you do me a favor and leave me alone for the rest of the summer?"

“Only if you leave me alone first,” I bark back. “And make sure you put that in the recycling bin; don’t just trash it.”

“Of course I’m gonna recycle it!” Ivan hisses. “God, you are the *worst*.”

“Just checking,” I hiss back. “And feeling’s mutual.”

Ivan has no response for that. He unlocks my door, yanks it open, and looks both ways before stepping out into the hall. The door is almost closed again when I spot it. One single, slender bottle of margarita mix half hidden by the door of my wardrobe. I’m not going through this again. Ivan needs to take this down with all the rest. Then we’ll never talk or even look at each other once for the rest of our lives.

Without anything else to hold the bottle, I stuff it under my shirt, holding it up against my back when I step out into the hall.

“Ivan!” I call out. He’s about to get into an elevator with a group of other students, but he hears my voice and stops. So does everyone else getting into the elevator.

“We, um,” I start. “You forgot . . . something.”

Ivan’s eyes light up in recognition. My strange posture, holding one hand behind my back like a cater waiter, clues him in to my situation.

“Right,” he says with a quick look at the six-odd strangers holding the elevator for him. “Let me just grab . . .”

Just what? He can’t come back into my room; people are watching. I also can’t slip the bottle into the backpack without anyone noticing. “No!” I call out. “I’ll come over there. To you.” I shuffle sideways along the hallway wall, not wanting anyone to see what I have behind my back. The hard part will be getting from the wall to the elevator. My grip on this thing isn't amazing either, so when I try to step forward I feel it slip an inch down.

I officially have about five seconds before it looks like I pooped an empty bottle of marg mix on the hallway floor. Ivan is there in three. He leaps out of the elevator, strides across the hall, and grabs me by my waist—or, no. It just looks like he does. His arms are around me, but his hands are occupied with steadying the bottle.

"Hold it here," Ivan whispers. "Look at me." I do look at him, and there they are, those green eyes in magnified close-up. I feel a puff of warm air on my cheek that moistens my skin, hear the whisper his breath makes as it comes up his throat, crosses his lips. Our faces are close enough that if either of us felt the urge to lean in and headbutt the other, we could.

"Oh my god, I knew she looked familiar." Someone in the hallway has stopped to look at us. I don't know what they're talking about because Ivan Hunt's face is near my face and Ivan Hunt's hands are slowly starting to move the glass bottle from the back of my shirt to the front.

"Hey—" I start to say.

"Shush." Ivan is calm and concentrating on moving the bottle. His hands are on top of my shirt, but as the bottle rolls it catches on my slightly sweaty skin. Still, he makes progress. It tickles a little, and the cold glass is giving me goose bumps, but I dare not move. Not like I would know how or where to go. This whole situation is fairly unique for me. For most people, I might assume.

"You're so right, it's her," a stranger says.

"Well, that's one mystery solved," adds another.

The bottle is now under my shirt and pressed up against my stomach. Ivan keeps one arm around my waist and uses the other to quickly flip the bottle from under my shirt to under his.

"It's not gonna work," I say, angling my head down to see the obvious bulge in his shirt. Now his breath is rustling the errant curls I tuck behind my ear, and I hear it come shallower than before. If he's this nervous, how does he think I feel?

"Got this," he mutters. His voice sounds slow and thick, an entire world of difference from the sharp, mean tones we used with each other back in my room. "Go."

Ivan pushes away from me, and I've never been more grateful to have my back against a wall. It's like the building itself is holding me up just when my knees were about to give out. A quiet gasp escapes my mouth at the sudden lack of his body, his warmth. At the way he holds a finger up to his lips in a conspiratorial "shh" as he backs up into the elevator. His arm is cradled around his waist in a way that could maybe mean he has a stomachache. Or a glass bottle held horizontally across his abs, which are pretty tight now that I've pressed up against them for a bit, which is irrelevant information.

"Hold on, I think I have the picture." Another stranger, another strange thing to say.

"Told you he was dating someone."

I watch Ivan, wide-eyed, until the elevator doors finally close. It's done. He has all the bottles. I'm safe, my room is clear, and he promised he'd recycle. It takes a few moments for me to remember I have feet and another few to clear my head enough to pay attention to the rest of the universe. Where someone is already pushing their phone toward my face.

"Zora! Hey, Zora! This is you, right?"

Of course it's Chaz. I flinch away from his screen, though not fast enough to avoid glimpsing whatever he's trying to show me. I expect some bit of nonsense to match with the nonsense people have been spouting since Ivan took the breath from me (bottle! I meant bottle). I don't glimpse nonsense, though. I glimpse myself.

Here is a video of two people standing together at the end of a red carpet. One is a boy in a shearling leather jacket, and the other is a girl in a long, black puffer coat. His arm is around her, but she yanks herself away and stares back at him in disgust. Okay, glimpse over. No need to watch any more of that. I know that story, and it sucks, and now I have to own up to the fact that Ivan Hunt publicly identified me as his groupie at Wizzcon.

"That's me, yeah," I admit. No use denying it, even though the cringe factor of reliving this moment makes me want to knit myself into a cocoon starting at my feet and all the way up past my head.

"For sure!" Chaz exclaims. "Yo, guys, I was right! I told you she looked familiar." He bends down to show his phone to the students sitting on the floor. A few of them shuffle forward on their knees to get a better look at the video, which loops back to the beginning.

I try not to watch it again, but it's hard not to. I try to think of the girl in the video as someone separate from me, a fictional character who happens to share my face, and then . . .

I see it. This time, instead of seeing my own seething embarrassment and wanting to cringe my neck flat, I see a different story entirely.

I see the boy, handsome and grinning like he's looked forward to this moment all week. I see the girl, flustered with surprise that they've run into each other outside. I watch them watch each other and imagine the bantering chemistry that bubbles up between them when she *pretends* to be embarrassed. When she pulls away from him, it's coy, not rude. The boy is in on the joke when he gently pulls her back. With that simple gesture, I see through the reality of that moment.

In real life I remember feeling humiliated, like I was nothing compared to the boy everyone was happy to see. But that was only *my* story. From Ivan's perspective, and from anyone else's, that blushing embarrassment could mean anything. It could be a love story. And it is, according to the video description:

**Sorry ladies! Looks like VANE made his Wizzcon return with a new gf on his arm! Does anyone recognize his mystery girl? DM us, anon or not!**

The group on the floor scrambles to their feet to get a better look at me. I've been stared at a lot today, but this is the first time I feel like they're doing it out of curiosity and not contempt.

"*That's* why he was waiting for her to arrive today," Chaz explains, right as Kavi walks over to see what the fuss is about.

"Oh my god, I'm so sorry," the girl I remember looking at Ivan in the lounge earlier apologizes. "When you told me to back off on Ivan I didn't know it was because he was taken. My bad, totally my bad."

"Were you guys seriously not going to tell anyone?"

"Wait, did he just come out of your room?"

"It's so cute how he switched seats so you can sit together."

"What's your name again? And wait, okay, back up; I *need* to know how long you've been together because I had this theory . . ."

I don't have a response for whatever the hell is happening right now, but I have to get a handle on it before it becomes another interpretation of me that I can't control. I'm so close to being stuck again, written by another hand, or many, many hands. When the only writer who should matter is me.

"I'm Zora," I begin. And why not sell it with a smile? "And yeah, you got me. I'm Ivan Hunt's girlfriend."

# CHAPTER NINE

I WISH I could predict which version of myself will emerge in times of crisis. There's the Zora from this afternoon, who publicly melted down under the pressure of, and let me check my notes here, saying *hello* to a camera one time. Then there's the Zora who took less than forty-five minutes to pull together a war council at the twenty-four-hour diner I found a few blocks down from the dorm. The first Zora? Not that helpful, but it's not like I bring her out on purpose. The second? She's the part of me that stays prepared for the worst because she wakes up every day expecting it to happen. I believe they call this anxiety.

This is not to say that I expected to end the first day of academy orientation with a monster-sized Ivan Lie that I can't take back. It is to say that the uncomfortable flutters I felt in my stomach the moment I laid eyes on Ivan this afternoon were definitely onto something. Second Zora wouldn't have helped him with those bottles. She would have kicked him out of her room and told him to get lost, margarita mix and all.

But she didn't show up to work on time, and now I'm here, dealing with First Zora's stupid little problems.

"You told them you were *what*?" Ivan's voice cracks at the peak of his disbelief. "What is wrong with you?" Make that First Zora's stupid big problems. Problem, really. Singular.

"What's wrong with me?" I snap back. "It's not like you left me with a ton of options!"

"Options for what? You didn't have to do anything."

"You're right," I sarcastically agree with an eye roll of planetary proportions, "I should have let you *Alien* face-hug me into a wall and breathe into my mouth in front of half the class with no explanation whatsoever."

"I only did it because your butterfingers couldn't hold on to an empty bottle."

"These butterfingers shot the horse out from under your butt in the match today, if I remember correctly."

"It was a unicorn, and he was important to me," Ivan huffs. "Felt like *Ghost of Tsushima* all over again."

"Don't you dare bring Nobu into this." I hate that I'm a little impressed that Ivan got that far in *Ghost*. It's one of my favorite single-player games, and I'd usually give someone major cool points for admitting they played, but not this time. And as always, big RIP to Nobu the horse. "Do *not* go there."

"Don't you mean don't go there, 'boyfriend'?" Ivan snaps.

"This is why they believed her, by the way." Trieu's voice snips the ever-tightening cord of tension between Ivan and myself. My stomach flutters cease in an instant, the butterflies suddenly confronted with increased gravity. "Like, you hear it too, right?"

"No, totally," Kavi agrees and gently guides me back into a seated position next to her in the diner booth.

"Hear what?" I ask.

"Nothing," yawns Trieu.

"Don't worry about it," says Kavi.

Kavi was my first war council recruit, though it's more accurate to say she recruited herself. After I somewhat impulsively told everyone Ivan and I have been dating for months, she all but tackled me back through my dorm room door citing "girl talk" again, which got me away from the crowd, where I could breathe and come up with a plan.

Trieu was my second recruit. He knows everybody, he's clearly a hell of a lot smarter than he chooses to let on, and, if I'm being honest, I needed a guy to intercept Ivan on the he/him floor before he returned to the party. Also no one else here likes me.

Cass did not pick up his phone, sort of. I didn't actually call him because talking on the phone is not normal behavior, but I did text him a few times. I texted him a lot, actually. Like ten times, but with no response to any of them. I hope when he wakes up he finds this funny instead of creepy, and by "this" I mean the entire situation I've gotten myself into. Just everything, all of it.

And yeah, I also have Ivan. I am devastated beyond belief that he showed up at the diner freshly showered, initially unbothered, and on time, because I'd love another couple reasons to despise him. I am capable of admitting that I need Ivan's help; I'll never admit to being happy to see him.

But I'm seeing him. Right now, in this moment. Sitting across from me in a booth seat held together with duct tape and hope, where his wet hair drips a little at the tips and looks much darker than it does in the daylight. Inky black instead of that shiny coffee-bean brown with highlights that look like a zoomed-in photo of a cocker spaniel's coat. And the scent I smelled while we were in close quarters is stronger now, cleaner. Nicer, uncut with street and sweat beyond what's mixing with the droplets from his hair and just now starting to run down the side of his neck—Good GOD, when I find out which part of my brain is coming up with this shit, I'm putting it in time-out for life.

"Two Cokes, a ginger ale, and a water?" The overnight waitress drops off four frosty glasses and a handful of paper-wrapped straws on the table.

"Thanks so much." Ivan sits up straighter and leans up to get a look at her name tag. "I'm Ivan, by the way. And your name is . . . Yekaterina?" He says it with a hint of an Eastern European accent, correct enough to gain points for trying but goofy enough to coax a laugh out of her. She smiles; he smiles back, brilliant and charming. "That's my mom's name."

"Really?"

"Yep. When I was little I thought it was the prettiest name ever. Still do."

"Aw." Yekaterina's face softens. It makes her look younger. "You're a sweetie, Ivan. If you need anything else, call me Kat," Yekaterina says, before leaving us to our drinks.

I wonder if he ever gets tired of performing. I know what it's like to keep a mask up so people don't think I'm nearly as weird as I feel inside, but his universal sweetheart act must take at least as much effort as my totally-normal-nothing-to-see-here show. And he doesn't need to do it for neurodivergent reasons. He just does it because he's manipulative.

*And I'm not?* a little voice, call her Zora 2.1, pipes up in the back of my head. *He's as trapped in my lie as I am. In this story I wrote to save myself.*

"Ivan." I grab my ginger ale and deliberately take a sip without a straw, allowing the ice-cold sugar to zap me awake teeth-first. "I need you to do something you've never done before."

"What is it?" Ivan's drink is water with extra ice. I award no points for his dedication to staying hydrated.

"I need you to put yourself in my shoes. A girl's shoes."

"Excuse—"

"Shush. You are you, Ivan Hunt," I continue. "People here know you, and for some reason I cannot begin to fathom, they are genuinely interested in your behavior. I am me. Just Zora. I am a total unknown, and the only reason people know my name is because I screwed up their first chance to endear themselves to the . . . ," I trail off. What's the word I'm looking for? Onlookers, but worse. Fandom, but derogatory. "Niche internet micro-celebrity microcosm of Wizzard diehards whose opinions determine our fate here, apparently, and for reasons I hate."

"Next time, just say nerds," Trieu points out. "We'll be here all night."

"Regardless of intention or how we got there, you and me, in the hallway with the wall and everything. It looked suggestive."

"Quite suggestive." Kavi backs me up again. "And Zora's hair is huge, so nobody could see what was going on behind all that. Just saying, you two looked cozy."

"That was not my intention," Ivan says quietly. Is that a note of apology in his voice? Nah, he must have a spot of brain freeze.

"*Regardless* of intention," I repeat. "By the time you left—carrying my backpack, which also looked a little weird—everyone around us had already made up their minds about what just happened. They cornered me."

"Uh-huh." Ivan takes another sip of water. "Cornered you into inventing a fake relationship that stretches back six months?"

"Only because someone pulled up a video of us together at Wizzcon, which was, count it with me, six months ago!" I explain. "You know, when you pretended to be dating me for a substantially dumber reason?"

"Wait, *what*?" Trieu turns in his seat dramatically, facing Ivan. "You didn't say anything about that."

"That is what we call 'burying the lede,'" Kavi adds. "What? I deal with PR people all the time. I know journalist lingo."

"I had kind of forgotten about Wizzcon," Ivan admits.

"Literally an hour ago we were talking about Wizzcon in my room."

"You right," Ivan admits again, this time truthfully.

Then, Yekaterina returns with a plate of fries we didn't order and places it between our drinks. "Another table didn't want these," she explains. "So they're yours now. On the house."

Ivan handles the niceties that come after an offer of free food, the are-you-sures and couldn't-possiblys, before he accepts what's offered on our behalf and she walks away. While they're talking I remember how hungry I am. Evening sushi with Cass feels like a lifetime ago. I try to grab a fry, but instantly recoil like I've been struck by a diner cobra. These fries are fresh and hot. There's no way Yekaterina had enough time to order them for a table, bring them over, find out they weren't wanted, and decide to give them to us without them losing some temperature. Suspicion confirmed. There was no other table. This lady just fired an order of fries solely because Ivan's mommy shares her name and he made her smile. And now he's smirking again.

"What's so funny?" I ask.

"Nothing's funny," he replies, with a chuckle.

"Something's funny," I press on.

"Fine." Ivan yanks the plate of fries closer to his and Trieu's side of the table. "It's just . . . my mom's name is Donya."

No wonder he's confused when I don't fawn all over him. From Ivan's perspective, I am a broken chatbot—spitting out negative responses to prompts he uses to great effect in every other encounter with similar software. I look back at the fries. Yeah, I'm not eating those. I'd feel dirty taking part in Ivan's fry lie. French Lies?

"So wait." Kavi slides the fries back toward us. "Hold up. Ivan. You came in here guns blazing like Zora was out of line for pretending you were dating, but *that's* what you were doing in that video?"

"Not to this degree!" Ivan argues.

"Still counts," Trieu adds apologetically. "Gotta be honest, I was Team Ivan coming in here, but no, you're both nuts. Talk about matching each other's freak." He pauses to breathe around a bite of fries—should have warned him they were hot. "I kinda love it."

“Me too.” Now that Trieu has broken the fry seal, Kavi moves to shake the table’s bottle of ketchup over the whole plate. Ugh, I hate when people put sauce on things willy-nilly. Now all the flavors are touching, and I have to pretend like it’s fine. I’m fine! Comparatively, this is fine. “Trieu, are you thinking what I’m thinking?”

“Yup.” Trieu eats another fry. “I think we could do it. You and me? No problem.”

“I mean, it would be a challenge, but we’re not starting from nothing here. This is Ivan Hunt we’re talking about.”

“Literally what is happening right now?” I ask. I’m lost again at my own war council.

“What’s happening is there’s really only one way to fight a rumor,” Trieu begins.

“With the truth?” I offer hopefully.

“What? No. What are you, five? You fight a rumor with another, more interesting rumor. Or, in this case—”

“You own it.” Kavi picks up the idea and runs with it. “Double down. It’s your rumor world, and you have to start living in it. Harness the power of the rumor. Control it. Mold it to your ambitions.”

“We’re still talking about the dating thing, right? Not, like, the Sith?”

“Same difference,” mutters Ivan. “Anyway, they’re right. Whatever both of us did to get here is irrelevant. If we show up tomorrow saying we’re not actually dating, I look like a girl-eating jerk again. I’ve come too far to slide back down there, reputation-wise.” Has he?

“We need to be dating tomorrow; it’s simple as that,” Ivan says, like anything about that is simple. Like he didn’t even give a second thought to the idea of using me to launder his reputation. But that's not how this is going to work. I am not a two-legged aura cleanse whose proximity grants a "totally not misogynist" buff to problematic white boys.

"Agreed," says Kavi. "Zora, what do you say?"

Gee, I don't know. What does one say in this situation? There is no fake-dating primer out there for me to download and peruse before making an informed decision. Obviously part of me thinks it's a terrible idea, but there's another part that remembers the way Brian Juno sized me up onstage, like he wanted to flip through the contents of my mind to determine if I was a good witch or a bad witch. What's odd is that even after my disqualification, I don't think he's decided which kind of witch I am. Yet.

All I know is Brian and Ivan have history. Positive history, considering how Brian openly favored him before today's match. If anything will change Brian's mind about me, it's allying with Ivan. So again, what does one say in this situation? Maybe it's easier to think of it like writing a cutscene. What comes next in the story? Got it. It's this:

"I'm not against the idea in theory," I admit. "I just want to be clear on what *I'm* getting out of this."

"Of course you do," Ivan scoffs. Really?

"What you get is a cheat code. A shortcut," Trieu explains. I think back to what Cassius told me earlier today, about my uncle Clive. *I get why he'd maybe have a thing against shortcuts*.

"Right now you're at the bottom of the academy food chain. Ivan and, let's face it, people like me and Kavi are much closer to the top."

And that is something else that's bothering me about this. I invited Trieu and Kavi to the war council, but mostly for advice on how to kill the rumor I started. I don't understand what they get out of helping me keep it alive. I make that my next question.

"Believe it or not, but this was kind of our strategy coming in," Kavi says.

"What?" I ask. "Your strategy was to wait for a complete social media Luddite to freak out in front of Brian so she gets disqu—"

"I need to stop you there," Trieu says sharply, but not unkindly. "But you talk in legit paragraphs, and if we let you start describing things, I repeat, we will be here. All. Night."

"Fair."

"Obviously Trieu and I have collabed before, but we've been trying to scout two or three other people to form a pod within the academy." Kavi eats another fry. Her nonchalance is admirable, but unlike Ivan it doesn't feel like a performance. She's just good at this, at conveying her thoughts in order. Maybe she's born with it. Maybe it's media training. "We'd keep an eye on each other, work together, cross-post to each other's accounts, co-stream, all that jazz. At least until the final week."

Ivan breaks the silence he's kept up for a few moments to heave a loud sigh. "Teamwork makes the dream work," he quotes solemnly. Very original.

"I mean, think about it." Kavi ignores Ivan. "The thing about battle royales is that you can't actually win them alone."

That doesn't ring true at all, but Kavi presses on.

"Katniss in *Hunger Games*," she says. "How did she win?"

I think about it for a moment. "She made alliances."

"The students in *Battle Royale*. How did they survive?"

"They formed an alliance."

"*Squid Game*?"

"They— Wait, no. That one doesn't work at all."

"Then it's a good thing we're not in *Squid Game*," Kavi concludes, arms crossed across her chest.

This was not how any of this was supposed to go. I was supposed to stay in my lane, start strong on the concrete work of winning, and keep my eyes on that number one win with Cassius at the end of the summer. I was supposed to be enjoying my first night away from home, a seventeen-year-old in New York City with minimal supervision and all the sushi she could eat. One *GLR* match, one party, a backpack full of bottles, and one massive internet coincidence later, I'm here. *Everything happens too much*, I think. *I wish today were over.*

Two blocks away or twenty, the long toll of a church bell rings loud enough for the sound to pass through the diner's glass windows. I guess that's the noise my wishes make when they come true. It's midnight. Today is over, and I'm starting my tomorrow in a diner with three strangers, two of whom I'm pretty sure are about to turn my problems into their personal summer renovation project, and one of whom is Ivan.

I look up at him again and see in his face that he's not kidding about going through with this. A fake relationship so neither of us spends the rest of the summer doing damage control on account of his green eyes and my big mouth.

"Please, Zora," he says quietly. "Give me another chance."

He is not begging; he'd never beg. But for the tiniest second, between the "please" and my name, I see something new. VANE's mask just slipped—there!—and behind it, the real Ivan Hunt waved hello. He is cleaner and he smells good, but he is just as young and exhausted and, let's face it, desperate as me. That desperate boy doesn't perform for no reason. He does it because it makes people like him, because he needs that, and it obviously works. Kavi and Trieu are literally enjoying the fries of his emotional labor.

I rub my eyes. God, I'm so *tired*. When I look back, Ivan's mask is back up, but my memory of what's behind it lingers like the phantom toll of the last twelve o'clock bell.

There must be a Third Zora in here somewhere. A secret Zora, one that left her tools out for someone like Ivan to find and use them to widen the tiniest of cracks in my defenses. I can only imagine how smug he'd be if he knew she existed and that he was making progress. I make a mental note here, right now, to never let him know. If we're going to fool the world, we have to perform like pros. Top of the leaderboard, the best to ever do it. So let's do it.

"Fine." I pick up the longest fry I can find and bite it clean in half. "But I'm not doing it for you. And we need to have some rules."

# CHAPTER TEN

THIS IS HOW we're going to play the game. Think of us like a party of adventurers in *Dungeons and Dragons*. I haven't played *DnD* with other people, that's what *Baldur's Gate 3* is for, but the concept is the same. The game has rules, we all have roles, we work together, and I swear to god if I have to explain this *one* more time, I will toss Ivan down a manhole and forget which one. So let's run this back.

1. Cass is in the party. He may have missed the diner meeting, but when I woke up a few short hours later, I'm the one who had, like, five missed calls and a text message chain I had to scroll way far up to read. At first he thought someone had taken my phone; then he realized it was me but thought I was kidnapped and posting under duress; then he realized I was (sort of) in my right mind and asked all the questions I assumed he would. Like "was that literally the only thing you could think of," "is this

what's going to happen every time I leave you alone for, like, ten minutes," and "How? How? What? Why? Zora. Zora! How?" And, listen . . . he's got a point. The good news is that he's not a snitch and he sees the logic in forming an alliance.

2. The alliance is built around what we have come to describe as "Zivan." That's me and Ivan. We are Zivan, and Zivan is us. While the structural integrity of Zivan is paramount, it cannot and will not be our only gimmick. This is as much about Kavi, Trieu, and Cass as it is about Ivan and me, so whatever story we're telling this summer will have to involve all characters.
3. Characters, Roles, and Expectations:
    - Ivan is our paladin. The shining hero, the good guy whose shield of pre-existing fandom hype and sword of Being a Hot White Guy lends all of us an aura of belonging. To borrow from the Emilia and Jake playbook, Ivan the paladin has a thing for girls who can kick his ass and now he thinks the sun shines out of mine.
        - Upon joining our party, Ivan gains a +10 "Changed My Ways" boost that mimics the abilities and reputation of a much less aggravating class.
    - Trieu is the wizard. He is in charge of maintaining the illusions that surround the party. We will wear what he tells us to wear, pose where he wants us to pose, post what he wants us to post, and I, specifically, will subject myself to his

polymorphic powers until I prove I can cast the spells on my own. Basically he gets to do my makeup, and I can't complain about it, and the only way out is learning to do it myself.

    - Upon joining the party, the wizard gains a Staff of Command, which summons a chosen party member to act as a model for his *Guardians League Royale*–themed makeup tutorials—now with special guest stars!

- Kavi is the rogue—she who works behind the scenes. She exploits the cheat code at the center of the game: that *appearing* popular and famous is the first step to actually *being* popular and famous. She has connections to the influencer marketing departments at companies most people could only dream about contacting, and if we start making content that looks important, people will start believing we are.
    - Upon joining the party, Kavi gains a buff that increases her range of influence beyond the bounds of her base power set. Aka, Kavi gets to dangle the rest of us in front of her followers and therefore expand her target demographic. This mostly applies to Ivan, since she already knows Trieu and I'm not cool enough to make a difference yet.
- Cass is a fighter, subclass TBD. He does what he wants. I can't ask him to do any more than that. This is my mess, my party. I hope at least he's happy to be invited. I know I'm happy to

have one person here who knows who I really am. Even as I take on the role of . . .

- Zora the barbarian. My stats skew toward strength and survivability, so even though the rest of the party is starting at a much higher level than me in this game, I'm still carrying a lot of the weight. Half of the weight, to be exact. Brian Juno may have disqualified my win, but everyone who played in that first match knows what a beast I can be on the field. I don't know how the Wizz-Algorithm works, but I do know *GLR*. I will teach my party members, train them in the art of battle. Share my strength to keep them in the part of the game we can concretely control.
    - What I gain upon joining the party is a fake boyfriend who gives me a fighting chance to win Brian Juno over to my side. That is my win state of this game, so I'll play it by these rules to make sure I get his good ending. And since Brian writes the endings, that makes him the Dungeon Master whether he knows it or not. His game, his rules, my victory.

It is Wednesday, and our party's first session starts now. Is everybody ready? No? Too bad. Roll for initiative.

"I think we need a name," Kavi suggests. "Something to make us feel more like a team."

"We're not a team," I say. "We're a party."

"Party, not team." Ivan overlaps my thought as he adjusts the collar of his T-shirt in the dressing room mirror. "Get out of my head, Zora."

"Can't," I snap back. "Without me in there, your chances of ever having a good idea fall ever farther below zero. We're talking negative numbers. Big ones."

"Well, if that's how it's going to be, I changed my mind. I can't do this," Ivan says with a dramatic huff.

Trieu, Kavi, Cass, and I go silent. Is he kidding? He better be kidding. Half this thing was his idea, maybe! Honestly after the whirlwind of Monday's disaster, Tuesday's continued player orientation, and this morning's crack-of-dawn wake-up call to get me—us, get *us*—ready for today's open scrimmage, I've forgotten who had which idea when. All I know is if Ivan thinks he can change his mind now, I'll . . . I don't know. He can't. It would be a huge dick move. Which, to be fair, I should have expected considering who I'm talking about here.

"What do you mean you changed your mind?" Trieu replies sharply. For all the energy in his words, his delicate grasp on the mascara spoolie he holds a millimeter from my eye remains steady. I don't know how Trieu knew there were actual dressing rooms in the other wing of the Wizzard Theater. I do know that we're probably not supposed to be using one as a staging area to prepare ourselves for the academy's first open lunch—a spectacle wherein selected content creators in the *GLR* fandom are invited to meet and mingle with us as players. I also know that Trieu does not care if we're allowed, it's better to ask forgiveness than permission, and that as nerve-racking as open lunch sounds, it's the perfect moment for Ivan and me to hard launch ourselves as a *GLR* power couple to the exact demographic of people who care. Or it was, until Ivan apparently *changed his mind*.

"I'm not cut out for the role," Ivan begins. I feel a flare of heat on the back of my neck. It's nerves or rage, too early to tell which. Kavi has stopped fussing with her eyebrows, her hand frozen in place by her forehead. Even Cass has stopped spinning on a stool by the door. "I don't think I can be . . . or even pretend to be"—Ivan pauses for effect—"a paladin. I think I'm more of a bard."

Our sighs of relief almost harmonize. Ivan's mirrored eyes glance toward the rest of us as he laughs. "Just breaking the tension. Feels like we're about to go to a funeral, not a meet and greet."

"That was a very bard joke," Cassius observes. "Motion to reroll Ivan's class from holy hero to comic relief whose main job is to fool people into thinking he's serious?"

"Seconded," I say. "I like that metaphor a lot better."

"Thirded. Stay still." Trieu unscrews the lid from a pot of lip gloss and scrapes a clean brush across its holographic, glittery surface.

"If we're enough of a team where our metaphorical class distinctions matter, then we're enough of a team to merit a name," Kavi says.

"*Phh-tmmm*," I mumble behind closed lips.

"Party," Cass translates. "But I agree with Kavi. A name makes it official. Binds us together."

You know what else bound people together? The One Ring. And look what that did to the Fellowship.

I'm not against giving this alliance a name in principle, but— No, wait. Yes I am. I am so much more comfortable going along with this when I view it from the distance of utility. Hence, convoluted *DnD* party metaphors. Teams are composed of people who work together for a group win. Parties are individuals with goals that dovetail until they don't. It's a small but crucial difference. If I'm going to win this thing, at the end of the day I'll have to do it alone.

Two things have me feeling a way about this. The first was the rest of player orientation on Tuesday, which thankfully separated all the five of us into different groups, so I didn't have to elaborate much on the Ivan Lie. I could tell that some wanted to ask—there were ten players in my group, and one of them was Chaz—but it's hard to be nosy when a Wizzard intern is leading your group through getting-to-know-you activities that volunteer plenty of information up front. "Where are you from?" "New Jersey." "What do your parents do?" "Beats me, I live with my uncle." "What does he do?" "Manages a sporting goods store. Very interesting, I know."

All the while, I took mental notes on my competition. Chaz liked to talk about himself, but kept bringing up the possibility of co-streaming with two other players in my group. Those players, Payton and Paxton, have an absurd amount of followers on WiTch, but their page is shared. Our new pages made for the academy competition are not. "That's gotta be rough," I said to Payton first, then Paxton later. "Are you guys going to try to split your followers or do you think they'll go with whoever streams first or, you know, better?" I could almost hear the geological crack of a fault line developing in their friendship. That oughtta keep them from teaming up, and keep Chaz occupied trying to choose which one's butt to kiss harder.

Some others in my group were just happy to be there. Three at least, by my count. They're not in the academy to win; they're proud of themselves just for getting in, a viewpoint far too psychologically healthy to be a threat to my goals. I belong to the *Guardians* series stan contingent, the deep-cut freaks who have their eye on going pro in the Guardians League or, like me, have their eye on Brian's mentorship. Those are my real competition. Those, and the four other people crammed into this dressing room.

"Team name, team name. What about . . . Team Fury?" Trieu suggests, with a cheeky eye on Ivan's reflection. I smirk at the dig, and Trieu takes advantage of the position to smear cream blush on the apples of my cheeks.

"That's not funny," Ivan says flatly.

"Team Z-TICK?" Cass supplies. "It's our initials."

"That's pretty good." Kavi nods. "If we want to sound like we're selling bug spray." Even though her makeup has been done since this morning, she's preening like a bird in the good dressing room light, touching herself up after this morning's academy presentation.

That presentation was the second reason I know I have to keep my distance. A senior Wizzard writer named Sarah gave a speech on how the core purpose of games is to create and sustain the player fantasy. In the team game *Guardians League Online*, that fantasy is to protect the spoils of an intergalactic gold rush from thine enemies. In *Guardians League Royale*, it's being a savvy space survivalist and dunking on sweats who can't shoot. Everything else—the action, the world, every scrap of text and visual effect—exists to keep that fantasy going. I'd never thought about games that way, as concrete pillars of code supporting something as weightless as an idea. My mind was blown.

After the presentation, someone asked the question I think all of us wanted answered: how did Sarah get started writing for Wizzard? I could have guessed what she'd say: she was a Brian Juno mentee. His first, to be exact, and the reason he started picking one aspiring game writer out of the ether to champion them for the rest of their career. If I play my role right for the next five weeks, I could be Sarah within the next five years. I hold the image of her onstage in my head and imagine myself in her place while Trieu dabs at the corner of my mouth with his pinky finger, removing an errant glob of lip gloss.

"What about Team Fantasy?" This gloss doesn't feel as heavy on my lips as I thought it would be, and it smells delicious. I poke my tongue out to see if it tastes as good as it smells. The answer to that question is no, it does not. Bleh.

"Sounds like an underwear campaign." Trieu sees me try to eat the gloss and gently shakes his head. All right, note taken. He worked hard on my lips, and like most products of artistic endeavors, it's considered rude to lick them.

"I like the concept, though," Ivan says and pulls his phone out of his pocket. That's almost like he's agreeing with me. Feels weird. "It should be something aspirational, something forward-thinking. Something that shows we have—"

"Done!" Trieu exclaims suddenly. He steps back from my chair and swerves from side to side, testing how the light hits my made-up face from different angles. "She was a babe to begin with, but when I'm good, I'm *good*."

Trieu spins me a quarter turn toward the mirror, and my reflection, bright, brown, and beautiful, bounces back into my disbelieving eyes. Which is strange, because I don't look all that different. I expected Trieu to go all out, with flashy eyeliner, fake freckles, and everything else I've seen makeup tutorial streamers do on their own faces, but that's not what he's done for me. It's my own face but glowy, like my skull is made of gold that shines through where the skin is thinnest. My almost-black eyes stand in higher contrast, with whiter whites and curling lashes that make me feel like a cartoon bunny, but not in a terrible way. I blink at myself a few times and feel the slight tickle of my lashes against my eyelids. I smile at Trieu, who smiles back. Then, on an instinct I should really do more to suppress, I check to see Ivan's first reaction.

"Vision," he says, both eyes trained on me. "Team Vision."

"I like it," Cass replies, and I'm not sure he's talking about the name. "Team Vision, I mean," he clarifies, though no one asked him to. "Name good."

I can only nod my agreement; I'm busy getting acquainted with the lady in the mirror. Her face looks capable of things I've never tried to do. Like being coy, for one. I flutter my eyelashes, just to test the theory. *How did Ivan and I meet? Ask him, he tells the story* so *much better.* Needs work, but with a little practice I think it could be convincing. How about a cheeky smile? *Oh, Ivan, you are incorrigible.* That's not as hard since it's true and he is. Now let's try humble surprise: eyes wide, brows up. *Of course I'll be your mentee, Mr. Juno!* Not bad, not bad at all.

Before my silent face journey can get awkward, Trieu's phone blasts out the staccato opening beats of the siren diss track from *Hades 2*. What's the name of that song again? I'm about to ask Trieu when he starts scooping up all the makeup he spread out on the dressing room counter. "That's five, let's get a move on."

"Thank you, five." Ivan's attention predictably returns to his own reflection for one last futzy moment involving the way his bangs fall over his forehead. I stand up and shake my own hair out—Trieu can do makeup, but it's more than I can ask of a Vietnamese stylist to learn how to do Black hair in a week, though he did offer to try.

"Aren't you forgetting something?" Cassius asks me. He mimes holding a camera in front of his face and clicks his tongue like a shutter. "For Clive."

"Oh, right." I told Clive I'd send him some pictures after orientation. "Kavi, can you come in for a selfie?"

"Oh, for sure, for sure."

I laugh in earnest. I'm not the only one who noticed Chaz has a catchphrase, and Kavi has an uncanny ability to mimic his tone.

"Our first selfie as Team Vision?" Trieu asks, excited.

"Nope, just girls," I explain. "My, uh . . . my uncle thinks I'm at an all-girls coding camp right now."

I hear Ivan snort from his place by the door. "And *I'm* the one who's full of it?"

Suddenly, for reasons I don't have to interrogate, I remember the name of that song. It's "I Am Gonna Claw (Out Your Eyes then Drown You To Death)." A Darren Korb classic.

Kavi comes in for the picture and takes the phone from my hands. I surrender it willingly; she's known me for two days and has a much stronger eye for my angles than I do. It's odd seeing Mirror Zora on the screen, but for once my wide-eyed confusion comes across photogenically. After taking a few pictures, Kavi taps straight into my messages and sets up a Team Vision group chat.

"Send it to all of us," she instructs. "We should take a few more today and cross-post to our WiTch accounts after the meet and greet. Presents a united front."

Sure, but before I do that, I have to text Clive.

*Hey unc, two days in and I already let my roommate talk me into a makeover. Ready for my close-up! Miss u.* Attach photo. Nerd face emoji. Hair flip emoji. Send.

"Okay, we're good."

"Team Vision on the move, let's roll." Ivan holds the door open for all of us, letting Trieu guide us like a mother duck through the narrow back halls of the Wizzard's less public-facing wing. Each turn takes us closer to the lounge, through better lit halls, across the crowded lobby, and finally through the double doors that lead to the Wizzard Theater's premiere performance space. And I do not mean the stage.

## CHAPTER ELEVEN

"HEY, WHAT'S UP, guys, this is MannyPlays here at the Wizzard Theater in New York Cit-ayyy." A twentysomething-year-old man with a broccoli cut and the rubber-faced enthusiasm of someone with a crippling caffeine addiction and a YouTube channel is sitting next to me on a couch. He's not talking to me as much as he is saying loud words at the lens of his camera setup while Ivan and I are both in blisteringly close earshot.

The last time I was in the players' lounge at the Wizzard Theater was at Wizzcon, and for a moment I'm not sure if it's still the same room. Six months ago every beanbag chair, every table and chair, every packaged snack and soda can set front-facing in the glass refrigerators was themed around Wizzard's actual games.

Now every item in the room is sponsored by some company or another in a horrendously discordant display. The chairs are printed with the logo of a VPN provider, and the couches are trying to sell me a new pair of headphones. The fridges are stuffed with an unreleased flavor of carbonated cold brew, and there are QR codes printed on banners that promise free tokens for new users of a sports betting app. It's all so ugly I almost flinch. One look over at Ivan tells me he's grossed out as well. Is this how Brian wants to use the academy? As a backdrop for cramming as many ads as possible into the retinae of everyone's combined followers?

"Relax," Ivan says without moving his lips an inch out of place from a toothy grin. I remind myself to add amateur ventriloquy to the list of skills Makeup Zora needs to pick up.

"I am relaxed," I mutter back. Thankfully MannyPlays hasn't given us personal mics, or rather he tried until he realized I was wearing a hilariously expensive jumper (Kavi borrowed it from a friend's older sister's job's sample sale). I had the choice between letting him unzip me to run a cord behind my bra and me taking his arm off like Beowulf; he should think about changing his name to Grendel.

"If you want to see more live-streamed content like this, don't forget to smash that like button and subscribe with notifications so you get an alert every time I post a new video and to get reminders for my weekly streaming schedule—"

"Okay," Ivan says again. "Then could you maybe stop squeezing my hand like a stress ball?"

I look down at my lap, where my hand is in fact holding his very tightly. It was Ivan's idea to hold hands when we sat down. No, wait. It was mine. Or, no, it kind of just happened; I don't know. It seemed like the right thing to do at the time. But now the tension in my fingers is turning his knuckles whiter; I try to wrench my hand away.

"Nup-up." Ivan holds my hand fast in his. "That part we have to do." He thinks for a moment, while MannyPlays continues to get through his intro, somehow. I don't think this man-ny has even stopped to take a breath since he started. "Unless you're uncomfortable with the contact. I won't—we don't—only if, you know, consent and—"

"It's fine," I say, mostly to get him to stop talking. Ventriloquist or not, this is Ivan's first video appearance since he disappeared after the *Guardians League Online* championship last year. His fans, and his not-so-fans, will be observing the heck out of his behavior. *And mine*, I realize. I wonder how many times I'm going to have to remember to act like I'm being watched before it's second nature. I look at Ivan again; this time he catches my glance and winks, face cheated at just the right angle so the affectionate gesture plays toward the camera.

"And of course to support the channel even more, there's a link to my Patreon in the description; paying subscribers get access to all kinds of awesome perks like early access to my streams, discounts on my merch drops . . ."

Actually, on second thought, no. I deliberately remove my hand from Ivan's and watch his fingers flex the moment I stop touching him. He must be relieved I've stopped squeezing.

"—and you even get to vote on which topics and players I cover every week including this surprise-drop power couple here to take Brian Juno's summer academy by storm! To start off with the obvious, VANE's back! That's right. What's up, man?" Manny holds his hand out for a high five, which Ivan uses his newly freed hand to slap. I tuck mine under my thigh and remember to keep smiling no matter what.

When I said "no matter what," I actually meant "until my brain crashes out halfway through lunch." Nonstop socializing, especially when I know I'm being potentially filmed by everyone in sight, is more hellish than I could have imagined. I am grumpy. I am tired, and Trieu is making the most of it by showing off how good my lips look when I'm pouting.

"I mix some of the highlighter into the lip gloss before I put it on," Trieu explains. "You can see the effect better on Kavi and Zora than you can on me." I pop my hip to bring my height down closer to Kavi's level, smooch my lips out obediently, and hear a chorus of clicks from people who don't know how to silence the sound effects on their phones.

"Make sure you get her good side," Kavi says proudly.

"All she's got are good sides," Ivan bluffs from the sidelines. And I swear to god, someone (not me) actually swoons.

"How do you spell your name again?" another amateur photographer asks.

"Zora like from Zelda," I say, "and Lyon like the city in France."

"Cool name," they reply.

"You have no idea," Ivan interrupts again, "how cool she really is."

My stomach flips, and I feel a familiar anger creep up to redirect my thoughts toward dislike. I know Ivan has to say nice things about me, but the more he compliments me and the more sincere he sounds, the more I hear the lie underneath it all.

"She's an incredible player too; just wait for the match later."

He must be making fun of me. That's how he's so good at this—he's turning me into a joke where only he knows the punch line. Why else would he be laying it on so thick?

My jaw hurts, which makes sense considering I've now spent two hours alternating between a huge fake grin and clamping my jaw so tight I could bite a chunk of coal and spit out diamonds.

Next to me, on another branded couch, with his hand on my knee and barely a droplet of sweat showing on his pearly skin, Ivan snort-laughs.

"My favorite thing about Zora? I mean, look at her, she's beautiful. But she also makes me laugh." He sighs dreamily. I lock my eyes at a spot on the wall to stop them from rolling. We're not even on camera this time, just chatting with some influencer while Kavi and Trieu shoot some B-roll around the room. Chatting and now standing so close together that I'm surprised the rules of surface tension haven't merged all the water in our bodies into one warm, angry droplet.

"Babe?" Ivan asks, his thumb brushing over my shoulder softly. I try not to shudder away from its phony comfort.

"Sorry, what?" It's harder than I thought, to pay attention and make right faces in the right order.

"I said you'd never forgive me if I went easy on you in *GLR*."

I can't stop myself laughing. I don't care if it's the right response or not. Ivan going easy on me? Is that the narrative everybody wants to read here? Hate that. Pass the game script; I'm doing a rewrite.

“That’s true, I wouldn’t forgive you,” I say. “But it’s not like I’m worried.”

“And why is that?” I can’t remember this influencer’s name. It’s Dennis.

“I knocked *him* out of the running for the academy at Wizzcon,” I reply. Immediately, I see panic rise up in Ivan’s eyes.

“Oh, is that how you two met?” Actually, wait, I think it’s Tom.

“Yep,” I say proudly.

“No!” Ivan says at the same time.

“And, wait, if you didn’t win at Wizzcon, how did you end up in the academy, Ivan?” Finally, Doug (?) is asking the right questions.

“Great question.” I nod. “How exactly did that happen, babe?”

I smirk over at Ivan, thinking this is appropriate revenge for him mocking me all afternoon, but something has changed with him. He’s fidgeting, and his hand is compulsively tucking his hair behind his ear. I don’t know what his problem is, but I’m not going to make it mine. I’m still looking out for number one.

“Excuse us,” Ivan says sharply, ostensibly to Doug, but I know his tone is mostly meant for me. “Great talking to you, Barry.”

Oh, wow, I wasn’t even close.

“That was unkind of you, Zora,” Ivan says the next time Team Vision regroups in the kitchen area.

"Maybe," I admit. "Wouldn't want you to think I was 'going easy on you,' though." Trieu is dusting at my jawline with a kabuki brush, so he's close enough that I hear the frustrated hiss he otherwise tries to suppress.

"What's the problem?" Kavi asks. "We were doing so well!"

"The jerk store called and they're out of her," Ivan grumbles. That was toothless, even for him.

"You do realize—wait! We got a bogie on our six." I notice a not-so-sneaky someone pointing their phone in our direction and straighten up.

"That's our three," Ivan corrects me. "Six would be behind you."

"Shut up and do what we practiced in the lounge."

On cue, we all fake a laugh in case they're recording something. Look at us, the cool kids. Cool kids being cool friends, cooling the day away.

"He's gone," Cassius calls out. I shake my hair out and continue the extremely sick burn I've cooked up for Ivan.

"You do realize," I start again, "that if the jerk store is calling you about a supply chain issue, it's because *you* are a jerk wholesaler late on delivery. In which case"—I clear my throat—"not only is your chosen business built on you generating a surplus of jerk, but you are also failing to fulfill your contractual obligations. Hell yeah, got 'em!" I hold my hand up for a high five, which Kavi discourages with a shake of her head in Cass's direction. He obeys and leaves me hanging.

"Has anyone ever told you that you talk like a serial killer in a movie?" Ivan continues. "Because you talk like a serial killer in a movie."

"No, nobody has ever told me that." I plop down on a kitchen stool, suddenly feeling the exhaustion I earned with Kavi's early wake-up call.

"What are you, a cyclops?" Ivan asks, trying and failing to keep his voice to a whisper. "'*Nobody has ever told me that*.' I am telling you that! Right now!" He stomps off; thankfully the crowd in the lounge is thinning out as today's action moves toward the theater.

We still have a *GLR* match to play today—the first one that will actually count toward our Wizz-Algorithm rankings now that our accounts are unlocked. I need something to perk me up or else I'm going to get grumpier, if possible.

"Gotta say, I don't get you." Trieu finishes buffing my face. "There are people who would pay money to hear Ivan Hunt say the kinds of things he said about you today."

"Like what?" I say, resisting the urge to touch my face again. I'm a good model, I promise.

"*Hello, world, have you met Zora? She's so beautiful and funny and talented, and I want to hold her hand and gaze into her eyes all day.*" Trieu's Ivan impression could use some work. I do not tell Trieu this.

"Come on, he doesn't mean any of it." I can't believe I have to explain that to Trieu, our wizard. He of all people should know how much work goes into pretending to be someone other people want to watch, let alone act like they're in love with.

"Sure he doesn't." He zips his makeup bag closed again. "For sure, for sure. We need to be in the theater in ten minutes."

"Give me five of those, please."

"She said five," Cass echoes and herds Trieu and Kavi toward the double doors across the room. That boy is an angel. I set my elbows on the kitchen counter and prop my head up on my fists. The more I think about Ivan, the more time I spend around so many people, the more tired I get. The least I can do for myself is sit in the lounge as it empties out—who knows, maybe someone will take a picture of lonely little Zora sitting alone and get a poignant candid that makes me look extra relatable. Maybe I should get into a better pose for that. I'll cross my ankles to be more ladylike, sit up and pin my shoulder blades together like Kavi told me to do for pictures. Spin around on the stool a little and— *FREEZING!*

Something icy presses up against my exposed back, making me shriek and twist around to see what frozen hell I've summoned in this jumpsuit.

"Gotcha."

Ivan holds two Red Bulls pebbled cold with condensation. One of them has a shiny splotch in the middle of the narrow can where he pressed it up against my back.

"Thought that would wake you up." He places the can I've already claimed back-first on the counter in front of me.

"Do I look that tired?" I ask.

"Not to the rest of them," he says and cracks his can open, then mine for me. "But just now, the jerk store thing."

"Ivan, I—" I'm not sorry.

"You were talking in paragraphs again, which you only do when you're actually upset. At least I think it's only when you're upset. You're always upset when I'm around."

"It's not just you this time." I grab my Red Bull and look at it. Sniffing it would probably be insulting. But how else can I test for poison? "It's everything. The lights, the noise, the people, the questions, the talking, the scrutiny, the comments."

It's called autistic overwhelm, and I am deep in its grip. But Ivan doesn't need to know that.

"Too many people and twice as many eyes." Ivan takes a sip and winces, probably much less familiar than I am with the fizzy sciencefruit strangeness of its flavor.

"What?"

"Too many people and twice as many eyes," he repeats. "Just something I think when I'm here. Or streaming or whatever." He sighs and takes another sip. A gulp, really. I watch his Adam's apple bob up and down when he swallows and note the obvious tension in his neck. He might be allistic, but it's entirely possible that Ivan is as stressed about this as I am. "Kind of like 'don't worry, it's worse than you think.'"

Ivan and I have been attached at the hip for an hour. It's on me that I didn't notice the details that give his game away. The neck tension. The wet darkness under his armpits, disguised by his dark green T-shirt. The massively overdoing everything because one wrong move could tank us both and we kind of forgot to calibrate our front-facing chemistry.

"It's wrong, though," I say. "Not everyone has two eyes. On average it's probably less, depending on the room."

Ivan stares at me a lot, but this time feels different. It's a warm stare; he is amused, and Real Ivan slips out from behind his mask again for a second.

"You," he says, "are so weird."

"You," I reply, "can leave now. Please. The match is in five minutes, I'll see you there."

"Fifteen minutes, actually. Brian is pushing the match."

"How do you know that?" That's two Ivan Mysteries that have come up this afternoon. First is how he got into the summer academy without winning a top two spot in one of the twenty-five *GLR* finals. Second is what the hell is his deal with Brian Juno? Something tells me those two questions are intrinsically related, as are both of their answers.

"Because the auditorium is closed for a lighting test," he answers. "And those take fifteen minutes."

Right. Not everything is about having supersecret inside information. I think about what Trieu said, and the Red Bull in my hand, and Ivan being suspiciously but undeniably kind to me, even after I wasn't nice to him.

Ivan and I have the same goals and are in the same mess. Would it be the worst idea in the world to trust him a little bit?

I mean, yeah. Obviously yes, it would. But if he can start pretending to like me so much, the least I can do is try to pretend back.

# HELLO, IVAN

# CHAPTER TWELVE

IVAN STOOD AT the edge of Brian Juno's VIP viewing box with the tips of his fingers touching a window so huge and clean he kept forgetting it was there. His brain told him that if he leaned forward he'd fall all the way down onto the stage and break his face, but when he tested the hypothesis, the reality of the cool glass met his forehead with a predictable *thonk*. Standing up straight, he saw the decoration his attempt left behind: a foggy sweat stain in the shape of the minimal space between his eyebrows. Art.

Behind him, the rapid-fire clicks of Brian typing on his phone came to an abrupt stop.

"Ivan, please. I just cleaned that window," the cofounder of Wizzard Games said with amusement. When not onstage or doing an interview, Brian's accent sounded much weaker. At first it had surprised Ivan to notice that Brian got noticeably less French Canadian in private conversations, but he'd spent enough time scrolling through fancams of Brian's impeccable suiting, interview zingers, and dance videos performed in the

Wizzard motion capture studio to understand that everything Brian Juno did was part of his effort to procedurally generate a wacky, beloved games industry patriarch also named Brian Juno. And if Brian Juno had actually cleaned the VIP window with his own busy hands, Ivan was a giraffe.

"No, you did not," Ivan corrected him.

"You are right, I did not." Brian's fingers resumed their clicking on the phone screen. "But someone did. Give me two minutes."

Unlike the players' lounge, Brian's VIP box was devoid of branding. It was dark and plushy and personal and red, like the inside of an animal, though the color only came from the light tests the arena team were conducting in the house below. Before Ivan's eyes the light coming through the glass changed to green, and Ivan knew for a moment what it felt like to stand at the bottom of a pristine lake. Then the light turned purple, which reminded Ivan of nothing specific, and red once again.

While he waited, Ivan tried to test his knowledge of the academy's PC arrangement. Ivan had been poring over the seating chart since Tuesday, when Brian sent him the PDF to ensure Ivan knew where each and every student sat and who their neighbors were. Would the information come in handy? Probably not. But Brian expected him to know, so he did.

From the last seat on stage right, Slays Brown's seat was three places in from Matt Travels; clockwise from them sat ShugZ, Payton and Paxton . . . Trieu, Kavi, himself, and Zora.

*Don't think about her*, Ivan demanded of himself. He'd done enough of that today, when he felt her react to everything he said with quiet horror, if not disgust. If he wanted to delude himself, he could say that Zora's upset stemmed from her being mean or naive, because of course he had to pretend to like people he objectively didn't, of course he had to lie on the spot ten times a minute; that's what this whole game was about. But the more uncomfortable she looked, the more visibly tired she became after listening to him talk and talk and talk, Ivan had begun to think that maybe instead of being cruel, Zora was being honest. Zora saw the person Ivan spent his entire life trying to distract other people from noticing, and it was unbearable. He thought about her black eyes constantly, looking straight through him. It didn't help that the girl-sweat-and-shea-butter smell he'd come to associate with her was clinging to him like perfume. The only way to avoid it would be for Ivan to stop breathing, which she honestly might prefer.

What did he *just* say? *Don't. Think. About. Zora.*

So Ivan returned to his brainteaser of a task, imagining the retrieval of information from his brain like stomping through his mind palace and tearing Post-It notes from the walls with more force than was probably necessary.

The next desk onstage belonged to Sola, a triple-threat streamer whom Ivan once considered a friend. She'd ditched him when the Emilia thing happened, once he was no longer a cool kid. Next desk after that was Chaz, and screw Chaz. After him . . . ugh. Ivan knew the next answers, but he gave up on mentally reciting them because somehow, the knowledge bored him more than doing nothing. He sheepishly tacked the Post-Its back on the walls of his brain and crossed his arms in front of his chest.

“Who are you talking to?” he asked Brian, only half expecting an answer.

“Editor of WizzFeed,” Brian replied robotically. Of course. After the scandal of last year’s *Guardians League Online* championship received some small critique from gaming news sites, Ivan had watched from the sidelines as Brian started scooping up a game journalist from one site, an editor and reviewer from another, and so on until he’d built a team large enough to run an entire site dedicated to news about the league. These were the people who took Brian’s suggestions and ran with them, crafting the program’s narrative one post, one video, one on-brand tweet at a time. And when the ethical quandaries involved in covering one’s own company as news clashed against the unprecedented access the WizzFeed writers had to the players themselves, the access won every time.

“Okay, VANE,” Brian said after another few seconds of clicking. Ivan turned around to see him slip his phone into the cupholder of his large, boxy leather recliner. Ivan thought that was Brian’s way of signaling that Ivan had his full attention, but he was simply swapping the phone out for a tablet, which he tapped at intently until a mirror of its screen appeared on all of the viewing suite’s many television screens. “Before we start, you got anything to report?”

Ivan dutifully launched himself away from the window and plopped down into the chair next to Brian’s. That was a mistake. The seat was nowhere near as soft as he expected, clearly some dumb new chair technology from someone who enjoyed modern art and had never sat down once in their life. It felt like he’d tip over the moment he got too comfortable in any direction, which may have been the point. As much as he admired Brian, "comfortable" wasn't a word he'd use to describe their working relationship.

"Couple things," Ivan began. "Someone tried to bring a bunch of booze to the first party after orientation, but I was able to clear it out before anyone could get it on camera."

"Thanks for that. Last thing I need is some kid getting alcohol poisoning on day one."

"No problem." Ivan knew what Brian wanted him to talk about, but it felt better if he led up to the whole Zora thing with some other useful information. It made Ivan feel like these reports were official, like Brian had hired him for a real summer job.

"Hired" was a strong word; "hired" implied that Ivan was getting paid. He wasn't, or at least not in actual money. When Brian approached him after his fiftieth-place loss at Wizzcon and offered him a spot in the summer academy regardless of his in-game performance, obviously Ivan had leapt at the chance. All Ivan had to do was attend the program and keep an eye on everyone on behalf of Wizzard Games. And also to "keep things interesting," no matter what. And to report back so the company couldn't be surprised by any twists in the academy's inevitable inter-player drama.

"Payton and Paxton are fighting," Ivan continued. He withheld the part where he knew it was Zora who sabotaged them. If Brian found out how good she was at stirring up shit, it would be her in his suite twice a week instead of Ivan. "That's something to watch. Friends to rivals or whatever."

"Nice." Brian nodded, far from satisfied. "And . . ."

"And"—Ivan swallowed thinly—"I've picked the front-runners, like you asked." It was far more accurate to say that the front-runners chose him, but Brian didn't need to know that. "Kavi Khurana, Trieu Vu, and Zora Lyon."

"Not Cassius Sharpe?" Brian raised a blond eyebrow. "You don't think the first battle winner is worth looking out for?"

"Nope." Ivan shrugged. "He doesn't have what it takes."

"And yes to Zora Lyon? Number fifty?"

"Yep. Trust me."

"Okay," Brian said with playful skepticism. "Let's see if you're right."

Brian fiddled with the remote until the TV screen showed what Ivan had come to see: the god's-eye view of the Wizz-Algorithm working in real time. Part stock market ticker, part rapidly shifting leaderboard, with every view, comment, like, reaction, and WiTch minute spent on each academy player's profile contributing to their standing in real time. Ivan watched the numbers and names flicker all around them, wondering if this was what it was like to live inside a computer. It was almost too much information for his brain to take in at once, until Brian paused the entire operation with a touch of his finger. The characters on-screen resolved into something more readable. Names, in a list, numbered from one to fifty. Ivan only had to look for five:

#1 Cassius Sharpe

#27 Ivan Hunt

#28 Trieu Vu

#31 Kavi Khurana

#50 Zora Lyon

"This is how we looked this morning, before the open lunch," Brian explained. "Now that your WiTch accounts are open and everyone's been posting . . ." He tapped the screen again, and the names swapped around.

#8 Ivan Hunt

#20 Trieu Vu

#23 Kavi Khurana

#30 Cassius Sharpe

#32 Zora Lyon

Ivan felt a wash of pride. He had been right. With the addition of audience scoring into the Wizz-Algorithm, everyone had trended positively except for Cass.

"Wait a minute." Brian squinted at the screen. "Zora Lyon jumped *eighteen* spots since this morning?"

*So did I,* Ivan thought. *That's not a coincidence.*

"Forget what I said about the Cassius kid; we're going all in on Zora. How did you do it?"

"So." Ivan steeled himself for the big reveal. "We kind of told everyone she's my girlfriend.

With a click, Brian turned off the screens, plunging the room back into red, then blue, then green again. He actually put his tablet down and, for the first time since Ivan entered the room, gave him his full attention.

"You're a genius," Brian said simply. "I knew I could count on you." He leaped up from his seat, clearly too excited to stay in one place, and paced toward the window and back.

"Just your presence was enough to get tongues wagging, but now you're going full romance subplot with one of our unknowns? She has no baggage, no footprint, which means she can be anything we need her to be." Brian brought his fingers to his lips and smooched them wetly. "Chef's. Kiss."

“About that,” Ivan began. No one had to tell Ivan that romance brought eyeballs to the league; he’d had front row seats to the development of the first one. “We’re not really a thing.”

Brian looked at Ivan as if he just told him he’d never learned to read. “You of all people should know it doesn’t have to be a thing to be a thing.”

“I know,” Ivan said. “Like, obviously we’re not really dating, but it wasn’t my idea to fake date her either.”

Brian frowned. “So you’re saying it was her idea?”

“No!” Ivan replied quickly. Honestly, it was a philosophical exercise to determine whose idea it technically was, but he didn’t want to give Zora any credit for surprising him. Again.

“Good.” Brian let out a puff of air in mock relief. “Because if that little girl got the better of you, then I should be talking to her in here, not you.”

The fact that Brian so directly echoed Ivan’s concerns about that topic contributed little to his sense of security.

“She didn’t get the better of me,” Ivan snapped. “I just”—his mind flashed back to two nights ago in Zora’s dorm room, a collection of moments that were colored a tense, dark blue in his memory—“was surprised she went along with it.”

“Why wouldn’t she? It’s a Cinderella story. Famous streamer falls for a nobody, she climbs the ranks, a new power couple emerges, you get your comeback—and your timing couldn’t be better!”

Brian looked expectantly at Ivan, clearly wanting to be asked exactly why said timing couldn’t be better. Ivan stared back patiently, with silence being his only real form of defiance in this situation. Brian stared back. Ivan blinked. Brian blinked back, and Ivan pretended not to notice. Brian blinked again. Finally, after an eternity:

"Wh—"

"Because the captain of our New York *Guardians League Online* team is leaving at the end of the summer." Brian nodded knowingly. "We both know battle royale isn't your bag. If you pull this off, I don't see why one of our biggest stars from the academy couldn't step in and take his spot."

This time, Ivan was silent because he couldn't process what Brian was offering him. Captaining his own team was something he hadn't even considered. It was a pipe dream, something he'd given up on last year when, well . . . when Emilia found out what Team Fury did, left them for Team Unity, and beat them at their own game.

Ivan didn't love thinking about that time, now over a year ago, but with this specific offer on the table, how could he not? Emilia joined Team Fury at the apex of their dominance. Ivan was only one of five players, but their unstoppable record made them the favorites to win the tournament that awarded one team a massive contract to play in the Guardians League. He knew that Emilia was part of that winning formula, but as the tournament progressed, Ivan began to realize she was more than that. She was their secret weapon. Some of his team members didn't like that. They did everything they could to ruin her life—kicked her from the team, put her public information online, and used her relationship with Jake to sic the worst of the internet on her family and friends. And Ivan did nothing to stop them.

At first he tricked himself into believing they were kidding about exposing her. When it was clear they weren't, he tricked himself again by pretending his hands were tied with the tournament contract. He still didn't think they would have listened to him if he had spoken up, but that didn't excuse the part where he didn't try. As far as Emilia knew, and as far as his actions showed, Ivan was just as in on the doxxing as the rest of Team Fury. Honestly, he'd been relieved when they lost. It was karmic, obviously, but part of him hoped that Emilia felt that all the shit they'd put her through was maybe, kind of, if you squint, a little bit worth it. She had the contract Ivan had dreamed about for years, and she deserved it more than him. She still shouldn't have had to live through that.

And now the dream was back. He could do it without the rest of Team Fury, and instead with an entirely new team that would never, ever hurt someone like Emilia ever again. He could be a leader, an example; he could change the way the game was played!

But, to get there . . . he had to fake date Zora Lyon. Which, now that he thought about it, was totally her idea to begin with. Which was smart, and since Zora was obviously smart enough to spot the advantages, who was Ivan to get in the way of her decisions? It wasn't like this was some elaborate scam. It was going to be a very, very simple scam. The only thing now was to commit to it. That made sense, right? Of course it did. Just stick with Team Vision for the rest of the summer and get his spot in the league that fall. Foolproof.

"Can I get that in writing?" Ivan spoke as if he was joking. He wasn't. Brian simply smiled.

"Later," Brian replied. "For now, work on generating some heat for the next battle royale. Don't be afraid to get cute. Emilia and Jake are great, but they could do with some competition in—"

"No." It came out of Ivan's mouth before he knew he was saying it. "Zora and I can handle our end, but I don't want to be compared to Emilia *at all*. That's not the story."

"Fine." Brian held his hands up innocently. "You're still touchy about that; I get it."

"Promise me."

"I promise." The cocreator of Wizzard Games saluted Ivan and headed to the door in the back of the suite. He held it open, clearly expecting Ivan to walk out on his own. "Scout's honor!"

Ivan nodded, took the hint, and left. It wasn't until much later, after he walked all the way down to street level, waited for the lighting test to end, and took his seat onstage that he thought to wonder if Brian Juno had ever in his life been a Boy Scout.

# ZORA

# CHAPTER THIRTEEN

I WAS TOO young to know what was going on when my Uncle Clive was drafted for the NFL, but I remember how my grandmother reacted when they called his name. She wasn't the most emotive person, actually she was kind of cold as far as grandmas go, but where anyone else would be jumping and screaming for their son's success, she simply . . . sat down.

I was the only one looking at her; the day was about Clive. There were too many people clustered around our TV and I didn't like the noise, so I had retreated to my favorite hiding spot under the dining room table. From under there I had a view of grandma and not much else. They called Clive's name and she sat down, looking more exhausted than I'd ever seen her. But she was smiling.

Six-year-old me concluded that grandma needed a nap before she could be happy, but now I think I know the real reason for that smile. She was relieved. The waiting was over, her work was done; all the years she spent sacrificing to give

Clive the best possible shot at his dream had paid off. She could finally sit down.

This kind of feels like that, except the opposite, and not at all, and worse.

"Zora . . ." Trieu warns me without looking up from his phone. He's still trying to troubleshoot the connection between his phone and the TV, specifically so we can watch Brian Juno reveal the results of the Wizz-Algorithm's week one calculations as if they're an NFL draft, a parody video idea that I neither supported nor shot down because if these people find out I know anything about football, they might put together that I'm related to Clive. I don't know why I care about that so much, but I do. I think I just want this summer to be something I do by myself, completely separate from his legacy.

Trieu follows up his warning with a command: "Stop. Picking. Your lips."

My hand freezes a few inches away from my face. Busted. I can't help it, though. I feel all nervous and zoomy inside and when that happens, I pick my lips. I've never been good at waiting, and with the Fourth of July tomorrow, this wait is unpredictably punctuated with the sharp *crack-pop* of fireworks echoing off the tar-sticky roofs of Lincoln Center. At least I hope they're fireworks. Great, let's add the bloated American specter of gun violence to the list of reasons I'm crashing out.

It was Ivan's idea to wait for the news in the lounge instead of at the Wizzard Theater with everyone else. He said it was to give our content a more "intimate vibe," which matches our brand as the tight-knit coalition where love can apparently blossom. I suspect there's another reason, though. I think he did it to spare me the crowd and knew I wouldn't ask for myself. Which is so nice, like, genuinely thoughtful, and that's really the heart of the problem.

Ivan Hunt is an amazing boyfriend. Or he would be, if any of this were real. I don't know if he went to Juilliard in a past life or what, but the boy can act. Objectively I know there's a difference between acting and lying, but it's hard to remember that when Ivan is waiting outside my dorm room door with a bouquet of bodega flowers (with Kavi rolling digital tape to cut the staged gesture into a WiTch clip). Or when he's holding his jacket over my hair when a freak summer storm catches Team Vision on our way up Broadway with fifteen blocks to go and my twist-out barely a day old (not recorded, but only because by the time we got inside all three of them looked exactly like those oily ducks on the dish soap bottles. My hair was fine, though.).

This morning, he said "good morning" to me, as if he cares if my mornings are good. Or yesterday, when Kavi showed everyone the outfits she pulled for me to wear for the ranking reveal today, he actually said "that one would look nice on you." What gives? Don't even get me started about him offering to pick up my lunch after our seminar with the *GLR* character designers on Thursday, like some kind of love-bombing charlatan.

And yet, for all his fawning attention, he's late to meet us here.

"There we go," Trieu's phone finally connects to the TV. A few taps later and we're watching the countdown to Brian Juno's first Saturday live stream from the academy.

"Can we see how many people are watching?" Kavi asks him.

"Fifteen thousand in the waiting room on WiTch. Getting bigger. Looks like they turned off the comments on the stream."

"That's fine," Kavi waves her hand dismissively. "Would have been nice to get a temperature check, though."

"Yeah, but our impressions are good. I know the comment section on WiTch is super modcrated but the tone has been trending up. There's excitement Ivan's back, *lots* of curiosity about Zora, and that *Kal Ho Na Ho* x *GLR* parody video you did on the Brooklyn Bridge is still circulating."

"Never underestimate the social sharing power of aunties," Kavi adds, looking pleased.

I just let them talk when they get like this. They might be speaking English, but I'll never know for sure. I have only known Kavi and Trieu for six days, and it amazes me how they are my age and run their whole lives like a business. Being a professional teenager is *work,* and now after a week of trauma bonding and after-hours scheming at the diner, two of the best ones are my . . . mentors? Fellow adventurers?

Friends. The word I'll settle on is friends.

"There's only like a minute left on the countdown," Cass says quietly from his spot on the couch. "Somebody should probably find Ivan. Not me, though."

"They should not. I come pre-found." Ivan announces himself with a flourish. "Sorry I'm late, I had to, uh . . ." He looks at me, arms crossed and not *not* pouting in the armchair. "I, um."

"Spit it out, dude." Cass, from the couch, completely monotone.

"I left something at the Wizzard. And Zora, you look nice."

I actually feel a shudder of pride at the compliment before I remember he's just performing. For whom, I'm not sure. It's just Team Vision in the room. Ivan takes his seat in the armchair opposite me and raises his eyebrows in some unreadable gesture.

*It's just a game*, I tell myself. *It's a story. You are a character in a story that ends with you as Brian Juno's favorite person ever.* And that's still not enough to stop me from feeling self-conscious around Ivan in a way that I've never experienced before. Which is worrying, because before this summer I would have sworn that my awkward self has experienced every kind of consciousness one can have about feeling weird in public. But, as it turns out, there will always be new lows for me to hit in that department.

The countdown ends with the grand, orchestral sting of the *Guardians League* series and tries to segue into the regular stream, but the video quality is so blocky it looks like a ten-year-old tried to recreate the Wizzard Theater in *Minecraft*. The sound isn't any better. It's choppy and disorienting, to the point where I have to jam a knuckle in one ear to mitigate the noise.

"Hey! Turn it off," Ivan says quickly. "Trieu, come on."

"Don't have to tell me twice." Trieu winces and stops screensharing to the TV.

"Is the stream any better on your phone?" Kavi leans over Trieu's shoulder.

"Nope." He holds his screen up to show us that the entire WiTch page for the summer academy is down.

Kavi throws her hands up. "Ugh! Brian, get your *shit* together," she hisses with a vehemence I haven't seen her express until now.

*Bing. Din! Bada-boop. Bzzt. Zoop.* Five phones, five email notifications coming through at the exact same time.

Team Vision exchange panicked looks. Without the stream, there has to be a way to communicate the results to the academy players . . . and I'm pretty sure that's happening right now.

This is it, the moment of truth. We haven't said anything out loud, but I think all of us are waiting on the results of the first week to determine whether any of this is worth the effort. I try to think of a number I want to hit, the cutoff after which I consider this a massive failure, and settle on the number forty-two. Get me above forty-two and I'm in for the summer. Anything below and I'm out. I'll find a new strategy, I don't care. If I'm going to make a fool of myself with Ivan, it needs to be quantifiably worth it.

See, now I got myself doing math. My game performance shouldn't drag me down. I crushed it in the match this morning—top five, baby!—but will my first match disqualification mess up those numbers? Is Brian averaging them? Do comments pull more weight than likes? I don't know how the Wizz-Algorithm works. No one does, and without that knowledge we're all just flinging romantic, interracial spaghetti at the wall and seeing what sticks.

Five clicks, five phones unlocked. I hold mine far away from my face, tapping the email open at arm's length.

*Dear Academy Players,*

*Wow, what a week. After a shaky start, our Summer Academy Royale is* blah blah blah, recap recap, whatever, I'll read this part later. Show me the rankings, Brian.

"Holy shit." Trieu actually puts his hand to his mouth and gasps. Spoilers! I scroll faster until I hit the bottom of the email and open the attached PDF and scan the columns only for the relevant information.

#8 Ivan Hunt

#20 Trieu Vu

#23 Kavi Khurana

#30 Cassius Sharpe

#32 Zora Lyon

Overshot my goal by ten. From the shocked, happy looks on Kavi's, Trieu's, and Ivan's faces, we're having the exact same thought. It's Ivan who puts it into words.

"Okay"—he nods at the screen—"so we're doing this."

"*Happy birthday to you, happy birthday to you.*" I don't normally sing when I'm getting dressed, but I like the Fourth of July. I don't mind fireworks when I know to expect them, and I love baking myself darker on the beach. It also turns the entire continental United States into an unlimited hot dog dispensary for twenty-four hours, which was more of a plus for me when I wasn't staying in New York, where hot dogs are legally considered a food group.

"*Happy birthday, dear America. Happy birthday to*"—an aggressive tap on my door cuts off the big finish—"Almost ready!"

"It's me," Cass calls from the other side. Odd. Team Vision is meeting in the lounge again at noon, but Cass has never come up early to see me first.

"Hey!" I open my door and step back so Cass can see I'm wearing the purple dress. It's not very patriotic, but it's the prettiest shade of plum I've ever seen and Kavi said to come looking cute. Which is *really* suspicious, now that I think about it. We agreed not to make #content on a holiday, so why did I put this dress on again?

"Hey-yowza." Cass stands up straighter. "Sorry, I'm looking for my friend Zora? I know you're a supermodel and everything but if you see her, tell her that Kavi asked me to ask her if she's ever played *Overcooked!*"

"*Overcooked!*? The co-op cooking game? That you play with a partner? And have to team up and work together?"

"That is what co-op means, yes."

"Well," I poke my head out of the door to see if I can spot Kavi at the end of the hall. Yup, there she is. Futzing around with the lounge TV again. Hopefully not trying to screenshare a stream this time. "I haven't seen this 'Zo-rah,' but I feel like she'd answer that question with a request for Kavi to take a *wild fucking guess*!" I shout the last few words loud enough for her to hear me—almost no one else is hanging out in their dorm rooms around noon on a holiday so I'm not worried about disturbing the peace.

"I figured!" Kavi shouts back with a laugh. "Just checking."

"So that's her plan, huh?" I grab my summer academy tote bag on my way out the door. "Making me and Ivan play co-op?"

"Not exactly," Cass answers. That perks me up.

"Making you and me play co-op?" I ask.

"Hard pass." Well, now I know how Kavi felt two minutes ago.

Ivan and Trieu are already assembled in the lounge when Cass and I make it down the hallway. Kavi's "look cute" memo must have applied to Ivan as well, since he's lightly dolled up in a patterned short-sleeve button-down and shorts. I lean forward to see what the pattern is—oh my god it's tiny flamingos, that is *adorable*—but snap back when I realize I've leaned right into Ivan's personal space. I can tell because I'm smelling him again, and I've been trying not to do that as much, because. Just because.

"Hi to you too, Zora," Ivan says with a smile I would classify as shy if I didn't know him.

"Right. Hi." I wave. Is it weird to wave when you're standing right beside someone? I did it without thinking but now I'm wondering if a wave is more of a faraway greeting. Is there an optimal distance between the two waving human points of a line that unlocks better social outcomes?

Ivan waves back.

"All right, love birdies, enough," Trieu calls from the kitchen table. "You two have a lot of work to do."

"We do?" Ivan asks. "I thought we were crushing this. Or at least *I* was."

"You crushed the trial run." Kavi feels around the back of the TV for a place to plug in an HDMI cord. "It was the first meet and greet, everyone was a little off their game. But the two of you—got it." The TV screen bursts into a riot of cutesy colors that form the menu for *Overcooked! 2*."

"What," Ivan asks flatly. "This is the secret plan? I thought we were going somewhere."

"It's a multi-phased plan," Kavi says. "This is just phase one. Also I didn't finish my thought," Kavi reminds us. She pulls two Switch controllers out of her bag and tosses them to Cass one after the other. "Calibrate, please. Make sure there's no drift." Cassius begins to calibrate the controllers.

"The two of you need to get on the same page. You slipped up on Wednesday with the 'how did you meet' thing. And by the end of the meet and greet both of you looked like murder was on the menu."

"So we're taking it off the menu," Trieu adds. "And putting something new on the menu. Food, if you can believe it."

Ivan takes a deep breath, like he needs to calm down before he speaks. "Kavi," he begins politely. "Could you perhaps enlighten me as to what exactly I'm doing wrong?" He looks over at me. What, for support?

"Sure." Kavi takes the calibrated controllers back from Cass and begins setting up a new co-op campaign while she talks. "Ivan, you're overcompensating. As for Zora, you are overthinking."

"I don't know what those words mean in this context," I whine.

"I'm only overcompensating because she—"

"*She,*" I defend myself, "can barely get a word in edgewise whenever he decides to—"

"To what? Carry this grift on my back like Atlas?"

"Does anyone else hear this?" Kavi interrupts. "It's the diner all over again. Am I the only one paying attention to the tools we have at our disposal?"

The room is silent; neither Trieu nor Cass look up from their phones. "Anyone. Nobody? Cassius?"

Cass frowns at her. "Yes," he says very deliberately. "You are the only one."

Kavi rolls her eyes. "Lie to yourself, Cassius," she says. "Not to me."

"Fine." Cass points to Ivan and me like he's picking us out of a police lineup. "You two have been literally obsessed with each other from day one. The only thing you talk about when the other one isn't around *is the other one*. You even finish each other's sentences. But none of that is coming across on camera because Ivan never shuts up and Zora always has this look on her face like she's solving a Rubik's Cube at gunpoint."

"Because it's all lies!" I argue. "It's really hard to control my face when I'm too busy staring slack-mouthed at the part where nobody notices Ivan doesn't mean a word he says, ever."

"Hey!" Ivan protests, but Cassius talks right over him.

"Zora, I mean this from the bottom of my heart: *Who cares if he means it?*"

"Zora, we talked about this before," Trieu adds. "Just because you think Ivan doesn't mean what he says doesn't mean you can't pretend it's not nice to hear it. Did that make any sense? Did I double my negatives?"

"I do mean what I say, by the way," Ivan says quietly. "Sometimes."

"How am I supposed to tell the difference? We only know each other through this whole, you know . . ." I wave my arms frantically around at the people in the room, hoping they'll get what I mean so I don't have to say *fake dating emotional fraud team alliance that's actually working* out loud.

"Exactly," Kavi interrupts with a smile. "Hence: *Overcooked! 2*. The only game out on the market that'll either forge bonds stronger than iron, or make you hate someone with the heat of ten suns."

"I have a question." I raise my hand.

"Yes, Zora?" Kavi answers.

"What if it's the ten suns?" A younger, more naïve Zora might've thought there was no way a game with such cute little cartoon animal chefs on the case could incite that much rage, but I've been burned enough times to know the cutest games are the most infuriating.

"Then we keep trying," Kavi says with a casual shrug, eyes narrowing. "Even if it takes all night."

"Seriously?" Ivan asks with a choked laugh. "It's the Fourth of July; shouldn't we—"

"Did anyone here have plans for tonight?" Kavi interrupts again. Trieu looks up from his phone long enough to shrug. Cass doesn't even bother going that far, just shaking his head as he returns his attention to power-washing a jungle gym on his OLED screen. I didn't have anything going on today, I literally just want a hot dog. And even though Ivan was the one who protested in the first place, he doesn't have a rebuttal. Or plans, apparently.

Kavi grins victoriously before settling back down on the couch and picking the controller back up. "I rest my case."

"If we're playing *Overcooked!* by ourselves, what are you guys going to do all day?"

Kavi walks over to the kitchen table, where Trieu has set up three gaming laptops. She reaches down and yanks a headphone cord out of its jack. The bass notes of the *GLR* theme buzz loudly against the tinny speakers. "Take a wild fucking guess."

I prepare my final argument. "Shouldn't we be . . . I don't know . . . playing *The Newlywed Game*, or something?

Asking about each other's favorite colors and social security numbers?"

"More relevant references, Zora!" Cass calls from the couch.

"Fine. Never Have I Ever?"

"Accepted."

"I'm not giving you my social security number," Ivan whispers out of the corner of his mouth.

"I've had it for *months*," I whisper venomously, clocking the slight tugging at the edge of Ivan's lips that means he's trying to smother a laugh. Well, I'm glad at least one of us thinks this is funny.

"Wait a minute—Cass." I've just realized something doesn't add up. "I asked you point-blank if the plan was for me and Ivan to play *Overcooked!* and you said no."

"Mm, not exactly," Cass answers.

"What do you mean 'not exactly'?"

"That's what I said, 'not exactly.' I didn't say no. Because what you actually asked was 'Is this Kavi's plan, to make me and Ivan play *Overcooked!*' And that's not true."

I groan. "Are you really going to *Um, Actually* me because we're technically playing *Overcooked! 2*?"

"Um, actually," Kavi pushes an invisible set of glasses up her nose. "He's going to *Um, Actually* you because this was not *my* plan. It's Cass's."

"It was?" I whip around to face Cass. I'm not surprised that he thought playing a video game would be the cure to all wounds, but I am thrown off by the fact he came to Kavi with a suggestion without talking to me about it first.

Cass shrugs, finally turning his Deck off to look up at me with an unreadable expression and a tone that feels both playful and chilly. Like a snowman. "Had to pull my weight in the party somehow."

"I was lobbying to send you skydiving," Trieu interjects from the kitchen. "Because I think neither of you will live a happy life unless you get to kick each other out of a real plane at least once."

"But that shit's expensive." Kavi hands us both our controllers. Ivan's is watermelon green and pink, mine is classic Switch gray. A peacock and a goat. "Now go make me some digital sushi."

# CHAPTER FOURTEEN

"DID YOU PREP the rice?" I ask as my chubby alligator avatar dashes across the screen to chop the fish for our sushi roll before time runs out on our latest order—the last shot we have of earning enough in tips to make it past this level.

That level being Level 1. Which we've played through four times already.

"I thought you were on the rice?" Ivan asks as his (raccoon? Wolf? Other gray mammal?) avatar washes the same dish I swear he's been washing for the past ten minutes.

I bite down on my tongue until I've calmed down enough to not breathe fire the second I open my mouth. "*You* said you'd be on the rice if I handled the fish and the seaweed."

"I meant just for that last order."

"Then you should've said that."

"I did," Ivan says through gritted teeth as a grating *ding-ding-ding* announces the end of yet another unsuccessful round.

"Great," I say with what I already know is too much bite as I toss my controller onto the couch beside me. "We were only a hundred dollars short this time."

"Better than two hundred," Ivan mumbles, every word dripping with sarcasm.

It doesn't seem possible, but this was our most productive round so far. We managed to serve three whole orders before we got derailed by Ivan's avatar careening off the side of the cliff our kitchen was conveniently built on, throwing off our entire flow for the remaining two minutes of the round.

"It shouldn't be this hard," I say, more to myself than to Ivan—my voice thicker than I expected it to be. None of this—the game, the academy, pretending with Ivan—should be so hard.

"Isn't that the whole point of this?" Ivan gestures to the screen. "Forcing us to work as a team?"

"And we're clearly doing an awful job." I hate the way my voice gets higher pitched the more I talk, but I especially hate the way I feel like I can't look at him head-on. Like it'll tip or break something inside me. And that feeling—that fluttering beneath my skin whenever I look at him for too long—is the most terrifying thing so far.

"All right. New game plan for this next round." Ivan nods to himself, like a coach running through plays in his head before calling his choice for the team. "What do you actually like doing here?"

"Like on Earth, or . . ."

"In the game."

"Not cooking," I say. "Too many little indicators for when everything's done."

"So that's dishes and serving for you. Stays the same every time. I'll do the cooking and assembly and call out orders."

"Is that what you like doing?" I ask.

"I'm working with what I got," Ivan replies, and clicks us back into a new kitchen.

"And you won't forget the rice?" I ask with a raised brow. Ivan forgetting about the existence of rice is what destroyed us in the last round.

"I will never again, for as long as I live"—Ivan nods before turning to give me a smile that makes my stomach feel like I just swallowed a bag of Pop Rocks—"forget your rice."

He is so full of it. Ignoring my traitorous desire to keep looking at him, I focus my attention back on the screen and tap in for the next round.

We play in silence at first. The round always starts off easy—orders coming in slow enough that we think we've got a handle on things.

"Orders one and two are ready," Ivan announces as he sets two completed sushi rolls on the counter opposite my avatar.

"Yes, chef," I reply, moving on pure instinct to get the food served and dishes washed and ready for Ivan to plate up the next order.

And that's the way it goes. Silence except for the occasional call out that a dish is ready to be served or that I've set a fresh stack of plates on the counter or that we need more sashimi to be chopped. Our movements feel strangely synchronized—like we're performing a waltz even while five feet apart. The subtle clicks of our fingers mashing buttons and sharp inhales as we race against the clock ground me like my own personalized ASMR soundtrack.

The sound of the timer signaling the end of the round catches me so off guard I almost leap out of my seat. I clutch at my heart like a damsel with her pearls as I will my body to stop trying to sabotage me every few minutes. By the time I can feel my heart slowing beneath my fingertips, our score has been displayed.

We haven't just made enough tips to pass the round, but also enough to earn us a perfect three gold stars. Our little chefs finally move up the path on the map.

"Let's go!" Ivan shouts at the exact same moment I jump into the air with a battle cry of "Yes!"

My adrenaline spikes with that sweet feeling of winning as Ivan whips around to face me, his smile as bright as the glow of Times Square. I swear I can see my reflection in his eyes—beaming like I've won it all. The final battle royale. The mentorship. The dream life I've always pictured for myself. And with the way my cheeks are aching from my ear-to-ear grin, I might even think it was real and not some kind of weird lens distortion.

Even with the round over, we still move in perfect synchronicity. Our hands fly up into the air, meeting in a high five so powerful it echoes through the room and sends a sharp sting of pain all the way down to my elbow. But for once it's the good kind of pain—the thrill of knowing you absolutely freaking crushed it.

We come down from the high together, as if we listened to Trieu and went skydiving instead, our chests heaving as we collapse back onto the couch. We've somehow gotten physically closer together since we started the round too, close enough that Ivan's knee brushes against mine when he flops back onto the cushions.

"Not so awful, huh?" he teases before I can linger on the fact that our skin is touching and I didn't spontaneously combust.

I bite back a snort and take the opportunity to pull my knees up to my chest—an extremely safe distance from any more unexpected contact. "Speak for yourself."

Ivan pouts and holds a hand against his heart as if I've wounded him. "That's not very fake girlfriend-y of you."

This time I don't hold back my snort of a laugh. And while normally I wouldn't care what Ivan thinks about me or the noises that come out of my mouth, embarrassment trickles down my spine until goose bumps sprout along my arms. "I'm off the clock."

If Ivan's put off by my laugh, he doesn't let it show. Instead, he smiles. *Really* smiles. Not the perfect shiny white smile he gives for the cameras or Brian or his adoring fans. Something softer and more intimate. More . . . real. The kind of smile you won't find if you Google his name or scroll through his socials. That, if I were a weaker person, I might think is special.

"So am I," he says, eyes lingering on mine long enough that the fluttering in my stomach threatens to come back full force if I stay here any longer than I have to.

"Next kitchen?" I propose, yanking my attention away to grab my controller off the couch between us—my pinky finger brushing against his. The contact lasts for barely a second, but it's still enough to send a jolt through me.

I can hear Ivan let out a quiet sound of amusement. "If you think you can handle it."

If I weren't actively avoiding contact, I'd shove my knee against his. Instead, I settle for sticking my tongue out at him moments before we load up the next round—a very civilized and mature response.

As expected, the next level is more challenging than the first. We've upgraded to burritos and the occasional fireball launching at us from out of nowhere. People aren't kidding when they say the service industry is hell. My stomach sinks when we miss moving on to the next round by a single order, a groan threatening to escape my lips, but I owe it to our fake relationship to be optimistic for once.

"We're just getting the lay of the land," Ivan says before quickly opting in for a second match.

Thankfully, for both Ivan's and my sanity, it seems like he was right. We're able to find our same rhythm from the first round now that we know what to expect. Dodging fireballs comes with its own set of complications, but with Ivan on meats, rice, and washing dishes and me on tortillas and serving, we're able to make it through the round with two gold stars and no bodily or mental damage done to either of us.

The silence is welcome as we move on to the next round, and then the next. Our routine gets more and more solidified with every passing round. Within just a few minutes we're masters of communication—at least when it comes to the virtual kitchen. Whether that skill development will carry over to our real-life interactions is still up in the air, but progress is progress.

"What's your favorite color?" Ivan asks midway through the fifth—or is it sixth?—level. We've upgraded to burgers, fries, and chicken tenders all at once. Guy Fieri would be so proud.

"What?" I ask, brows furrowing as I focus on dashing toward the fryer to grab the chicken before it can burn.

"You strike me as a red type," Ivan continues, effortlessly gliding across the screen to deliver our latest order. From the lack of frantic button-mashing sounds, he's not nearly as focused as I am. "But I could see blue."

Unlike him, I need my full attention to concentrate. Once we've finished off the level, barely making enough to move on to the next stage, I work on processing what the hell he just asked me. "Why?"

For all I know he could be trying to find new ways to throw me off. I wouldn't put it past him to have a spreadsheet of people's favorite things on the off chance he runs into them on the street. Just a trick to make them feel special, like he remembered. Then again, if they do end up feeling special, does it matter how he remembered? I don't enjoy this line of thought.

"Because it's what you said we should be doing?" he responds as he sets his controller down. So much for moving on to the next round. "Learning each other's favorite colors and swapping social security numbers?"

Leave it to him to make my own words come back to bite me. "I didn't *actually* mean . . ." I trail off, not sure how to finish that sentence. Because I'm not sure what I meant. Sure, getting to know each other feels like a pretty important part of pretending to date each other, but is anyone actually going to quiz us on basic facts about each other?

Was I just looking for ways to get out of whatever Kavi had planned because the thought of having to spend more time with Ivan than I have to sets me on edge in a not altogether unpleasant way? Definitely still unpleasant, on some levels. Even when he's not "on," he's got a certain level of snark, which I would admire in someone who I wasn't actively trying to work with. But more than that it's the nagging fear that I won't hate this. That I'll start believing what he says. That I'll end up letting him make me feel special, and forget it's all a lie.

But, since he's off the clock, it might be kind of novel to hang out with Ivan. Not VANE, not the Ivan Hunt thousands of people love and adore and, more recently, love to hate. Just . . . Ivan.

Not that I'd ever say that out loud.

"Purple," I finally respond, after I've been quiet long enough that Ivan has been eyeing me like I might explode any second.

He seems taken aback, but also amused. "Really? Why?"

"Because I look dope as hell in purple." If my hair wasn't tied up in a messy "I need to concentrate" bun, I'd flip it over my shoulder.

Ivan chuckles as he takes in my purple dress "Point taken."

Well, I'm not sure how I expected him to respond, but it definitely wasn't that.

Heat floods my cheeks until I feel like I've come down with the world's most sudden fever. Goose bumps blossom along my bare arms even though the room is a perfectly pleasant temperature. I stay laser focused on the screen, busying myself with adjusting the game's display settings to give myself something to do while I struggle to both process Ivan's response, and think of a way to reply that isn't equally loaded. It'd only be fair if I threw a bomb back into his court, but I think if I attempted to match his energy with a sly compliment or a wink, I might break my brain in the process.

"And let me guess," I finally say once the game's settings have been thoroughly tinkered with. "Your favorite color is the same as whoever you're talking to, because you have *so much* in common and should be best friends forever."

Sarcasm, our forte. Or mine, at least. Something I know I can match blow for blow and puts us firmly back into neutral compliment-free territory.

"I'm not *that* manipulative—have a little faith in me," Ivan replies with another laugh. He's just full of those today, isn't he?

The problem is, now my interest is actually piqued. I'm able to bite my tongue as we start up another round, but curiosity gets the better of me about a minute in. "So . . . favorite color?"

Ivan doesn't respond at first, focusing on tossing burger buns to my half of the kitchen before replying, "Gray."

"That's just as—"

"It's a cross-season neutral!" he interjects immediately. The fact that he already had an excuse prepared just proves my point, though.

For once, I decide to have mercy on him. As much as I'd love to continue down this color rabbit hole, I'm willing to meet in the middle. It already seems like positive progress that we're able to effectively run a virtual kitchen together, and if I can resist the urge to banter with him to avoid meaningful connection, then we'll have made more progress in an afternoon than I thought we'd be able to make in a month.

"Favorite ice cream flavor?" I ask instead of pushing him to defend his (incorrect) favorite color more than he already has. Because I'm listening and learning. "Mine is cookie dough."

"Mint chip."

"Favorite video game character? Mine's Bayek of Siwa."

"Whoa, whoa, whoa," he says, pausing the game and tossing down his controller to hold his hands up in the air like he's under attack. I freeze in place—what did I do? I rack my brain, trying to remember the last few minutes, but all the brain spits out is *GLR* trivia and the squeezy, uncomfortable feeling I've done something wrong again. "Don't you think we're moving too fast?"

I unfreeze when Ivan leans toward me, his expression morphing into that teasing, cocky smile that would be almost very cute if he meant it. But he doesn't.

"No?"

"But . . . my favorite character is Sonic the Hedgehog."

My jaw drops.

"So we gotta—"

"Gotta go fast!"

The joke wasn't even that funny really, but it breaks the tension better than anything we've tried before. Within seconds we're doubled over, tears clouding my vision until Ivan's just a blurry outline. It just feels so good to have some kind of release. To let everything out in one long, cathartic, gasping laugh. Slowly, all of the stress that had built up on my shoulders throughout the day melts away. The pressure of knowing I'll be watched by thousands of viewers. Performing for them—to be not just likeable but the perfect girlfriend as well. My senses chill out for once, and I'm somehow calm even though Ivan paused our game two frames before my alligator was about to get hit by a taxi. For a blissful few seconds, it's just me, Ivan, and our laughter echoing through the room.

A familiar ringtone cuts the fun short, though. It's like I've plunged into an ice bath when I realize that Clive is calling, not even needing to look at the screen to know who it is.

"Shit," I mutter, pulling my phone out of my pocket to confirm what I already knew. I don't have time to dwell on how Ivan and I managed to close the gap between us again—our arms pressed together and knees touching as if they're drawn in like magnets—as I lunge off the couch.

"Everything okay?" Ivan whispers, sticking close behind me as I head back into the main student lounge area.

"It's my uncle," I murmur to him before standing directly in front of the TV to get the rest of the party's attention. "It's a video call!"

Cass sits up as soon as he realizes the direness of the situation. Kavi shoots me a nod before taking my place at the front of the room, wordlessly gesturing for everyone else to shut the hell up while I step out into the hallway and finally accept the call.

From the bright light when I pick up, I can tell that Clive is taking one of his many walks around our neighborhood in East Orange on this stunning summer afternoon. Even with his knees, he's terribly conscious of staying in shape. He's also doing a terrible job holding the phone steady as he walks, which is why I don't get a good look at his face until a few moments after he picks up.

"Hey, sorry, just got out of a seminar. What's up?" I don't have to pretend to be breathless—the rush of trying to get everyone into position ASAP does that for me.

"Just wanted to make sure my niece didn't vanish off the face of the planet, since she hasn't been answering any of my calls," Clive says, his tone more concerned than angry. He would prefer for me to call him more often, but he also knows how much I hate talking on the phone. Of course, I also could be texting him more often, but I keep getting so caught up in my days that two or three go by before I realize I haven't sent him so much as an emoji. Also, every time I text him, I'm perpetuating the lie that I'm at coding camp, which should feel less icky compared to everything else I'm lying about this summer, but doesn't.

"I know, I know, I'm sorry," I say to cover my bases. And I don't need to do much pretending there either. Lying was one thing, but actively avoiding having to talk to him is another. Complicated relationship aside, I didn't mean to make him more worried than he already was about sending me off on my own. "Our schedule's just been super hectic; we barely get any time to ourselves."

"That's good," he says, voice still unreadable. "Means you're learning new skills to make you more competitive."

"Exactly." He has no idea how right he is.

Awkward silence is better than anger, right? I'd offer up some other tidbit about "coding camp" except that throwing in more unnecessary details will just open up more possibilities for me to mess up later down the road.

"Well, I won't keep you. Just wanted to check in and make sure you were doing okay," Clive says. This time there's a softness to his tone that signals that everything is still okay between us. That he hasn't managed to see right through me from a barely twenty-second conversation.

"I'm doing great," I reply, my lips pulling into a smile without me even having to try. I look over my shoulder at the entryway to the student lounge—Kavi's hand clamped around Trieu's mouth while Ivan is practically red in the face from trying to hold in his laughter. Probably laughing at his own jokes. I've noticed he does that, but only when he's being especially corny. If it's a real stinker, sometimes he can't even make it to the punch line without cracking himself up. The same feeling from earlier—the warm flutter in the pit of my stomach—ignites as I take it all in. My friends. My party. "Better than great."

"You sure? You know you can always call me if you need anything," Clive insists.

"I know, Unc, but I really am fine. I swear."

"Got any plans for the Fourth of July?"

"Uh." I look around the hallway, hoping someone may have written a good excuse in Sharpie on their door. "Not really. Might get a hot dog, watch the fireworks."

"All right. Well, I'll let you go, then. Just be careful, okay? Be smart in the city."

I roll my eyes. New York City is already a lawless place on a daily basis—I can't imagine patriotism is going to suddenly skyrocket the crime rate.

"I will," I reply with as little sarcasm as possible, because I know in Clive's imagination I may as well be parkouring through the sewers to fight crime with four turtles. "Happy Fourth."

"You too, kid."

As soon as we end the call, my body sags against the wall behind me, what feels like a thousand pounds worth of panic melting off me as I close my eyes and work on slowing down my racing heart.

Somehow, Kavi has Trieu in a headlock by the time I'm back in the lounge. Ivan is rooting through the lounge's kitchen fridge like a truffle pig, and Cass has taken up the mantle of an abandoned laptop and started a *GLR* match on the sly.

Leave clowns unattended, come back to a circus. Hey, I like that. It's going in the scratch pad.

"What are you doing?" Ivan asks over the chaos.

I want to say "none of your business," but the reflex to be snarky is weak. Halfway between "it's nothing" and "just notes" I end up saying simply:

"No."

"Are we in the clear?" Kavi asks through gritted teeth. She lets go of Trieu as soon as I nod, and he makes a show of collapsing onto the floor and gasping for breath.

"Perfect!" Kavi claps her hands together and puts on a smile so wide you'd never think she was just trapping someone in a headlock seconds earlier. "Then we can move on to phase two."

"Phase two?" Ivan and I ask at the exact same time. He lets the fridge swing closed and stands up straight. Maybe Kavi's plan is working better than we thought.

"I *said* it was a multi-phased plan," she responds with an eyeroll. I squint in thought as I rewind back to our earlier conversation, my shoulders slumping when I realize that she's right. We were sufficiently warned.

Ivan and I exchange wary looks as Kavi physically collects first me, then Ivan from the kitchen area and loops back to escort us out of the student lounge.

"Now that you've learned how to work as a team, we can address the next glaring issue," she says as if it's common sense, but based on the look on Ivan's face we're both lost.

"Which is?" I ask as Kavi comes to a stop at the elevator bank.

She does the honors of pressing the Down button before standing back in front of us. "Coexisting *without a video game.*"

"We don't—"

The chime of the elevator arriving cuts me off before I can explain that while maybe Ivan and I aren't best friends, it's not like we're actively trying to hadouken each other whenever we're left alone together. Except we're never left alone together, so there's no way Kavi could know that. Before I can pick up where I left off, Kavi places a hand on each of our chests and gently nudges us back until we're inside the elevator.

"Your next mission is to spend one, o-n-e, night in the city together. Alone. No party involvement."

"What're we supposed to do?" Ivan asks as he scratches the back of his head. A fair question. New York is full of activity, the options are limitless—we could use some guidelines.

"Explore. Go get dinner, or see a movie, or ride in one of those horse-drawn carriage things."

"But those exploit horses!" Ivan interjects.

"Ivan." Kavi's patience is wearing thin. "It's the Fourth of July in New York City. If you can't figure out something to do with your fake girlfriend that doesn't exploit horses, then what is the point of you?"

"Wow," I mutter. "She questioned the point of your *life.*"

"But—"

Kavi cuts off Ivan again, hopping out of the elevator as soon as she presses the Lobby button.

"Have fun! And don't come back until I've given you explicit permission via text. *Ivan.*"

The doors close before either of us can argue with Kavi's logic. Forcing us to work together as a team was, admittedly, not a bad idea. But what does making us wander around aimlessly through New York City do to advance the party forward?

"So . . . ," Ivan begins with a shrug as I slump forward, my head resting against the cool metal of the closed elevator door. The rumble as we travel down the ten flights between us and the lobby is oddly calming. "What do you want to do?"

"We don't actually have to do this," I say as I pick my head up. The urge to press the button for our floor and just crawl under my bedsheets and call it a night is extremely strong. "It's not like they're watching us."

"This is Kavi," he responds. "She has eyes everywhere." He has a point. She's probably checking under my bed right now.

I sigh dramatically as the doors *ding* open on the first floor. There's a surprising amount of bustle in the lobby area leading out into the city. People coming and going like they're running late for a meeting, the security guard at the front desk hardly able to keep up with the number of people tapping their IDs against the scanner as they enter the building. There's a distinct smell of summer in the air. Sunscreen lotion and aloe vera, and beyond the doors the usual New York smell of honey roasted nuts and barbecue grills.

"Well, what do *you* want to do?" I ask as we step off the elevator.

Ivan shrugs and shoves his hands in his pockets. "Whatever you want to do."

I scoff. Gee, thanks, Ivan. How very helpful. "Stop trying to appease me and make a decision."

"I would never try to appease you. I'm just saying, I asked you first."

Ugh, he's right. I bite down on my tongue to hold in a groan loud enough to pierce the ozone layer. Before I can come up with a suggestion, my stomach lets out a growl that I swear makes the ground tremble beneath me.

Yeesh. I know I've been serving up some very cute animated dinners on screen for the last couple hours, but my body didn't have to act like I've been depriving it of sustenance for a week.

Ivan at least has the grace to not belly laugh in my face at my body's inability to control itself. He's holding his laughter in just like he was earlier as he nods once, then starts walking toward the exit. "We have an answer, then," he calls out over his shoulder.

I look around in confusion, as if he left the explanation of his plan behind with me. I jog to catch up to him just as he steps outside, the humidity hitting me like a water balloon to the face. "Where are we going?"

He gestures to the city with a wide, inviting arm like he's Willy Wonka beckoning me into his chocolate factory. "I'm taking you to my favorite hidden gem in the city."

# CHAPTER FIFTEEN

"I CAN'T BELIEVE you thought you discovered Veselka."

I know it's mean to make fun of people for not knowing New York-y things, but Ivan's hidden gem is literally the most famous pierogi restaurant on the East Coast. I've been wheezing since we turned the corner on Second Ave and I saw him bound up the sidewalk like a cocker spaniel to show me his super cool, indie dinner pick: Veselka's pierogies.

"Well, have you been before?" Ivan spears one of our pierogies—we've already forgotten what filling is in any of them—and bites it in half. A dark green tendril almost makes it impossible to get a clean break. Filling: arugula and goat cheese.

"No."

"And are they now extremely delicious?" He points his fork at the pierogi that's currently en route to my mouth.

I wait until I've finished chewing enough to decipher the filling to respond. Bacon, egg, and cheese. Weird, but satisfying. "You make a good point."

"A compliment!" Ivan exclaims with so much enthusiasm he drops his fork. "Hell must've frozen over! And in the middle of July—a miracle."

I hide my chuckle behind my hand—both to not give him the satisfaction of knowing he made me laugh, and to save him from seeing a mouthful of half-chewed food. "My uncle and I visit the city a few times a year, and he's always saying we should try this place out," I clarify. "I figured I'd come at some point this summer, but I haven't had the chance yet since fake dating you is a full-time job."

"And I don't even come with health insurance." He raises a brow before helping himself to what I'm pretty sure is . . . yep. Definitely braised beef. "So what's up with you and your uncle? You didn't tell him you were at the academy?"

I swallow hard around my last bite. "It's complicated."

"Well, there's no agenda for this outing, and we have . . ." Ivan gets a text on his phone and glances at the message while responding. "Infinity hours to kill."

And I'd love to *not* spend all of that time talking about my relationship with my uncle, but in the spirit of trusting Ivan a little bit more for the sake of the bit, I relent. "Fine. So, my uncle is kind of . . . Clive Lyon."

"Ha! Knew it," Ivan says. "I didn't want to be like, 'Hey, are you related to this other Black guy,' just because you have the same last name, but, man, Clive Lyon. That's nuts. You live with him, right?" Ivan's voice is too curious for comfort. "What's that even like?"

There's a challenge somewhere in the way he's pushing his luck right now. At first I sense it's because he wants me to talk about some of the things I hide from him, but that's not all of it, I think. He wants me to stop wanting to hide things from him. He wants me to stop manufacturing this distance, to stop building my wall so he can stop digging a tunnel under it. I don't know why he bothers. If I were going to ask Ivan a personal question, it would be why he hasn't given up on trying to get to know me yet. I'm not asking him a personal question, though, he's asking me one.

Ivan breaks the silence before I do. "Sorry," he says. "You don't have t—"

"No, it's fine." I stab another pierogi as fuel for the rest of the conversation. "He used to say it's one of the easier famouses to be. The only people who recognize him now are deep-cut football nerds and the occasional Netflix documentarian looking for their next ninety-minute sob story."

"Do they find one?" Ivan asks, his tone kinder than I expected.

"Not really. He doesn't dwell on it for himself. Kinda pathologically dwells on it for me, though."

"Like how?" Ivan puts his fork down and gives me his full attention. I see an opportunity to steal another pierogi. He notices, but says nothing.

"Like how when I said I wanted to write for Wizzard Games, he immediately pushed me toward, like, coding and engineering because they're safer bets than creative work. And I get it, I'm going to need those skills too, but he wants me to go through life expecting the worst, and would it kill him to let me, I don't know. Dream a little? Aim high? Go for the Brian Juno mentorship to just *see* if I can do it? Not everything has to have a catch."

"Was there a catch to you coming to the academy?" Ivan asks.

"Yeah. You," I reply before helping myself to a long gulp of water—the perfect excuse to not say more than I have to. "Anyway, my baggage isn't exactly first date conversation."

Ivan stills. The fact that he didn't have a snarky retort locked and ready to go immediately sets me on edge. The corner of his lips quirk into a smile as he leans in closer to me. Whispering so quietly I almost don't hear him over the chatter of the densely packed dining room. "So, we're on a date?"

If Ivan expects me to earnestly answer that question, he's overestimating the amount of goodwill he's earned tonight by having good, if obvious, taste in Ukrainian food. I down another huge gulp of water to buy myself some more time to respond, only to blurt out the first thought that comes to mind when the timer I've set for myself is up. "You don't talk about Emilia, ever."

"Wow." Ivan leans back in his chair. "That was the clumsiest attempt at deflecting I've ever seen. I expect more from you."

"Sounds like a you problem." I bite into another mystery pierogi now that I'm out of water. Sauerkraut and mushroom. Not top three, but still good.

"Incredible. It's like talking to a wall." I expect that to end this leg of the conversation, but Ivan persists. "Is that why you've never liked me? Is Emilia the only reason you screwed me over at Wizzcon?"

I think back. "Don't forget the groupie thing."

"Fine, okay. And the groupie thing."

"And you stole Cass's desk at orientation."

"He's right-handed!"

"*And* the 'go easy on me' thing."

"Zora." Ivan scootches his chair closer to the table and conspicuously leans in. I imagine he's enjoying this and wants a better seat for my rare and unusual performance of vulnerability. I'm starting to regret saying anything. Wait—oh. He was just scraping some sour cream onto his plate. He's fine. I'm fine. "There's something I want you to know."

"Okay." This is as good a place as any to stop talking and start listening. Mainly so I can stop talking. The longer I talk to Ivan, the more I end up wanting to talk to him, and that is terrible. I don't want him to think he's cracked me open for real. So I'll let him have his moment and slide into a nice, tense silence.

"You remind me of this guy I used to know. He was an asshole."

"You've mentioned that about me, yeah."

"No, that's the thing." Ivan puts down his fork. "You're not an asshole. The guy I'm talking about, he was my captain last year, when I—when Emilia and I played together on the same team. We played really well together, by the way. She was a great partner."

No shit, Emilia Romero was a great partner. She's one of the greatest *Guardians League Online* players to ever do it.

"All Emilia ever did was make our team better, and this guy *hated* her for it. It was nuts to watch. The better she did, the more he was convinced she was out to get him, but all she wanted was to be his friend."

"See, that's where she messed up—"

"Shush. I know that. Now. He got what he deserved in the end, anyway." Ivan wipes his hand down his face and exhales loudly.

Oh, wow, this might actually be a deep cut from his past. We've stepped into the mirror universe where Zora and Ivan can go out to dinner and talk to each other. Damn, I guess Kavi's multi-phased plan really did work.

"I don't want you to end up like him," he says. "So I'm going to ask you right now, for real. What is your problem with me? Consider it a . . . performance evaluation. You don't have to tell me now—in fact, take some time to think about it. Check please."

That last part is to our server, who's been hovering around our table expectantly. This is Veselka on a summer holiday evening, after all. She dashes back to the kitchen to print our check.

My head is still spinning from Ivan's regrettably on-the-nose analysis of why he actually grinds my gears. I don't think he's out to get me, per se, but if—and this is a huge if—he's really trying to be my friend, then I am the asshole who hates him for trying.

# CHAPTER SIXTEEN

I PUT MYSELF under a lot of pressure to understand people's motives. It's how I protect my confused little heart, and that's the only way I know how to be. I think of that anxious pressure, the constant second-guessing what people mean versus what they say, as fuel, like steam powering an engine, but the way Ivan describes me, it sounds more like I'm a time bomb. He is obviously wrong here. Pressure is good. Pressure makes diamonds. Ivan thinks letting go and surrendering control is freedom. I know it makes me an easy target for the catastrophe I can't see coming but need to prevent regardless.

"Have you heard back from Kavi?" I ask after our server sets down our bill and Ivan has tossed down a wad of cash—who carries cash anymore?—more than enough for the bill and a generous tip. My phone has dangerously little battery left, so we let Kavi know to text him whenever we're cleared to return home.

Ivan checks his phone. "Nope, not yet. Give it a few more hours, I guess?"

This time it's my turn to check my phone. A quick Google search confirms that we have about an hour left until the fireworks start, and who knows how long before Kavi deems us adequately bonded.

"If we leave now we can catch the 6 train that's coming in five minutes," I announce, already grabbing my bag and heading for the door.

"Where are we going?" Ivan calls out, nearly tripping over a table leg in his rush to keep up with me.

"I'm gonna take you to *my* favorite hidden gem in the city."

Summer in the city is incredible. I mean, yeah, everything smells like hot garbage, and those gross oily puddles that never, ever evaporate show up in every intersection after it rains, but the light is unlike anywhere in the world. Central Park is full today, of joggers and bikers and tourists milling around to enjoy the Fourth of July outside.

It's one of those memorably perfect summer nights where the sun does us a solid and sets slowly over the river, like it's treating us to extra time in the park before the fireflies come out and the open hydrants lose all their water pressure. And on this evening, glowing gold in the sunset, I bring Ivan to the tower in the center of the map.

"Is this—"

"A legit castle in the middle of Central Park?" I twirl a few steps ahead of Ivan, gesturing to the castle looming above us like I'm a game show host's assistant presenting a brand-new car. "Yes, it is. Belvedere Castle, to be exact."

Ivan's lips quirk into a shy smile. "I know. It's where the X-Men watched the fireworks with the Teen Titans."

"Wait, what? When?" My arms drop back down to my sides. I guess it shouldn't be out of the realm of possibility that Ivan is a legitimate nerd on top of playing one on the twenty-first-century equivalent of TV.

"One of the comic runs, I can't remember. An alternate Earth, but they had a castle just like this one, right here."

Marvel references aside, Belvedere Castle is still an iconic New York landmark. It kind of feels like an offense against nature—a grand, old stone castle that looks pulled out of a fairy tale plopped right into the heart of a city that smells like hot dog water. Squealing kids climb along the rocks at the base of the castle—heads poke out of the castle's windows to wave at cameras waiting to capture the perfect shot from the ground. Over the tops of the trees the sun has just started to set, painting the sky the perfect orange-dusted shade of gold.

"You know what else it reminds me of?" Ivan trails off as he blinks up at the castle with what I'm assuming is the same awe I had in my eyes the first time I came here. "The tower from *GLR*. The one in the—"

"Middle of the map." I— Yeah. That's exactly what I wanted him to see.

"Exactly."

Ivan shifts slightly—something unlocking in his shoulders as he tears his gaze away from the castle to look back at me. "Your favorite starting-position-slash-execution-ground. Maybe I shouldn't have brought that up."

"I'm sorry." It comes out before I can stop it. "For Wizzcon. Beating you fair and square is one thing, but I let you think you were making a friend and used it against you. And even though I still think you shouldn't have—"

"Grilled cheese sandwich, I remember."

"—it was shitty of me. *Guardians League Royale* is tough enough without adding a psychological metagame."

"Hear, hear." Ivan brings his phone out of his pocket to check the time. "And for what it's worth, apology accepted. I'm sorry too, for the whole groupie thing. I don't know what I was thinking there; I was trying way too hard to look good and didn't think about how that would make you feel. So yeah. I'm sorry. Really sorry, actually."

My heart stutters the same way it did when he asked me if our dinner at Veselka was a date. I seriously need to get that checked out. For all we know I could be dying of some rare heart fluttering disease. Very dangerous.

"But, if you think about it, Frank should have known I was bluffing." The smirk is back. I prepare my eyes for rolling at whatever ridiculous joke he's about to come out with. "You're clearly out of my league."

"There it is!" I have been mentally working on my post-Veselka fake girlfriend homework by reflecting on what my problem with Ivan is, and that is the perfect segue. "That's what bothers me."

"That you're out of my league?" Ivan asks, confused.

"That you say all these super nice things all the time. I guess it's to get people to like you? And since you're always saying whatever you think they want to hear, it's *impossible* to tell if you're just lying to get your way. And since I can't tell—I'm autistic, by the way—I kind of . . . think you're full of shit and that you're making fun of me all the time."

"Jesus." Ivan's eyes are wide with concern. "I don't know what to say to that." Good. That means he's already incorporating the feedback. "But, Zora, I'm not making fun of you."

"How am I supposed to know?" I say softly, my eyes trained on the broad stone façade of the castle.

"Because I take you seriously. I take what you want seriously. I always have."

He's got a point there. Ivan may have gone about it in the most boneheaded way possible, but the day he met me, he only interfered because he thought he was helping me get what I wanted. The back of my neck suddenly feels warmer than it should in the shadow of the castle.

"Thank you for doing that," I mutter.

Based on the way Ivan is gazing dreamily at the sunset, it's unclear whether he heard my response. I can't help but linger on the look of him like this, bathed in fading sunshine. I'm able to shift my attention to a very intriguing rock beside my foot when he whips around suddenly, an overeager smile on his face that just screams trouble.

"Let's take something to post on WiTch," he suggests, already pulling his phone out of his pocket. In a blink, the dreamy moment is gone and I remember what we're doing here in the first place. Getting to know each other outside the game so we can pretend to be into each other later. For an audience. To beat an algorithm. Now is actually the perfect time to post something on WiTch.

"What are you thinking?" I ask, resigning myself to striking some poses and grimacing for another camera.

"Let's do a few selfies. Extra cute, extra gross?" he responds with a raised brow.

I bite my lip as I run my hands along my smooth, bare arms. "I'm not in my Kavi-and-Trieu-approved Zora Face," I explain, tossing my arms into the air and letting them fall limply back at my sides.

Another key aspect of social media: you only ever post when you look your best. And from what I saw in the reflection of the subway door a few minutes ago, the humidity hasn't been especially kind to me.

"You still look great," Ivan says so easily, even though it knocks me back like a shove. I'm able to keep my ground, but just barely. Since when does Ivan Hunt—and not the Ivan Hunt who's actively pretending to date me—think I look great?

"But—"

"You look like you," he adds before I can protest that my hair is not a fan of the moisture level in the air. "It's perfect."

I'm not sure if he means that me in all my messy hair and makeup-free glory is perfect, or if the façade is. That we can still be the happy, beautiful, adoring couple even when I'm not wearing enough makeup to make me feel like I have a second skin on. But my heart doesn't care about the difference. It kicks into hyper speed, beating so fast and loud I'm sure everyone within a five-mile radius can probably hear it.

Before I can decipher the who, what, and how of my heart palpitations, Ivan's hand is in mine, tugging me toward the edge of the castle. The world is a blur as we weave through crowds of sweaty tourists until we reach a free patch of grass right in front of the rockface along the side of the castle. The perfect angle that when Ivan holds up his phone, we can capture both the castle and the lake at the base of it in frame.

"Try to not look like hanging out with me gives you chest pains," he says as he quickly fluffs his hair.

I hear the click of a camera shutter seconds after I laugh, my cheeks flushing as I whip around to look at the camera. "I wasn't ready yet!" I protest, attempting to fix my hair as quickly as possible.

Ivan pockets his phone and makes a little rectangle out of his fingers and peers through it to frame the landscape around the castle. "Now let's do a video, wait—I got this. Let's tell a little story. It's going to be awesome. Can you walk toward the castle's stairs?"

I used to think Ivan was arrogant, but when he says something will be awesome, he can craft an entire universe out of words and smiles and pointed little gestures to make sure it's actually awesome.

"Okay, Richard Avedon. Relax. What's the story we're telling right now?"

It's only now that I notice Ivan hasn't followed me up to the castle. I've crossed a footpath and am two steps up, but when I turn around, he has his phone out and is filming me walking from behind.

"Ivan!" I call to him. "Warn me!"

"No!" he says with a very un-Ivan giggle and slowly moves across the path to keep his camera shot smooth. I don't know what's got him so giddy. Maybe this is what he's like when he's got some endorphins in him after performing light cardio. Maybe Veselka's pierogies induce mania in those unused to their doughy perfection. Or maybe he's . . . no, is he really having fun? Am I having fun? The thought stops me in my tracks and I make a confused enough face for Ivan to lower the phone and stop taking video.

"You okay?"

"I'm fine." I'm potentially fine. I'm fine.

"That was pretty good up until the end. We can cut that part out, though. Here, look."

He shows me his phone—ugh, his screen is cracked; that always gives me agita—and taps the video he just took. From where Ivan was standing, the sunset over the park makes my whole right side glow, and I looked half-golden when I turned around and spotted him filming. Even without the emphasis of Trieu's makeup, I can tell my lips aren't in the annoyed, angry purse I thought I remembered making. *"Ivan! Warn me!"* I say in the video, but it sounds different this time. I don't recall laughing when I said it a few moments ago, or my laugh being what made Ivan break into a corny snicker behind the camera. But that's what I'm seeing on-screen.

"Oh, favorite part. Right here," Ivan says. The camera moves closer to me, still a bit shaky despite his attempts at being a human Steadicam, and the closer angle makes a lens flare halo around my head. The fuzzy curls in my four-day-old twist-out catch the light in shimmery C-shapes that dance when I shake my head as Ivan gets closer. And here comes the part we're definitely cutting out. The quick change from my huge, sunlit smile to an immediate frown would be comical if I didn't remember what I was thinking when it happened.

"That looks . . . ," I trail off. I look amazing. Ivan wasn't kidding.

"Good enough to post," Ivan replies smugly. He can be smug about that one; he deserves it. "Even on our day off."

Well, no. That doesn't make any sense.

"We can't," I explain. "You're barely in it. This video is just about me, and we all know it's the two of us people care about."

"Look again." Ivan cocks his head at me like he's not taking that for an answer. Fine, I'll stop being stubborn and watch it again. "But remember who took the video." He cues it up from the top, and after a few moments I see exactly what he meant.

That video does tell a story with pictures, not with words. It's a story about a boy who likes a girl so much he can't help capturing the little moments that make her extraordinary in his eyes. When he's behind the camera, everything she does looks more magical than reality should allow. She pretends to shy away from his lens because she doesn't see what he sees, but the way she smiles makes it clear she's grateful someone notices she's special. She's especially grateful that he's the one who notices.

It's a solid, if cheesy, narrative. No wonder the internet likes it. Silly fantasies like that don't happen in real life, but Ivan and I have gotten miraculously good at making it seem like they can.

"Let's do one more," I say. "Another candid, but it's your turn."

"Fair is fair." Ivan hands me his phone and scrambles up a few more steps.

"Rolling!" I call out. "Do something cool, Ivan. Do a flip."

His laugh is cut short when a dark shadow appears at the top of the screen.

"What is—"

"Shit," Ivan shouts, careening down the stairs and jumping so far back he nearly goes toppling into a bush. I reach out to grab his outstretched hand just in time to pull him back to safety.

Just as soon as he's safely on land, the same dark swirl reappears out of the corner of my screen. Then another, and another. A flock of pigeons storming in to pick at the remains of an abandoned pretzel. A few feet away, a mom consoles her toddler as the birds chip away at what must be the remains of their dinner.

Another pigeon flies past Ivan's shoulder, and he doubles over to avoid getting hit by a rogue wing. He's practically curled up in the fetal position on the ground, holding there for a beat before lunging out of the pigeon's hunting ground. For the second time today, I'm doubled over from laughter, my sides aching from the force of my laugh. It takes a Herculean effort to straighten myself out enough to chase after him. A few more birds hop along the ground near him, and he leaps into the air to avoid them like they're made of toxic waste.

"He's afraid of birds!" I wheeze, spinning the camera into selfie mode. "Pigeons almost took him out! Tell the world! I'm dead!" Tears brim at the corners of my eyes and threaten to spill down my cheeks as I finally catch up to where he's collapsed onto a nearby bench.

"Pigeons are flying trash cans!" he says extremely quickly and extremely defensively.

I'm tempted to stand up on behalf of pigeons—which are as iconic to New York City as the Empire State Building—but decide to let Ivan live in his fear without judgment. For now, at least.

"I got that on video!" I wheeze once it seems like we're in the clear. The pigeons are distracted by their feast, and Ivan doesn't look like he's one wing flap away from passing out. My arm hovers on the bench behind him, my fingers twitching to reach out and try to console him somehow. Y'know. Like a good fake girlfriend would.

"Of course you did," Ivan mutters and runs a hand down his face. He shakes himself off like a dog on the beach, his hair an effortlessly cool mess. Completely unfair. He grabs his phone on his way past me and slaps at the screen until we hear the telltale beep of a stopped recording.

"Play it back, Ivan."

"No."

"You gotta."

"No!"

"For me?"

"Fine." He cues the second video, and I see his panic morphs into a genuine smile.

Ivan is grinning like a madman at first, silhouetted across the darkening sky like a giant as I call out to him. He looks so pleased to be there, even if I'm teasing him, but his impressive on-screen figure morphs absurdly fast into a panicked blur charging off frame.

Then, pure chaos. Belvedere Castle spins on the horizon behind us as I tried to catch up to Ivan's movement, until all becomes a whirl of sunset colors. We hear cooing, squawking, the crash of a boy into a bush. Cue my face and my uncontrollable laughter. Despite the massive building shielding us from the sun, the golden hour still manages to cloak me in the softest warm light. Even without makeup, my skin is lit up like there are a dozen flecks of glitter just beneath the surface. My smile is radiant. Honest. *Real.*

I can't tell if it was an accident, or Ivan continuing to attempt to get a candid moment even under duress. But it doesn't matter. Because it's perfect.

"I'll let you post this one," Ivan says, nudging his shoulder against mine. Before I can protest that we should post one where he's not just a screaming blob, he's already texted it to me along with a sunshine emoji. "If you let me post the one of you. Also, buy me a Popsicle."

Ivan Hunt's kryptonite revealed to the world and all I have to do is buy a Popsicle? This is the deal of the century.

"Why do you take what I want so seriously?" I finally blurt out the question that's been weighing on me all week when Ivan gets up from the castle steps to toss our Popsicle sticks in the trash. "To the point of being weirdly cool with pretending to date me?"

Ivan sighs and leans back against the steps like he's trying to crack his back. When that doesn't work to calm him down, he settles for another classic Ivan ritual: running his hand through his dark hair.

"I've been in situations where being me helped me get away with stuff. Avoiding consequences. And I know that people like you—don't look at me like that; you know what I mean—don't have that to the same degree, I guess. So if you decided you needed to use me, or what I have, to get ahead . . . I wasn't going to stop you."

"I didn't need—"

"And maybe I'm kind of using you too? Beyond the algorithm stuff."

"Oh, I have *got* to hear this." I cross my arms and lift a brow. "How? How are you using me outside of the competition?"

"To feel better about myself." He shrugs. "Helping you because I didn't help someone else."

"Why?"

"Why?" he repeats. "I . . . don't know? I have this need to like myself. I want to be the good guy."

"You want to *think* you're the good guy," I agree. "That's different from being one."

"Fair. But yeah, maybe it's just that. I want people to like me, so I try to be a person people like."

"Wow," I say. "As far as I'm concerned, you *really* shat the bed on that one."

"I said people, not *you*." His tone is light as he nudges his knee against mine. Our bodies are closer together again, like two magnets that can't resist their pull. "I stopped trying to get you to like me long ago. Talk about a lost cause."

"I didn't make it easy for you." I pause, then make a rewind motion with my finger. "Don't. I *don't* make it easy for you."

"And yet I persevered. And maybe succeeded."

"Only when you're not trying," I point out.

"Eh." He shrugs. "That's what I like most about you. Not having to try when I'm with you. That and how good you look in purple."

Before I can reply to that *very* loaded statement, an explosion makes us jolt off the steps in surprise. We step out from beneath the shadow of the castle to get a better look at the sky. A crack, then a high-pitched whirring sound, a boom, and a dramatic shimmery clatter that turns the evening light on the East Side bright green for three long seconds. The fireworks.

I read somewhere that the body and the brain don't always agree on what certain signals mean. When someone is scared, for instance, their body responds to the situation by pumping them full of adrenaline and getting their heart rate up, but those symptoms don't go away when the danger does. Those leftover homemade happy drugs need something to do, so the imperfect machine that is the human brain will start associating them with whatever is nearby. And that thing—or, sometimes, a person—will start to make them feel happy and safe.

I am not afraid of fireworks, but I do startle easily. My adrenaline is up, that's for sure.

"Look at that one!" Ivan points up to the sky, where a bolt of red explodes into a shimmering cascade of sky glitter. He looks so cute, with his arm stretched up like a little kid trying to touch the sparkles as they fall.

"You know what?" I turn to Ivan, shouting to be heard. His light eyes reflect each new color in the sky as they burst, crackle, and fade. "I think you might not be the worst thing ever."

A lull in the fireworks makes that last word too loud, which makes us giggle, which brings us closer together on the steps.

"You sure about that?" Ivan asks. Slowly, dramatically, he pulls out his phone and shows me what's on his screen. His text messages.

*KAVI: Mission complete!! You guys can come back now.*

*KAVI: Guys???*

*KAVI: Seriously it's been like three hours are you dead*

*KAVI: Did you kill each other??*

In the time it takes me to read the texts, Ivan's body has shifted close enough for me to smell his neck again, and I am *this* close to . . . fully collapsing into a puddle, if I'm being honest.

"When did you get these?" I ask, though I can't seem to get my voice up beyond a whisper.

Ivan shrugs. "Oh, like, halfway through dinner. I was waiting to see how long it took you to notice."

Above us, the sky explodes in red, blue, and sparkling white.

"You motherfu—"

I think the first time he kisses me it's to make me stop talking, which works. The second kiss is because the first one overwhelmed every sense I've ever noticed having and has me dragging Ivan closer by his shoulders, his shirt, anything I can do to stay suspended in the center of that perfect, too-much feeling of everything. The third is just for fun. And, well, with the fireworks and all, let's say we'll have a very happy Fourth.

# CHAPTER SEVENTEEN

AFTER THE WORK she's put in this summer, Kavi deserves to be the youngest winner of the Nobel Peace Prize. Hold on, let me look something up. Never mind, second youngest. But my point still stands.

After the Fourth of July, the party that rolled up to our next academy match was an entirely different entity. Sure, the clothes and makeup were the same, but our party actions suddenly worked in ways I didn't even know were possible under this ruleset. In fact, we may have graduated from the definition of party. In just a few short weeks, we've become what I thought I wanted to avoid but now realize I desperately needed: a team.

Everything is a performance when there's an HD camera in your face, a ring light beyond your monitor, and a couple hundred strangers watching us play a *GLR* match live, but now it feels like it's all clicked into place. We took a sledgehammer to the wall I built up between us, and it's so much easier to play my part now that I'm not afraid of seeing Ivan. Fully.

"Nice shot, babe," I praise Ivan as he manages to take down someone attempting to snipe us from a nearby tree. I even commit the cardinal sin of *GLR* and look away from my screen long enough to shoot Ivan a smile IRL, my heart swelling when I realize he's looked away from his screen too, as if he was waiting—no, hoping—that I'd look at him.

Between us, Cass doesn't bother hiding his gag.

I consider taunting him on camera, but decide against it when a distant explosion forces me to focus on the game again. Real feelings aside, this is still a performance. One that Cass isn't a part of—at least not today.

With the sniper finished off, VANE covers my back while I pick off the remaining chests in the forest clearing we landed in. We split up the goods—a couple of grenades for me, and a chainsaw for him—before a chime announces the shrinking of the safety zone.

"Meet at Belvedere?" Ivan asks, immediately matching my pace when I start sprinting to the east side of the map—straight for the tower.

"You read my mind," I reply with a smirk, memories of our own adventure at a very familiar castle making my cheeks feel hot despite the legion of cooling fans keeping our computers safe onstage.

Out of the corner of my eye, I spot an influx of heart emojis coming into the chat—the usual flood that comes in anytime Ivan and I do something remotely couple-like. Part of me should probably feel weird about the fact that people are cheering on what are now genuine interactions between me and the guy I . . . well, I'm not really sure what we are now, but the point is, there's more to our performance now that there's a layer of reality involved.

"Thanks for the subscribe, OpieDopie11," Ivan calls out as we make our way across the map. "Make sure you check out the new emotes and keep the hype train running!" As much fun as I'm having, Ivan's better at keeping the crowd engaged. This boy could sell spaghetti Popsicles in a bridal shop, and he makes everyone in chat feel special just for showing up.

If I'm being honest, I'm kind of, maybe, starting to like playing *GLR* for a digital crowd. It's difficult to keep my eyes on the game and the chat at the same time—especially when they're not just spamming emotes—but I watched enough anime with subtitles in high school that the quick-reading skill is coming back to me a little more each stream (shout-out to *One Piece*, straw hat for life). At this point it barely matters if people are watching the match on Ivan's WiTch or on mine; we're both getting the same boost from the Wizz-Algorithm.

A laser beam goes flying past us, narrowly missing VANE's head by inches.

"Shields up," I announce, my jaw set as I scan the horizon for any sign of our attacker. Ivan and I each employ our respective shields, exchanging a thumbs-up emote before wordlessly splitting up into separate, but still close by, areas of the map. While it might not be as exciting for the fans watching, sticking together basically makes us walking targets.

I keep a careful eye on where VANE winds up going, taking note of the rock he's crouched behind while I dash for a cave to my left. I have time to flick my gaze toward chat while I haul ZORA up on top of a dripping green stalagmite and see that the hype train Ivan mentioned is losing steam. On a whim I decide to maneuver myself in the direction of Ivan's hiding spot and mash the blowing a kiss emote in-game. And . . . the crowd goes wild! Hype train picks up again. Suckers, all.

Our attacker doesn't take any more shots at us once we've settled into our hiding spots. I pull out the binoculars I snagged from the last loot chest and take a closer look at the horizon from the safety of my cave refuge. Suddenly, I see a flash of something from behind a cluster of trees—the edge of a laser gun peeking out from behind a tree trunk. My breath hitches as I try to gauge the distance, whether they're in close enough range to hear my mic.

"Third tree from the left," I whisper cautiously, shifting my camera to get a better view of VANE. He shoots back a thumbs-up emote, and I know we're prepared to attack.

Slowly, carefully, we get into position. Leaving our hiding spots and inching toward the trees without putting ourselves in our hidden attacker's line of vision.

"Charge!" I yell into my headset as soon as we're within range, and the chat spams bow and arrow emojis. Calling out our attacks is kind of my thing now. Ivan would usually respond with something cute like, "I'm with you to the end of the line," or "Where you lead, I will follow," but this time we focus on our plan of attack.

Ivan distracts the attacker, zigzagging his way across the clearing leading up to the trees while I perch up on a nearby rock, ready my bow, and take aim. The arrow goes flying as soon as a flash of an arm is in sight, and I've got another loaded and ready to go before the first one has even made contact. Never let them catch you off guard.

But the second arrow isn't needed. My first one misses, but VANE reaches the tree line in time to swipe his chainsaw through the air and cut down both the tree and our mystery attacker. The body bursts into a flurry of pixels as they fade out of the game.

PLAYER CASS HAS BEEN ELIMINATED BY PLAYER VANE.

Shit.

I look up from my screen to see Cass whipping off his headset and tossing it onto his keyboard with a clatter that makes me wince.

"Cass, I—"

"Zora, look out!" Ivan calls out, snapping my attention back to the game.

An arrow comes barreling toward me, and I manage to barrel-roll out of the way in the nick of time. VANE takes a shot at whoever came after me and misses, but successfully distracts the attention away from me. Long enough that I'm able to make a dash for a nearby hill to get some leverage. From this vantage point, I'm able to pull back my own bow, take aim, and fire.

PLAYER ZION HAS BEEN ELIMINATED BY PLAYER ZORA.

"My knight in shining armor," Ivan praises once he's caught back up to me.

"C'mon, damsel," I call out to him before taking off to the new safety zone. "We've got a match to win."

Ultimately, the match isn't ours to win. Ivan gets taken down by a rogue rocket launcher midway through our sprint to the new safety zone, and I wind up placing third after a fierce melee battle with a girl I vaguely recognize seeing on my floor before. Still, it's an improvement from our match earlier this week—both in terms of placement and viewer reaction.

"Thank you guys so much; this was fun," I say to chat as a flurry of heart emojis pile in at the end of the match.

"Seriously, you're the best," Ivan adds. "After Zora. Zora's the best, then you guys."

"I thought you said you were lactose intolerant?" I say to Ivan, who looks over at me with confusion. "But today you're extra cheesy," I finish, to a barrage of laughing emojis and all-caps messages in the chat.

Ivan rolls his eyes and brushes his hair out of his face in a way that we both know drives his love-stricken fans wild—his own chat says as much. We, along with the rest of the academy, sign off from our respective streams with a final goodbye to our viewers. A weight settles uncomfortably on my shoulders as soon as the red light above my camera blinks off, reality setting in now that I'm no longer on my virtual stage.

"I thought that went pretty well," Ivan says, appearing beside me in record speed.

"Zora, can we talk?" For someone so tall, Cass is surprisingly good at sneaking up on me. He didn't used to be, or maybe I never used to let myself get as distracted as I am these days.

"Yeah." I make sure my headphones are unplugged and roll my chair around to face him. "What's up?"

"You had that shot on me and you didn't take it. You gave it to *him*." He gestures toward Ivan with a look of pure disgust. "The Zora I know would never do that."

"Cass." I lower my voice. Is he being serious right now? "You know it's just for the stream."

"Yeah. That's worse," he says. "I can't do this."

By now, Kavi and Trieu are out of the game and are tuned into our conversation. It's rare enough to see Cass on this side of the stage—but to have him look at me like I'm a coiled-up cobra is extra rare.

"What do you mean you can't do this?" Kavi asks. "We still have a week to go before the final rankings come out."

It's been neck and neck between the five of us, but now that Ivan's truly on my side, I'm not as worried about winning the academy. Top five would be great, top two amazing, but I have my in with Brian Juno regardless of what happens. Or at least that's what I told myself when Trieu and Kavi pulled in front of Ivan and me in the rankings last week. Which doesn't make a ton of sense, but the Wizz-Algorithm works in mysterious ways.

"I mean I'm off the team. Leaving the party, whatever. Good luck with the rest of the academy, but I can't contribute to"—he takes a pause to look at me, then Ivan, then back to me—"whatever this is."

"Cassius, please—"

"Zora!" a voice calls out before I can say anything else—a voice that makes me rocket out of my seat. Cass hears it too and rolls his eyes.

"See you on the map, guys." And with that, Cass exits stage right.

"There you are, all of you." Brian Juno doesn't have to wait for the crowd of teens onstage to part for him to have a clear path to our cluster of desks.

"Hi, Brian!" My voice is high-pitched enough to summon a pack of dogs as I stand at military-precision-level attention. Ivan's arm wraps lazily around my shoulders—the weight of him grounding me is comforting, despite my general aversion to touch.

"Fantastic job today," Brian praises as he approaches us with a childlike bounce to his step. His cheeks are flushed pink like he just got in from a snowstorm. That, or he has rosacea.

My knees threaten to buckle, but Ivan thankfully tightens his grip on me when I wobble slightly. "Thank you so much," I reply quickly, resisting the urge to jump up and down. Approval!—praise!—from Brian Juno!

"Kavi, Trieu." Brian nods at them each in turn, and I hear Trieu in particular fail to restrain a thrilled squeak. "Do you mind if I borrow these two for a moment?" The two to which he refers are Ivan and me. "Walk with me." Brian's already walking past us, gesturing for us to follow him by curling his index finger. I've never walked so fast in my life—practically leaving behind a dust cloud as I race to keep up with him.

We weave through the hall with ease, all of the other academy members parting for Brian like he's Moses in the Red Sea. I can't help but preen over the quiet gasps and whispers surrounding us as we head for the closest exit on the right side of the room—leading toward the Wizzard offices we've never been allowed to visit. Before, being the center of attention felt like a curse. Dozens of eyes watching my every move, pulling me apart. Today, a rush of pride washes over me as Ivan and I are escorted out of the room by Brian Juno himself. Proof of what I've known since I got here—that I have what it takes to make it to the end. To be the best of the best.

"Your streams have been doing excellent numbers," Brian says as soon as the door to the hall swings closed behind us. "No surprise, our audience loves a good star-crossed lovers story."

My heart rockets into my throat at the idea that *we* might be the next Wizzard staple couple. Emilia and Jake. Zora and Ivan. I've gotta admit, it has a nice ring to it. Ivan shoots me a discreet knowing look, giving me a thumbs-up first before sliding an arm around me again. Without thinking, I lean into his touch. The smell, the warmth, the feel of him making this all the more intoxicating.

"I see a lot of really exciting opportunities for you two. And if you keep up the good work," Brian says as we turn a corner to a sleek gray hallway—office doors with vaguely familiar names listed on the doors. Wizzard execs, I'm pretty sure. I'm practically vibrating from the high of Brian Juno praise. If I wasn't so determined to see this through to the end, I might even say I could die happily right in this moment. "Ivan mentioned you might want to throw your hat in the ring for my creative mentorship program this fall?"

I glance over at Ivan, who wiggles his prodigious eyebrows at me. He really wasn't kidding. I am basically already in with Brian!

"I absolutely do," I say with a little too much enthusiasm—my voice echoing back to me in the weirdly sparse hallway. "Thank you so much, Brian. I—"

"That's great." Brian stops in his tracks so abruptly I almost walk right into him. He turns on his heel in front of his suite at the end of the hall, his own name written on the gold nameplate beside the doorframe. "Ivan, do you mind coming in here for a minute?"

There's a pause as Ivan looks over at me with a look that's either panic, confusion, or both. My brows knit together in confusion as I glance between Ivan and Brian and back again.

"Y-yeah. Sure." Ivan's smile seems forced as his arm falls away from my shoulders and he takes a slight step away from me.

Brian still has enough energy to power Times Square, though, as he gives me a megawatt smile. "Thank you, Zora. Again, really good work today."

"Th-thank you," I stammer out, managing to stop myself from bowing at the last second and taking an uncertain step back instead.

Brian and Ivan disappear into Brian's office in the blink of an eye, the enthusiastic lilt of Brian's voice carrying even through the thick wood of the door. I stay rooted in place for longer than I should, unsure if I should leave or hang around and wait for Ivan. We *did* say we wanted to debrief after our match today—go over any moments where we might've slipped on camera, or things we can do to improve for next time. And then there's the whole Cass thing, which I'll need to sort out at some point. My head spins just from the thought of having to face that conversation.

Still, something keeps me rooted in place. The softly muffled sound of Brian's voice. Of Ivan saying something I can just barely make out. I take one step toward the door. Adrenaline and curiosity pushing down my conscience and pulling my body forward. Then another, and another. Until, finally, I'm close enough that those muffled sounds begin to take shape. And I can hear exactly what's on the other side.

# IVAN ALL ALONG

# CHAPTER EIGHTEEN

THERE WERE WORSE places to be than inside Brian Juno's cushy box at the Wizzard Theater. Worse places like the minuscule town in Ohio in which Ivan's parents decided to have their daughter, the minuscule house where they raised her, and the minuscule bedroom-slash-office they converted when a second child arrived twelve years after the first. Even as a kid Ivan knew that he was somewhat supplementary to the plan his parents made for their lives, and for his sister's, so he endeavored to spend as little time in that house as necessary, and he succeeded.

The trick to staying out of the house was to make as many other people as possible desire his company. When he was a kid, Ivan maintained a packed schedule of sleepovers, spaghetti dinners at the neighbors' houses, camping trips, and anything else that kept him away from the borrowed feeling he felt whenever he crossed the threshold to his childhood home. Invitations were his currency, and invitations only came when people wanted you around.

To his peers, Ivan radiated the kind of nice-guy coolness that makes teachers and authority figures disbelieve the stereotype of popular kids. He knew everyone's birthday, their favorite color, what games they played and how to beat them, and prided himself on making at least one person feel special every day. To his neighbors he was a Good Kid, attending church on Sundays with one family, Saturday service at his town's only synagogue with another, complimenting each casserole-bearing doyenne when they shyly unfolded the tinfoil lids keeping their post-service luncheon hot in the basement or meeting hall. He found if he was pleasant enough and asked people questions that got them talking about themselves, no one minded when he declined to participate further in their religion because as far as Ivan was concerned, God was bagels.

Ivan grew up cooking with moms, memorizing all kinds of sports statistics to chop it up with the dads, smiling at the girls who rarely got smiles, and holding court with guys who weren't sure if they wanted to kick him, date him, or be him. He was good at being liked almost wherever he went, shapeshifting from one paragon to another, and it was fucking *exhausting*.

Rather, it had been exhausting. Recently Ivan had caught a break. A huge, Zora-shaped break. A girl, a whole, complicated, brilliant, outrageously hot girl who saw exactly who Ivan was underneath the countless layers of people-pleasing character work. And she liked what she saw. Eventually.

He knew when he met Zora that she was someone special. At the time he assumed "special" meant "put on this earth to test me," but looking back there was something else he'd felt when he first looked into her clever black eyes: he felt seen.

Back then the feeling was terrible—nothing he said or did charmed her or convinced her to give him the little bit of leeway he'd been cultivating with other people since he learned to talk. Christ, she literally met him once before she decided to shoot him in the face, and *he deserved it*!

The night of the Fourth, when the fireworks had finished and the two of them walked back toward Lincoln Center, Ivan admitted to Zora how shook he'd been that day.

"I wasn't kidding when I said I thought about you," he'd said. The hundreds of people leaving Central Park after the fireworks had caught up with them, cocooning both Zora and Ivan in the cozy anonymity of a summer-drunk (and probably drunk-drunk) evening crowd. "After Wizzcon. Couldn't get you out of my head, really."

"Same," Zora admitted. "Usually after I beat someone, I don't think about them ever again, but you got under my skin like a splinter. At first I thought I just had a wildly overdeveloped sense of revenge—"

"You do. Iñigo Montoya–ass."

"—but that wasn't totally the reason why. The memory just stayed frozen up there in my head. When you touched my shoulder, when you looked at me. I was just so . . . I thought it was angry? Though now I realize it was probably something else. Horny-angry. Horngry."

That was the least sexy thing Ivan had ever heard, so he kissed her.

"I can't pretend around you," he'd said later, as they idled outside their building, too caught up in the heat of the day and each other to head inside just yet. "Scares the shit out of me."

"I can tell," Zora replied. "It's hilarious." Ivan laughed at that, imagining a sign attached to the left side of Zora's chest. *Do not enter*, it read, invitingly. "I can't pretend around you either. Or anyone, really. I'm a single-speed bike."

"It's the best speed. My favorite speed, my only speed. If it's over the speed limit, I'm getting a ticket."

"Relax." Zora hadn't meant it unkindly. She'd swung around on a No Parking street sign and used the momentum to kiss him again. "And, yeah, I do see the irony of my uptight ass telling you to relax."

"Watch it," Ivan said in the thankfully brief moments when her mouth wasn't interrupting his mouth. "Just because you're my fake girlfriend doesn't mean I won't fight you for talking shit about my fake girlfriend."

"Oh." Zora pulled away and tilted her head thoughtfully. "Right. That. Should we maybe —"

"Narrative consistency," he'd reminded her. "Is just 'girlfriend' fine?"

She had sighed, rested her head on his shoulder (which, by the way, top five physical contact moment EVER), and grumbled into his shirt. "I guess. So now we're *real* dating for clout? That's . . ."

"Convenient," Ivan admitted.

"I was going to say 'worse,'" Zora corrected. "But sure."

After slipping back into the dorm along with the massive rush of fellow students, they wound up on the couch. The only light in the common room was coming from the illuminated menu screen for *Super Smash Bros.*, which they would eventually play that night—now that they'd mastered working as a team, they could get right back to destroying each other.

Just not right then. There was more to talk about, and more important questions to ask.

"How did we not figure this out sooner?" Zora whined, quiet despite them having the dorm to themselves for the rest of the night.

"We're dumb," Ivan reasoned, his words partially muffled on account of his lips being pressed against Zora's long, beautifully brown neck. "We're so, so dumb."

"The dumbest," she'd agreed. "Kiss right above my collarbone."

"And you're *bossy,*" was one of the many words he'd said against her skin that night.

Ahem. But Ivan digressed. It was so much easier to maintain their romance hustle when it wasn't a hustle at all. The chemistry between himself and Zora hadn't necessarily changed, but the whole vibe of their #content was totally different when they weren't wasting time fighting the metaphorical moonlight. They played better as well, with the Wizz-Algorithm skyrocketing both of them up in the ranks. In short, absolutely everything was coming up Ivan. At the end of August, Ivan looked forward to Zora taking her rightful place as Brian's mentee, while he happily ascended to the captaincy of the New York *Guardians League Online* team. Where his team would compete against Emilia and Jake, to whom he and Zora would continue to be compared, which would be bad because Ivan knew Emilia deserved a very wide berth when it came to him.

Nope. That was a tomorrow problem. Today, Ivan had leverage, ideas, and he had Zora.

"We need to talk," Brian said within seconds of Zora closing the door behind her, leaving Brian and Ivan alone.

Well, that was never a good sign. Nevertheless, Ivan's optimism refused to wane. The fact that Brian had asked Zora to join them on their walk to his office was a positive sign that things were going the way he'd hoped. Captaincy for him, and a mentorship for Zora, if they continued playing their cards right.

And assuming Brian Juno wasn't about to do something wack, like right now.

Brian had a rolling table set up in front of his usual leather recliner and was hunched forward in his seat to tap at the keyboard of a Wizzard-branded laptop.

"You shouldn't sit like that," Ivan advised, eager to defuse the unusual tension in the room. "Terrible for your back."

"I tell you what to do." Brian's voice was flat. Uncompromising. "Not the other way around."

Ivan held his hands up. "Sorry, sheesh. Just looking out for your spine."

"Look out for yourself," Brian said, still short and cold. Ivan felt a sharp twinge behind his stomach. If everything was going as well as he thought, why did it feel like Ivan was about to get in trouble?

His answer came when Brian turned his laptop screen around. "Care to explain?"

Ivan squinted at the screen, his eyes not totally adjusted to the darkness from the brightly lit main hall, and made an informed guess: this was the backend of the summer academy members' social accounts, which were technically owned by Wizzard. Brian had pulled out some data and auto-visualized it in a chart that showed some line or other trending slowly down.

“Explain what?” Ivan asked.

“Explain why you and Zora’s metrics have been trending toward the toilet since the first week of July.”

“They are?” It was news to Ivan. “But our rankings have barely dipped.”

“And then there’s this.” Brian clicked around and pulled up another window, this one with comments on Ivan’s latest stream.

```
> Is anyone else kind of over Zivan?
> I miss when they kinda sniped at each other
> Booooooring.
> Are Zora and Ivan bad at science? Because
  they're failing chemistry
```

“That last one’s clever,” Ivan flattered sarcastically.

“The problem,” Brian began, in a tone that suggested Ivan must have failed more than just chemistry, “is that we’re in the last week of this program and things need to start heating up, not cooling down.”

“Okay.” Ivan wasn’t sure if Brian wanted him to pitch suggestions or what, but the focused look in the CEO’s eyes threw him off his guard. “How about if we expand this story beyond Zivan? Cook up some rivalries between us and some of our other friends at the academy? Kavi and Trieu are—”

Brian hummed loudly before Ivan could finish, but Ivan had a feeling in his gut that it wasn’t in thought as he pondered this suggestion. "Not enough," Brian replied with a sense of finality that told Ivan his gut instinct was on the money.

"Then what do you suggest?" Ivan asked, resisting the urge to throw his hands up in the air in defeat. If Brian had an idea from the jump, why didn't he just get right to it?

"I'm glad you asked," Brian said, quickly enough to signal he'd been expecting Ivan to ask that exact question at this point in the conversation. "You need to dump Zora."

"What?" Ivan spoke louder than he intended. "Why?"

"I don't need to tell you why," Brian said dismissively, but the glare of his cold eyes never left Ivan's face.

Ivan didn't buy that for a moment. "But you're going to anyway."

"Four words." Brian waved his hand in front of him as if cleaning off a chalkboard and punctuated each word with a flourish. "Battle. Of. The. Exes."

"You," Ivan said, realizing something he should have clocked far earlier in the summer, "are a lunatic."

"Maybe," Brian replied. "But all of our market research points to building these last few weeks up toward something huge. And since you and your fake girlfriend are by far the biggest breakouts from the program, I've decided a break*up* is the simplest and most effective way to make sure we have maximum eyeballs on the academy's grand finale."

"I won't do it," Ivan said, barely hearing the rest of what Brian said after "fake girlfriend." Considering Brian's bizarre obsession with the personal romantic lives of minors, he didn't care to divulge that the "fake" part of his relationship had tipped significantly toward the real—especially since that inflection appeared to be the point at which he and Zora stopped giving the masses the drama they clearly and mathematically craved. "You can't make me dump her."

"Might I remind you that the only reason you even have a second chance at a Guardians League contract is because I put you in this position? You lost. Twice." Any trace of the forced camaraderie the two of them played at was gone from his voice. This was usually a situation Ivan could fix with the right words and reassurances, but that only worked if the other person had anything to lose from dropping the act. Ivan was suddenly aware of how young he was compared to Brian, and how few people he had who he could count on. It became clear to him just how much Brian didn't need to count on other people's company. He *had* a company. And this shiny-eyed, calculating adult was looking at Ivan like an asset that wouldn't even merit a write-off. "I didn't pick you because you're the best player for my games. I picked you because you'd do whatever it takes to win again, and for a while that meant dating Zora Lyon."

That was a vastly simplistic interpretation of Ivan's motivations at the beginning of the summer . . . but not too simplistic. Ivan suppressed a wince at the possibility that Brian was right.

"Your win conditions have changed," Brian continued. "Get over it and stick to the plot."

"No," Ivan said quietly. He didn't want to be that person anymore. He'd never hurt Zora the way he hurt Emilia. He would not abandon her and once again become a villain for something he never wanted to do in the first place. "I won't do it. And it doesn't even make sense. I'm a better person than that. People have to know that by now. I won't throw away a year of progress to satisfy your story requirements."

Brian leveled his gaze at him for a long moment, with a silence that would have turned Ivan's insides to jelly at the beginning of the summer. But Brian didn't scare him anymore. There were more important things than the official recognition of the Guardians League and Wizzard Games as an organization. There were his friends, there was his own hard-fought reputation. There was Zora. More than anything, there was Zora. And in any situation where he had a choice between being with her or propping up Brian's propaganda machine, he'd pick her any day.

Then Brian surprised him. After staring at a spot over Ivan's right shoulder for a few long seconds, he . . . smiled? "Okay," Brian said with a shrug. "So much for that idea. I can't force you to dump her."

"That's right," Ivan said tentatively. His victory over Brian's will felt oddly perfunctory, and happened altogether too quickly to be trusted. "You can't."

"That's true, I can't," Brian sighed. "After all, it was your idea to use her as a walking rehab for your image after you shat the bed last year with Emilia Romero. You just needed a girl, right? Any girl to vouch for you. Well, preferably a brown one; that was just extra points. Someone to let all the others know you've *changed*. You're *safe*. You're one of the good guys."

"That's not what—"

"But it helped. And let's be real, you needed the boost. Admit it."

Ivan suddenly knew what it felt like to be cornered. It sucked, especially because he had no idea why Brian was acting like this. He'd always been kind of a prick, but this was genuinely scary. Ivan felt his frustration build up behind his face, threatening to burst forth as anything ranging from tears to yelling to outright running away from this horrible office. He did none of those things. He simply froze.

"I mean, yeah, it help—"

"Did you get that?" Brian asked, his voice suddenly loud, as if trying to reach someone on the other side of a wall. Turned out, he didn't need half that volume to make his point. Ivan looked over his shoulder toward the back of the box and felt his stomach sink when he saw who was standing in the doorway.

"Loud and clear," answered Zora. Her calmness was ten times more concerning than if she had come in guns blazing.

Ivan felt like one of those expensive architectural LEGO sets, if someone had just dropped it from a balcony and onto a concrete slab. Thing was, if he had actually been one of those, Zora would at least be compelled to look at him. Today, framed in the door like a full-length portrait of a vengeful Fury, she looked straight past him, straight past Brian even. Ivan mentally followed her gaze to the view of the stage through Brian's huge glass window. That was where all her attention was focused, and Ivan felt another load-bearing LEGO pillar snap into pieces inside his brain.

With each piece came a question—what? How? When? All the big ones really. But all Ivan could eke out was, "What is she doing here?"

# ZORA

# CHAPTER NINETEEN

FIRST OF ALL, to clear things up, yes, I was eavesdropping. I was dropping eaves so hard no one could ever pick them up again, and that is *not* the problem here. I was simply curious as to why he was having a one-on-one meeting with Brian Juno, and why I could very distinctly hear *my* name being said by Brian. Because, hello, I'm here to make an impression. Who wouldn't want to know what the person they've been trying to impress all summer was saying about them? So, I listened. And maybe, *maybe*, I was a little curious about Ivan's role in all of this. Because despite how incredible these last few weeks have been, weeks where I felt like I could finally unlock the Ivan box in my head and let the contents spill over into every corny, cheesy, heart-eyes manifestation of actually liking this dude, a part of me still wonders if I can really trust him.

"What is she doing here?" Ivan asks, sounding about as desperate as I'd imagine he should be considering the situation. And it's in that same desperation that he's asked the wrong question entirely. It's not about what I'm doing here. It's about what I'm about to do here.

Ivan's eyes are wide, their whites almost glowing against the dim light in this terrible, man cave–ass office where Brian Juno apparently watches our matches and hatches his freaky little schemes like the wizard of Wizzard. "I . . . I can explain. It's not what you think."

"It's not?" I ask. Something about getting my inside angry outside has made it easier for me to control my voice. Instead of exploding outward at the absolute insanity of the TV Trope conversation I overheard, I stay completely still in the doorway. Going by Ivan's face, I think this scares him more than if I was yelling. "So you didn't cheat your way into the academy by agreeing to be Brian Juno's spy on the inside, and you haven't been working with him the whole time to stir up drama, up to and including dating me? And now that interest is waning, he doesn't want you to break up with me and make me look like an asshole because he has the literal prerogative and power to do so?"

"Okay." Ivan has his hands held out like a zookeeper carefully approaching an escaped tiger. "So it is, technically, what you think, but—"

"So you, what? Flagged me on the first day as an easy mark? Capitalized on the fact that I had no idea what I had gotten myself into? Realized you could use me as a shield to deflect whatever strays you were still catching for what happened with Emilia last year?"

"Wait," Ivan says, "you do remember that the fake-dating idea was yours in the first place, right? I'll admit where I'm wrong, but I'm not going to suck up the blame for something I didn't do, not again."

"Because that's what you think this is about. Assigning blame. Ivan, you—we. I thought . . ."

"I know." Ivan looks up at me, more serious than I've seen him all summer. "That part was true." I see him shift his weight uncomfortably and try not to look over at Brian. Ivan's right if he's assuming that Brian has absolutely no right to hear this conversation, but apparently Brian's been the third wheel all along, so I'm not inclined to feel bad for him right about now. "It's still true; I really care about you."

"No," I interrupt before he can say something even more stupid. The only thing I can think to do with my words right now is to let him know just how close he is to losing me, somehow even harder than he's losing me now. "I don't believe you. Say something else."

"I can't!" Ivan says, like he has any right to be exasperated. "It's true, I like you. I don't, like, one-hundred-percent get it either, but you are the only person who expected more from me. I don't know when it changed, and I don't think you do either, but we're better together. I'm better. You've made me realize that it's possible to want things beyond what this asshole"—he gestures to Brian ("Hey!")—"can offer."

"I don't want to make you better," I reply. "I don't want you to *feel* better because of me. I would honestly hate to leave you with the impression that your self-improvement, or your reputation, or how you feel about yourself, is anything close to my priority." If that makes me sound like a serial killer in a movie, so be it.

"So what is your priority?" Brian Juno asks. It's the first time he's addressed me since I crossed the threshold into his awful corner office and started ripping into Ivan.

"What?" What kind of question is that? My entire summer just got tossed in a blender and set to puree, and he wants to know what my life priorities are?

"Do you still want your contract or not?" he asks, more deliberately. The pronoun catches me out—*my* contract. Like it's already there and waiting. Is it?

"But the algorithm—"

"Let me handle the algorithm. There's nothing in those numbers I can't change on the backend. And have been, by the way. So, you know. Welcome to the show," Brian finishes for me, and I feel the wrong kind of weightless. That's all this place has ever been. For show. "I'll make some adjustments," he says with a careless wave of his hand. "Get you into the top slot, if you want it."

"I don't—" I look over at Ivan, who is finally starting to look less terrified and more pissed off. Scared Ivan is useless to me; angry is at least something I can understand. "Would we still have to do the breakup?"

"Zora, no," Ivan says in disbelief. "You're not seriously thinking about going along with him."

"Why not?" I snap back. "Is manipulating people with Brian's help something only you're allowed to do? Why not fake break up, Ivan? It's not like we were ever fake together in the first place."

"That's not true."

"I don't care." I turn to Brian. "Okay, let's do it. Battle of the exes, sure, it's on. We position the breakup as Ivan screwing up, and me getting a chance to kick his ass up to God for what he did to me."

"Are we still talking about *GLR*?" Brian asks with a knowing smirk.

"Does it matter?" I answer. Somewhere in my emotional mire of betrayal and seething rage, I've managed to find some boldness. And why shouldn't I? I'm just as valuable to the academy as Ivan is now; I should absolutely have a say in my own storylines.

"Not really." Brian shrugs. "But I think we have room to negotiate. We have to work quickly if we're going to build it big enough for the finale next weekend, though. We'll need some pictures, some social media posts, get Kavi and Trieu in on it—good idea to work with them, by the way—maybe a little in-game beef . . ." He ticks the necessities off on his fingers. I can't help but feel a little pleased that I've managed to parlay this into Brian inviting me into the inside track. Now that I know said track exists. I mean, I knew Ivan was hiding something, but I didn't think it was this blatant.

"No," Ivan says. "I'm not going along with it."

"You can't veto getting dumped, dumbass," I snap back.

"Dump me all you want, but I'm not playing along anymore. I'm out. Brian. I'm *out*. I'm not going to be the guy everyone hates again."

Of everything I've heard in the last ten minutes, that's the one that finally sets me off.

"That's your objection to this? You don't want to look bad in front of everybody again? When the other option is throwing me to the wolves. You know what people would say if I'm the bitch who crushes *your* precious little heart, and you're fine with me suffering those consequences if it means people think you're Wizzard's golden boy?"

"I'm saying neither of us have to do anything we don't want to do."

Part of me wants to march out of Brian's office right now and leave both of them behind forever. As far as I'm concerned, Ivan can go suck an egg and Brian can squeeze the chicken. But that's a lot of hard work wasted. I think back to how I felt at the beginning of the summer, or even further, to how angry I felt back in January when I thought Ivan was using me, and realize that my first instinct was right the whole time. I was angry, and angry gets shit done. It served me well before I ever laid eyes on Ivan Hunt. I welcome it back now. I welcome it back and let myself be angry, because Ivan has done the one thing I can't forgive. He made me look stupid.

This whole time I felt like I was in control of this relationship—it was my idea, I set the terms, and I had an equal if not outsized say in how things developed between us—but I wasn't in control at all. I was a kid sitting on a couch, thinking they're playing a video game, but their controller isn't even hooked up to the system. Worse, Ivan knew he was following Brian's script and still encouraged me to feel like I had any say whatsoever in what happened to me. It's patronizing, it's humiliating, and it makes me the butt of a summer-long joke. Slowly, I let my gaze slide back over to Ivan's horrible, handsome, lying face. I don't think I've ever hated anyone this much in my entire life.

All I have to do is break Ivan's heart, step over his corpse, usurp his place as Brian's fly on the wall, and have my pick of places in the Guardians League. That, and ally myself with someone who's been trying to puppet me all summer despite him being an ostensible authority figure because he's obsessed with controlling the private lives of teenagers for money. But I'd get what I want as a sure thing.

"What I don't want is for all of this to have been for nothing," I say. "But I'm out. Sorry, Brian."

"Are you sure?" he asks, his face plastic-still in the dim box. "Think this through."

"Put it this way: when I find myself walking in a parade where all the flags are red, I don't think there's much else to think through besides getting off the route."

"Thank god," Ivan says. "Let's ditch this and just *go*. Mr. Juno?" He turns to Brian. "I'm dropping out of the academy, effective now."

"Sure, sure." Brian swats his hand in Ivan's direction. One hundred percent of his attention is focused on me now. "Ms. Lyon, do you really want to do the same?"

"I really d—"

"Funny how history repeats itself. A Lyon, the chance of a lifetime, and one bad choice that takes it all away. May as well wave a white flag on your dreams."

Ivan catches what must be shock on my face and speaks up. "Do you see who he is now? He'll say anything to get what he wants."

"SO DID YOU!" I scream, pause, and swallow. My entire throat feels coated in ceiling plaster and sawdust. That moment of paying attention to my body again brings with it a wave of other sensations I simply stopped noticing when I followed Ivan up here this morning. My ears click as I swallow thickly past a jaw I now realize is far too clenched. My neck feels tight and high, my shoulders achy, and my hands are balled in fists so tight the tips of my knuckles are lighter than the rest of my hands. Everything is tense, everything hurts. I take a deep breath, close my eyes, turn my face to the ceiling, and try to relax everything. I suck in a breath that feels almost too big for my compressed lungs and let it silently whoosh out from between my lips as I bring my head back down, and open my eyes again. This time I don't bother to look at Ivan. He wants me to quit, to give up on my dream just because I'll have to get a little dirty to do it. I can't believe how wrong he was about me. By the time I'm done, he'll definitely believe it.

"Fine. I'm not going anywhere. Let's do this," I say. "But that mentorship is *mine*."

I'd rather wave a red flag than a white one.

When I send an all-caps EMERGENCY MEETING text to the party—well, what's left of the party—they know I'm being serious. Within seconds of sending out my proverbial bat signal, I can hear Kavi's and Trieu's footsteps racing down the hall to my dorm room. I whisk them in quickly, locking the door behind me like I'm pulling them into a speakeasy.

"What's going on?" Kavi asks while I press my ear to the door to confirm that no one is lingering in the hallway. I've learned the hard way just how easy it is to eavesdrop through a closed door.

Once I'm sure the coast is clear, I turn to face my captive audience.

And my mind goes completely blank.

"I . . ." All I can do is stand there with my mouth gaping open like a fish out of water. I'm not sure where to begin. How to package all of the hurt and anger and betrayal rushing through me into an easily digestible anecdote.

"Ivan lied," is all I'm able to come up with, the words coming out quiet and meek and so unlike me it makes me want to scream. I hate how much it hurts. How deeply Ivan had managed to sink beneath my skin. I'd let him in—I'd thought he was different. One of the few people to like me for *me*. But I was just another pawn in his manipulation game.

"What?" Kavi and Trieu ask at almost the exact same time, but I can't find it in me to respond to them yet.

My shoulders tremble as I cross my arms and duck my chin to my chest, urging myself not to cry. Not in front of them. "All of them lied," I say once I'm sure my voice won't crack. "Him. Brian. Everything about this place is a lie."

Trieu takes a hesitant step toward me. "Zora, what do you mean?"

"You remember how I beat Ivan at the qualifier? How he shouldn't even *be* here?" I look up in time to see the two of them nod. "Brian brought him because he wanted him here to *watch us*. To trick the rest of us into playing into his game."

"Brian?" Kavi asks with a wrinkled brow. "As in Brian Juno?"

I nod stiffly, gritting my teeth so hard I'm sure they'd crack and chip if I wasn't so committed to my flossing routine. "None of this is real. There's no academy—not really. No algorithm, or at least not one Brian can't just change if he wants."

"So, all of these matches we've been doing were for nothing?" Trieu asks.

"What about the streams? All of our new subscribers?" Kavi follows up immediately after.

I shake my head, clenched fists trembling. "None of it mattered."

Didn't I already know that? Isn't that why we were doing all of this in the first place? To get ahead—because we knew we'd never win if we played the game fairly?

"But you asked *him* to fake date—how was that part of the plan?" Kavi rubs her temples. I can't blame her—this is the kind of situation that would give me a Level 10 headache if I wasn't so focused on taking Ivan down.

"He went along with it to rehab his image, and because Brian saw that it was boosting our popularity." I inhale sharply before continuing, lower lip quivering slightly, "And as soon as he saw a dip in the ratings, he held a meeting where he told Ivan to dump me."

Trieu guides me to the edge of my bed when I start to tremble, sitting down beside me and waiting until I've sniffled my way through yet another almost tear attack to ask, "How did you find out?"

"I listened in on their conversation like a creep; how do you think?" Just the thought of it slices at me like a knife. "He wanted Ivan to break up with me so we could be the final match. A battle of the exes."

Kavi's eyes go wide as saucers. "Wait, so you're going to be in the final two? Officially?"

I scoff. "If Ivan actually shows up." While I doubt he'd pass up a chance at a moment of glory, I don't technically know if he'll hold up his end of the bargain and come to the battle. Stranger things have happened—like me falling for him. "Ivan said no."

"But you said yes?" Kavi asks, looking pointedly at Trieu before turning back to me. "You didn't try to fight back against this idea?"

"Why should I?" I practically spit back, so bitter and pissed I don't even bother to soften my voice. "They were always going to pick whoever *they* wanted. We've known since the minute we got here that none of this was about merit. If it wasn't going to be me, it was just going to be the next best option. None of this is fair, so I might as well get a win out of it."

"Zora, calm—"

"Don't tell me to calm down!" I shout at Trieu, and instantly regret it. They're not the ones to blame here. Brian and Ivan are the real villains—the only people deserving of my rage. But in that moment of blinding anger, all I could do was let the rage out. There was no time to think about who it was aimed at—how hurt they might be by me lashing out.

"We're just trying to help you!" Kavi shouts back loud enough that I wince. Both from the volume rattling my eardrums, and because I know I deserve it. "That's all we've done this summer—try to help you!" She gestures to herself and Trieu—whose cheeks are as pink as the sunset sky beyond my window. "And I guess that was for nothing too then? Since you're so willing to take the top slot without even standing up for the rest of us?"

"Kavi, I—"

"Forget this." She throws her hands into the air before I can apologize, shaking her head before turning on her heel and going toward the door.

I go to protest—to throw as many pleas for forgiveness as I can at her—but the door slams before I can. I slump back onto my bed like I'm deadweight, head hung so low it makes my neck ache. Trieu is unmoving on the bed beside me. I close my eyes and wait for them to leave too. To be the last member of the party left standing. Everyone gone, all because of me.

But there's no creaking of the floor or squeak of the stiff-as-a-board mattress springs. Just the warmth of Trieu shifting in closer to me. To his arm wrapping around my shoulders.

"I know how it feels," Trieu says, making me look up from the ground so quickly I give myself whiplash. The tears clouding my vision begin to fade as I straighten up, eager to hear what he means. "I know what guys like Ivan can be."

There's a sadness in his tone that makes my heart break. How could anyone possibly break someone as pure and good as Trieu's heart? All of my own sadness is replaced by a fierce need to get out of here, hunt down whoever hurt Trieu, and kick their ass into the next century. Trieu must sense my righteous anger, laughing quietly and pulling back just enough to take out his phone.

"But you can't trust Brian."

"I know," I sniffle miserably. "But what choice do I have now?"

"Oh, none, girl. You're fucked." Trieu pulls out his phone. "But there's someone you need to talk to. Like, now."

My brow furrows as I watch him scroll through his contacts, my breath hitching as a familiar name and face fill the screen once he hits Call.

# CHAPTER TWENTY

WHEN WE REHEARSED for our live stream from the theater earlier this week, the air on the academy stage had to be artificially cooled with fans in the wings to better protect the dozens of computers whirring just a few feet away. Today those rigs are stored backstage and the warm, bright spotlight beaming from the ceiling's iron catwalk is melting me like a candle. That's the bad part of being alone onstage. The good part . . . I'm still trying to figure that out.

I'm not entirely alone. Past the curtain I can hear the rumblings of my academy peers settling into their seats in the auditorium. Backstage, there's approximately twenty people hovering just off camera waiting for Brian to call out a demand to surge out and swarm like those colonies of bees that cook spiders with their own body heat. I'm temporarily blinded when the spotlight we'd been testing shuts off once people start streaming into the auditorium. Greenish-black circles float in front of my eyes as they adjust to the significantly darker room, but I don't need eyes to hear Brian's team buzz on toward me with makeup brushes, spray bottles, and tablets outstretched.

"She's shiny, don't you think she's getting a little shiny?" a woman with mid-'00s hipster glasses asks the man next to her. He nods silently. "Okay, so powder. Powder, right? We should give her a little powder?"

"*She's* right here," I mumble under my breath. No one notices, and another handler steps up with a compact in one hand and a thick, fluffy kabuki brush in another. He pats the brush into the powder, taps it against his arm, and begins to dab the shine-slaying material on my forehead, down the bridge of my nose, at the tip of my chin. He doesn't ask to touch me first. No one's asked me that yet today.

My vision begins to clear at the same time I feel the blunt poke of a pick in my hair, methodically lifting my curls away from my scalp to restore some of the volume I've surely lost to time, sweat, and gravity.

"We're all clear to go live in ten." Of course the first thing I see through the fog is Brian, expertly swerving around a light being wheeled offstage, clipboard in hand, to come stand beside me. "Don't forget to give it a little more emotion this time," he reminds me, as if I could've forgotten the note he gave me multiple times throughout rehearsal. "We threw in a few extra lines." He hands me an updated script, my speech challenging Ivan to show his face and clear his name now significantly longer. "We'll get the teleprompter updated, but you can take or leave these. Go with the flow."

"You got it," I reply dully. I'm saving my energy for the cameras and the crowds.

"Just remember," he continues, "you hate Ivan. He wronged you, abandoned you, and you've got to convince him to come back for one final confrontation. I need more fire, more fury. More righteous anger!"

You'd think drumming up those emotions for show would be easy, considering I actually do hate Ivan because he wronged me, abandoned me, and I need to convince him to come back for one final confrontation. It's not easy—it's life imitating art imitating life, spinning around and around until I can't remember which of my feelings are real and which ones I'm generating for a faceless audience of thousands.

The makeup crew takes a few more minutes to dab highlighter on my nose and cheeks, reapply my lipstick, and blend the line of my makeup down toward my neck. Someone appears behind me to slide my jacket up my arms a little rougher than I would have liked. It's a small comfort knowing that Brian agreed to let Trieu do my makeup for the battle instead of someone on his payroll who probably doesn't have the right color of foundation. That I'll at least have one person on my side before the biggest moment of my career—maybe even my life—so far.

What's *not* comforting is the realization that in seconds I'm going to be parading in front of the entire academy student body—including people who don't exactly love me right now. Kavi. Cass. And who knows how many other people I've managed to piss off since I got here.

"Places, people!" a production assistant whispers forcefully into their headset, sending the backstage area into a flurry of activity. The makeup artists flocking me finally disperse to the wind, and the various lighting rigs are all shifted back onto their marks.

Brian takes his place at the center of the stage, straightening himself up and putting on the cheerful smile everyone knows him for. I really wish I'd noticed before now just how forced it all is—his positivity, his charm. Everything that makes him the most wholesome guy in the gaming world. What an awful joke. I already fell for someone else's façade once this summer. Now here I am again, realizing someone isn't who they said they were. Fool me twice, shame on me . . .

Past the thick red curtains, someone manages to get the academy's attention until the chatter falls to a hum, and eventually to silence. A rumble begins backstage as the crew falls silent too—the opening notes of the song Brian chose specifically for this momentous occasion. Epic and loud and perfectly covering up the way my heart is threatening to hammer right out of my chest.

"We're live in three, two . . ."

I don't hear the PA a few feet away from me get to "one," but the roar of applause as the curtain pulls open to reveal Brian at center stage fills in the gap for me. Brian basks in it—the spotlight, the roar, the excitement. He matches their enthusiasm effortlessly, bouncing around to high-five the players closest to the lip of the stage as the song plays on. His cheeks are flushed pink as he returns to his mark, beaming like he just won the lottery—and, in a way, he has—as he addresses his loyal constituents.

"It's been an amazing summer," he begins, looking directly at the camera placed at the front of the stage.

It's easy to lose focus as Brian drones on and on about how grateful he is to everyone who came to the academy. Who dedicated themselves to making *GLR* as amazing as it could be. Blah, blah, corporate-approved spiel to make everyone misty-eyed before he crushes their dreams. Because everyone sitting out there still thinks they have a shot at winning this thing.

"It's my pleasure to announce the top two of the first-ever Wizzard Games Summer Academy Royale. Who'll be moving on to our epic battle royale next week . . ." Brian pauses for dramatic effect and gestures to the screen hanging above his head. Chairs creak, and shoes squeak against the floor as everyone shifts to the edge of their seats. In the reflection of one of the makeup artists' mirrors I can see the animation of all of our names appearing on-screen, shuffling rapidly before two names rise up to the top in time with a jaunty royalty-free tune.

"Our very own summer academy lovebirds, Zora Lyon and Ivan Hunt!"

The room breaks out into polite, but still pretty salty, applause. I can't blame them for not being enthusiastic about having lost the one thing they worked all summer for. I consider running away as I'm cued by a nearby PA to take my mark, preparing for Brian to call me out onto the stage for my grand reveal, but my body moves on instinct. Disconnected from the rest of me. Without even realizing I'd taken a single step forward, I'm standing on the black duct-taped X on the ground, my brain whirring with the lines I memorized, the pounding of my heart, and a dozen questions I still want answered.

Namely, *will this be enough to get Ivan to show?*

"But not everything is as it seems for our academy lovers," Brian says, and my back arches from a noxious combo of nerves and disgust. He's liking playing the game master to this teenage love story *way* too much.

"Zora, do you have anything to say to Ivan?"

With a gentle push from the PA, I'm stepping out of the darkness and into the spotlight. The silence in the crowd is broken by hushed murmurs. The news of our breakup hasn't left the bubble of the party yet. Despite walking away from us—well, me—Kavi didn't break her vow of silence. Thankfully, the crowd is completely invisible beneath the hot glare of the spotlight. All I can see are dark, faceless shapes—killing any chance of me finding Kavi or Cass in the crowd and buckling before I can even open my mouth.

Over Brian's shoulder, just above the lens of the camera, the teleprompter displays the speech we'd rehearsed. Packed with drama and metaphors and what I'm 99 percent sure is literally a direct quote from *Game of Thrones*.

*It's just another performance*, I tell myself. But as I stand there, baking in the heat of the spotlight, the words written on the screen might as well be in a foreign language. It doesn't feel right—none of it has. But especially this. Playing some lovesick girl when I really did have my heart broken. Everything might've been a lie from the start, but that doesn't change that Ivan *did* hurt me. And that doesn't change how hard it's hit me—no matter how much I wish it didn't.

Brian side-eyes me when I don't take the offered microphone from him as planned. He laughs nervously, tugging lightly at the collar of his button-down as he glances at a PA off camera to try to come up with an escape plan for me developing a massive case of stage fright.

"Well, I guess we'll just have to—"

I grab the microphone out of Brian's hand and look straight at the camera in front of me—not at the teleprompter. If I'm going to do this, I'm going to do it on my own terms. In my own words.

Besides, Brian *did* say I could take or leave the new script.

"Hello, Ivan," I begin. "I have a question for you: How did you think this was going to end?" I feel myself pacing across the stage; it takes a tiny moment for the spotlight operator and the camera to follow me across. "You must have thought about it. All the time we were together . . ." I trail off, trying not to think about those moments where I let myself fall for his poisonous charm. *How could I have been so stupid? I'm never ignoring my gut again.* "I'm sure you had a plan to finish the game. I'm equally sure that whatever your plan was, I ruined it. Not sorry.

"You played me," I say, with shame coming up to choke the words halfway up my throat, "and I was naive enough to like it. I liked the way your hair was always in your face. I liked the way you pressed your lips together when you were barely holding back from saying something you knew would piss me off. I liked your crazy white teeth and your wolfy little smile. I miss—" No. "I liked when the sun hit your face and I could see the swirls in your eyes. And the way you laughed at me, whether or not I knew I was being funny." I feel an ache in my hand and realize I'm gripping the end of my jacket's sleeve so tightly the metal buttons are almost cutting into my palm. "All of it. I liked all of it. The whole time.

"I was sick with you, but now I'm sick *of* you. Trust me, I have almost no interest in seeing your face again, but somewhere in that almost is the part of me that wants to bring you back and make you feel the way I felt when you left. The game isn't over.

"Come back, Ivan. Please come back. I deserve an ending." I raise my eyes to the camera and imagine Ivan watching this, imagine my vulnerability reaching out through the camera to stroke his ego and lure him back. "More importantly"—I lift an eyebrow and dead-eye the lens—"I deserve a chance to whoop your ass. Don't make me wait too long." I stretch my hand out and let the microphone drop from my palm. Somewhere off to the side, I hear a half-whispered "*nooooo*" from someone over by the sound booth. It's the only noise in the room.

Then, a clap. And another. It's Brian, who's looking at me like he just discovered El Dorado in human form and applauding his own discovery. Slowly, almost nervously, the rest of the crew join in. Then, the entire academy. I can't see much past the darkness, but I can tell some of them—maybe all of them—are on their feet. Suddenly, I have a change of heart and wish I could see their faces. Search for Trieu in the audience to keep me grounded as the applause rings in my ears and makes me vibrate all the way down to my toes. They start up a chant of my name, loud enough to make the stage start to shake beneath my already unsteady feet.

I don't get to revel in it for long, though. The curtain whips closed, and the spotlight flicks off, green-gray dots clouding my vision again. I welcome it this time, though. For a few seconds, I'm able to disconnect. Focus on getting my eyes adjusted instead of reality. That I just poured myself out onstage to who knows how many thousands of viewers. To the people I spent all summer with.

Finally, I was everything they—Kavi and Trieu, Ivan, Brian—wanted me to be. Charismatic and passionate and watchable. The best-packaged product on the shelf.

It was always easier to play my part when there was an inkling of truth in it. Especially when it came to falling for Ivan. As much as I'd like to think that was all performance out there, I know in my gut that it was just as real as what Ivan and I were. Or, what I *thought* we were.

A warm tickle on my cheek is all the warning I get before a tear slides down my face and drops to the floor, unnoticed in the din by everyone but me. Is it sad that I'm grateful it only came out once the curtain closed? Ivan doesn't get to see me cry and neither does anyone else.

"And that," Brian announces to the crew with his megawatt smile, "is how you reel in the fans."

There's another polite round of applause from the crew before they get to work on resetting the stage. Brian's half compliment is the only contact he gives me before heading off toward the offices, flanked by his business-casual cronies.

"Brian!" I call out, jogging to catch up to him before he can disappear. He stops just before the door that leads off the stage and into the maze of hallways toward his office, and dismisses his minions with a flick of his hand.

"I just wanted to know if you've been able to get me a copy of the contract so I can look over it," I say, half out of breath.

The more time to persuade my uncle to sign it, the better. Especially considering my current status as an academy student transitioning to the league is kind of in a legal gray area since Clive didn't actually sign my permission form. But Brian doesn't know that yet. I think.

"You'll get the contract when it's ready," Brian assures me. "In fact, I was thinking of making a show of it. Have you sign it onstage after the battle."

"Right, but if Ivan doesn't show up—"

"When he shows up," Brian corrects me.

"And if I end up losing the battle—"

"If you think you're going to lose," he says, "then you've just wasted a lot of everyone's time here."

"I just meant, you know, on the off chance. Won't it be kind of anticlimactic to sign me after I hypothetically get my butt kicked?"

Brian's visible confusion compounds. "What do you mean? If you get your hypothetical butt kicked, there won't *be* anything to sign."

"Wait, what? That's not what I agreed to. I thought all I had to do was get through this battle and I was in the league."

Brian shrugs. "You said it yourself. That's anticlimactic."

"So what will you do if I do lose?" All this thinking about losing is chipping away at the confidence I managed to fake onstage. And with each chip I feel more . . . tired and alone, I think. Now I can't even say that's the cost of success, since I apparently have one more hurdle to clear before I can call any of this a victory. There have been so many double crosses and verbal agreements involved in all of this that I'm starting to feel trapped instead of triumphant. No, not starting.

I am trapped. In a cage I built myself, with Brian's tools and materials.

But, hey, I get to play *GLR* onstage, right? I have a gimmick all my own. Mission god damn accomplished. Now on to the next level, complete with new enemies, rules, and win conditions. Is that just what life is like? Or is the video game metaphor only apt because of my specific situation? I don't know. I'm seventeen. I won a game at a fan convention, and now I have a makeup team and an evil ex-boyfriend (or I'm the evil ex-girlfriend, determination TBD).

"Same thing I do with any other investment that doesn't work out," Brian says, as if he were talking about penny stocks and not my literal life and future. "I cut it loose before it starts to become a drain on profit."

This is what I've allied myself with. This is who Ivan's driven me toward. It's almost a good thing that my only way out is through Ivan. He put me here, and I need to make him pay for that.

# CHAPTER TWENTY-ONE

OF COURSE IT has taken until today, the last day of the summer academy, for anyone to admit that the dressing rooms we've been using on the down-low are fine for us to use for privacy, if needed. As in "if I need a space in which I can have a modicum of privacy while still being a part of this bastard cornucopia of ethically questionable communications and entertainment enterprises." They didn't tell any of us that this was an option, which makes sense because if Brian had told any of us that we could opt out of being on display for five minutes, we'd obviously have taken that option.

In consideration of how I wound up at the end of it all, it's debatable whether or not I would have taken that chance. Would I trade everything I've achieved so far for a few moments alone, to think clearly and not be "on" for a handful of minutes? I'm not sure, though the evidence points otherwise. Maybe right now isn't the best time to think about it. I don't know how much longer Brian can delay the start of the *1v1* debut when one of those ones hasn't shown up yet. So if

I'm going to torture myself about something, it's going to be what happens when I sit down in my ergonomic gaming chair with electronic height control and adjustable footrest, boot up my all-new *GLR* edition of Claricom's latest PC rig with custom decals and rainbow coolant system, and play the soon-to-be-released one-on-one duel edition of *Guardians League Royale*, revealed for the first time on this very live stream and available to upgrade on the Wizzard Online Game Launcher starting midnight tomorrow. Did I get that right? I'll have to check my notes.

If all of that sounds expensive, it is. It's also my problem to promote it, and that problem only goes away if *he* shows up. That is the one factor I cannot control right now, and the only reason I'm okay with that is because I've already done everything I could to control it. I've recorded my promos, posted my thirst traps, vague-posted my guts out, and anything else it might take to lure that boy back to the Wizzard Theater today. My real feelings, used for a real fight in a fake, expensive world. My world.

Hence the irony in how I traded my interiority to get everything I've ever wanted, but now they offer privacy. Well, somewhat private. Thankfully I haven't alienated *every* single person in my life. If it wasn't for Trieu, I'd be making my grand battle of the exes debut in a messy ponytail, T-shirt, and jeans, which, while it would be an excellent fuck you to Brian and the toxic, aesthetic-based popularity contest that is social media, I'm more grateful to not be totally alone right now.

"Pout your lips," Trieu instructs as he carefully flits around me like a Disney-approved fairy godparent. The gloss dabbed on my lips is less grossly sticky than the one he used during my first makeover session, after he noticed I kept wiping it off every chance I got. I appreciate him for a variety of reasons—especially today—but his commitment to finding sensory-friendly makeup products is currently at the top of the list.

"Grip that any harder and you might not be able to use that hand," he says as he points a makeup brush at my fist clenched around the rundown that Brian's assistant brought to me when I first got to the dressing room. My knuckles have gone pale brown, my entire body vibrating from the tension of trying to keep the dangerous cocktail of nerves, anger, and concentration flowing through me from boiling over and igniting anyone it touches.

"Sorry," I mumble, sighing and finally taking in my face now that he's finished touching me up.

The mirror is so old that my reflection is speckled with dark bronze marks where the silvery bits have scraped off. At first the spots were all I could see, but now that I've been here for a minute or two, my brain is learning to correct and ignore the imperfections and only serve me a reflection of what I know my face to look like. It's not the most recognizable version of myself—I'm honestly a little surprised Trieu went for a darker eyeshadow. I'm told it's better for the stage, as opposed to looks that serve my features on camera or in person. It's uncanny, almost. From a speckled distance I feel completely unfamiliar, but the longer I sit with myself the more the white liner on my bottom lash line looks less obvious and my eyes just look bigger. The contour on my cheeks looks less like dirt and more like the natural shadow lurking under my cheekbones, my nose less cartoonishly outlined and more naturally thin, the V-shaped space between my boobs less dusty with powder and more bronzed to force my minimal cleavage into false perspective. My final polished-for-the-camera form.

"You don't have to apologize to me," Trieu replies with a shrug as he tosses the tube of lip gloss into his makeup bag.

I bite my lip, only to immediately release it. Leave it to me to mess up my gloss within ten seconds of it being applied. "Thank you again for being here," I say as he stacks all of his makeup and hair equipment on the vanity table. I know he has to leave soon, but I can't help wanting him to stay for just a few minutes longer. "I know I've . . . ," I trail off. I've done a whole lot of shit I'm not proud of, but we'd need a whole lot more time to unpack all of that. "Messed up," I finally settle on.

Trieu shrugs again. Some of the tension melts from my shoulders when he sits down on the lip of the vanity. He's not leaving just yet. I don't have to be alone with my racing thoughts—not yet. "I can't blame you."

"Really?" I ask, arching my freshly sculpted eyebrow.

"I'd be pretty pissed too, if I was in your position." He frowns, crossing his arms. "I mean, I *am* pissed, and I'm not even the one who got to have Ivan Hunt as a fake boyfriend."

*Real boyfriend*, I think, but don't say out loud. Dissecting the validity of our feelings is not something we have time to unpack right now. Or maybe ever. Once all of this is over, I can shove all of my memories of Ivan—good and bad—into the box of repressed memories that's currently collecting dust in the farthest corner of my brain.

"I get it," Trieu says after I don't respond, eyes fixed somewhere in the distance. Lost in another world I'm not a part of.

"Ivan has this . . . magnetism about him. Makes it feel like you can't possibly say no to him."

I swallow hard and nod stiffly. That's putting it lightly. But it's good to know I'm not alone in that feeling—falling for Ivan's magnetism.

Trieu stands up and tucks his finger under my chin like they do in the movies. "You're amazing. And stop blaming yourself for believing in everything he said." Trieu's smile is the most heartbreaking kind of sad. So raw and vulnerable it makes me want to hug him tight and promise nothing will ever hurt him again. "He's really good at that kind of thing. Making you fall a little bit in love with him."

Before I can ask him to expand on that—or give him the bone-crushing hug he clearly deserves—a knock at the door makes both of us jump.

"Guess that's my cue." Trieu grabs his various bags and heads for the door, an endless black void of a pit opening in my stomach. Is it time for the match already? Did Ivan show up?

Trieu pulls open the door expecting to find one of Wizzard's various production assistants, but we both stiffen at the sight of Cass standing in the doorway, hands in his pockets.

"Is Zora here?" he asks, making me sit up straighter in my chair. This is certainly a plot twist.

Trieu glances over his shoulder at me, keeping me carefully out of view. I nod, giving him the all-clear, and he pulls the door open wider so Cass can step in and he can step out.

"Break a leg, Zora," Trieu calls out as he steps into the hallway and Cass takes his place in the dressing room. "You can do it."

I give him a wave to calm my nerves, but the motion doesn't do anything to stop my hands from shaking. Something that only worsens when Cass closes the door behind him, and we're left alone for the first time in what feels like eons.

"Let me guess: you're only here to wish me luck?"

"Little bit." Cass scuffs his foot against the dusty carpet. "So this is where they store their superstars." He scans the room quickly and doesn't look particularly impressed. That's fair enough. It's not particularly impressive.

"Yeah, it's an all-new perk," I say flatly. "Sorry if I overwhelm you with all this glitz and glamour."

"You know me," Cass jokes. "I'm just a simple country boy from Delaware."

"Livin' in the big city," I add.

"Alone," he says, coldly.

I sense the shift in his attitude and look up at his face. For the first time this summer, I notice that Cassius's face and arms are tanned gold instead of his usual indoor white-boy shade of pale. His hair looks lighter, like he's been spending time in the sun. It's a more dramatic effect than he'd get just walking the twenty blocks between here and our dorms twice a day—has he been spending more time outside? With who? Doing what? I suddenly imagine him doing something teenage and sporty, like climbing around on the glacial rocks in Central Park with a crew made up of academy students whose names I forgot to learn while I was messing around with Ivan on the internet. Taking the Q down to Coney Island on a weekday to ride the Cyclone and sharing a folding paper bowl of crinkle fries smothered in salty cheese. Curled up in the sun on the fake turf they set up in front of Lincoln Center, getting sweaty and gold with his earbuds in. Having the summer we were supposed to have together, in another universe.

"Hey, come on. I was . . . ," I begin defensively. Sorry, force of habit. I can tell Cass is mad at me, but that doesn't mean he deserves the sharp side of my tongue today. He's right to feel left behind, just like I'm right to feel . . . whatever I'm feeling right now. I have to think about it for a moment. I feel . . . very little, now that I think about it, like the space where I kept my feelings is locked or just empty.

"You were . . . ?" Cass echoes me. He's not going to let me get away with a nonanswer.

"I was busy," I admit, "being a single-minded asshole who fell for a legit teenage con man?"

"Yeah, when you put it that way." Cass nods agreeably. "I don't really know what else I expected. That is the opposite of new behavior, coming from you.

"I think . . . I just thought, I don't know." He shrugs. "I really don't know. I thought that I was different to you. I thought the whole reason we did this was to be independent together. But you just—"

"Shot ahead instead?" I ask, hoping he'll at least acknowledge what I achieved by ditching him.

"Shot *away* instead," he corrects. "You pissed away our plans to end up where? Waiting to see if this guy shows up so you can make him the villain you need to be a part of this whole *deeply fucking weird* experiment Wizzard's conducting on all of us?"

"I guess, man! I fucked up, I'm sorry. It sucks."

"No, what sucks is you leaving me behind to put all of your energy into someone who doesn't care if you get what you want. From day one, you put all of your chips on him and let him drag you around dancing to his tune."

"That is one hell of a mixed metaphor."

"*I know*. Know what else I know?"

That's rhetorical, right?

"I know that if it were me with you all summer, you wouldn't be waiting for me to show up today. I would be there, here. Whatever. I would have done anything to help you, but you made everything so much harder for yourself. Why, when we could have done it together?"

"Because you didn't need me! All you have to do—all people, all boys like you have to do—is show up, get good, and nobody sees any problem with you! You get to be standoffish and unapproachable, and I don't have that luxury. I have to bend and twist myself into the exact right shape or people are going to assume the worst while *insisting* it has nothing to do with what I look like. Your default is belonging. Mine is proving. Ivan understood that I didn't make things hard for myself. He knows I have to be anything and everything all of the time and it still might not work."

For a moment, Cassius is silent. Then, quietly, he speaks again. "It's not like I asked for it to be like that. It's not like that's my fault."

I stifle a yawn. Not because this is boring, but because doing something normal like sitting in a chair and arguing with Cassius reminds me of how few energy-sucking things I actually did with my time before I came to the academy. It strikes me, for the first time today, that I am tired. No, not just tired. I'm exhausted. Keeping this up, pretending with Ivan, getting betrayed, fueling this grudge . . . it's all so much more than Before Zora would have attempted to juggle. This is the most normal I've felt in months, and like a marathon runner stopping halfway through the course, everything in front of me looks so much harder than if I'd not taken this time to sit and talk—I should have kept running. Stopping is what hurts. Stopping and this conversation.

"I think, for me," Cassius begins, sounding like he's about to change the subject, "the hard part was seeing you with him all summer when you knew how I felt."

"About what?"

Cassius levels his gaze at me, his eyes daring me to continue to treat him like he's stupid. "You know," he says.

He really is so honest, his feelings so straightforward. Maybe that's exactly why I never did anything even though I knew, and yes, I'm realizing now I definitely knew, that he liked me that way. Of course I fell for Ivan instead of him. I'm a winner, and I can't win if there's no game to play in the first place.

"I do know," I admit. "And I know I said sorry before, but that was kind of flippant, so I'm sorry. For real this time. You deserved better from me, as a . . . friend."

I let the word settle between us, imagining it trying to get cozy in the silence like a dog scratching at a blanket before lying down to sleep. I take full responsibility for being a bad friend, but I won't apologize for not wanting Cassius back. God knows I have enough to apologize for besides that.

"Okay." Cassius nods. "Thank you," he adds. "I should go."

"Are you sure?" I ask, though I think we're both aware that I'm the last person he wants to talk to after I dropped the rejection bomb.

He nods instead of answering me. With a few leggy strides, he's back at that too-small door, ducking under the frame to save the top inch of his skull. "Hey, Zora?" he asks before closing the door.

"Yeah?"

"Good luck today."

"Thanks."

"And for what it's worth . . . I think he's going to show up."

"How do you know that?"

"Because *you* would," Cass says, cold and correct. "And you two are exactly the same."

Ouch. I think he knew that would hurt me, but didn't say it only to accomplish that. Cassius isn't cruel, he's honest, but that doesn't necessarily mean he's right—am I just like Ivan? Would I show up today if the roles were reversed?

It's an impossible question to answer. I would never have been in Ivan's shoes in the first place. I would never—what? Find an unorthodox way to get what I want and pursue it single-mindedly? Trick strangers into liking me with lies? Align myself with a soulless executive in exchange for a shortcut to the top? Yes, I would! I absolutely, 100 percent would, and have, and Cassius is right once again.

Ivan and I are exactly alike, and that means he's going to face me onstage today. And he's going to be exactly as angry, driven, and focused as I am. I'm staking my future on boxing my own reflection, and I truly have no idea which one of us is going to win the match.

*Knock.* I briefly wonder if this is the Wizzard employee with the news I've been waiting for, but something about the confidence behind the knock makes me think maybe no. But who else would come to visit me today, here?

"Come in?"

Similarly tall, but otherwise different from Cassius in every way. Uncle Clive's summer beard is gone, hiding the patches of premature gray that speckle his face and making him look as young as he is to my eyes, for once.

"Hey, little sis," he says. It's nothing he hasn't called me before, but it hits especially hard today. My mom was estranged from her family by the time she had me, so I never got a good look at what Clive looked like as a kid, but I imagine they looked alike when they were younger. Which means he—and she—looked like me. We have the same narrow black eyes, the same squared-off chin. Now that he's beardless, I notice his ears are connected like mine, his bottom lip is dark like mine. I've tried so hard to distance myself from whatever family connections I have, mostly because they don't seem to last that long, but something about seeing Clive now, for the first time this summer, really reminds me that blood can cross any distance I attempt to make. No matter where I go or what I do, I'm undeniably Clive's family. And he's mine.

Or something like that, I don't know. I'm feeling mushy today. Vulnerable. I blame Cassius, and I hope I can snap out of this before it's time for the match. But in the meanwhile . . . while I'm sitting here and Clive is staring at me from the doorway . . . and while Cassius is mad at me and Ivan abandoned me and Trieu and Kavi both aren't really supposed to talk to me right now and Brian is counting on me and I'm so, so close to being who I wanted to be all along but light-years away from being who I want to be when I get it . . . I could really use a hug. From my family.

I don't think Clive is surprised when I spring out of my chair and fling myself at him from across the room. If anything, he anticipated it, seeing as I come in contact with a solid wall of uncle, with both feet planted on the ground, as unmovable as one of those rocks I imagined Cass clambering over in the park. Bad knee or not, my uncle still has the rooted posture of a football player when he wants to.

"I know, baby girl. I know," Clive says soothingly. He even rubs my back for good measure.

"You're here!" I repeat, briefly too overwhelmed to thread more complex thoughts together. "Wait—how are you here? What do you know?"

"Whatever this one told me about your little summer stunt, which was wild. Even for you."

Clive gestures toward the door. In my excitement over seeing him, I somehow did not notice Emilia Romero hovering right behind him. No Jake in sight, though, just the queen who needs no king.

"How—"

"Trieu called me," Emilia says, "and we called Cass, Cass called Clive, and before you ask, yes. Your uncle is grounding you for the rest of your life, and I know exactly how you feel. God, it's like looking into a mirror." Emilia does look into the mirror then, pausing to tap at the concealer under her cheek. "Or using a time machine."

"What do you mean?" I'm still shocked that she's even here, and extra shocked that the call Trieu said he'd make had such an immediate domino effect.

"You do remember you're not the first person Ivan Hunt screwed over and left hanging, like, days before the biggest gaming event of her life, right?"

Of course she's right. At least Ivan is consistent.

"Where is Ivan?" Clive interjects. "He needs somebody to kick his soul back up to God, and I'm ready."

"Don't." I smile at his protective instincts anyway. "Your knee."

"Fuck my knee; what else am I supposed to do when someone breaks your heart?"

I don't have the energy to refute that Ivan broke my heart. Normally I would, but I have too much to think about today to add the weight of another lie that accomplishes nothing.

The not-so-excellent soundproofing in the dressing room strikes again when I hear an extra loud fanfare rising from the direction of the theater. I can't make out exactly what the announcers are saying—could be anything, at this rate—but the immediate commotion outside my dressing room makes it much clearer within a few moments.

"He's where he's supposed to be," Emilia continues. "Walking to his dressing room on the other side of the stage."

"He's WHAT?"

"He's here!" shouts a Wizzard intern as they speed past my open door down the hallway.

"VANE is in the building," wheezes another, going the opposite direction.

Emilia is back to checking her makeup again, but this time there's a telltale smirk tugging at her lips.

"How did you do it?" I half whisper, even though the only person who will know if she tells is Clive, who deserves to know a lot more about this summer. And to whom I am going to spend the next seventeen years of my life explaining my reasoning.

"Easy." Emilia turns to me with her smirk still in place. "I told him the only way I was ever going to forgive him for sacrificing my reputation was if he sacrificed his for you. But for what it's worth, I think he was going to do it anyway."

"Poetic." Clive nods. "Still gonna kick his ass."

"Not if I kick it first." I've imagined the moment I'd hear Ivan show up today a million times in my head. I pictured myself strutting out onstage, staring straight past him, and taking my seat with every ounce of photogenic grace Kavi taught me this summer. I wouldn't let my hate lure me into saying anything; he doesn't deserve to hear my words ever again. Then I would destroy him and take what's mine. The acclaim. The title. The mentorship. The shortcut.

But now that it's within my grasp, I don't think that's what I want anymore.

Another soaring acknowledgment from the crowd reverberates through the theater walls, signaling that Brian Juno has taken the stage. That gives me about five minutes to get into place—he has a whole highlight reel with standout moments from the summer planned. Payton and Paxton's feud is in there, so are a bunch of Trieu's makeup looks. I asked Brian to put the pigeon video in so Ivan looked like a dork, but I haven't watched to see if Brian listened.

Then, I hear the crowd laugh, which morphs into the telltale group-booing noise people make when the bad guy appears on-screen in a cult classic movie screening. Guess Brian put the pigeons in after all. I wonder if Ivan knows they're laughing at him out there. I wonder if he still cares what they think.

This is the guy who broke with Wizzard Games because they asked him to betray me.

To be clear, that was after he'd already betrayed me. And after I stabbed him in the back in January. And—

"I'm going to give you a few minutes with your uncle, Zora," Emilia finally says. "Good luck out there."

"Thank you, Emilia." I think I could spend the rest of my life thanking her for a whole host of things, but looking out for me from the start of this summer is definitely the big one.

Emilia is halfway out the door when she stops herself—"Oh, wait. One more thing. Ivan asked me to tell you something before I left."

"What was it?" Clive asks, fists clenched at his sides. I think my uncle might actually try to kill Ivan?

"He said, 'Too many people and twice as many eyes.'" With that, she leaves, and something like a plan takes shape in my head.

Clive takes that in for a beat. "Your generation baffles me."

"We baffle ourselves," I agree. "But we're trying our best."

"I was too, you know," Clive says, suddenly serious. "Are you really going to take that mentorship after this? After—"

"Hey, Unc." I stand on my toes to give him a kiss on his newly shaven cheek. "I got this."

For the first time this summer, I know exactly what's going to happen when the cameras turn on.

# CHAPTER TWENTY-TWO

IF MY WALK to the top of the Wizzard Theater were a third-act movie moment, here's how it would go:

Cue "The Final Countdown" with its sick synth riff. Roll the camera, red RECORD light nice and steady up top, gliding in front of ZORA on a dolly. Catch the movement in slow motion as I rise from my chair and walk the bright halls of the Wizzard Theater to hit my mark at the top of the amphitheater's left-side aisle. Each time I pass a thematically significant location from this summer past, cue a split-second flashback: static, sepia reminders at the overlook to the black marble lobby where I dropped the VIP Wizzcon lanyard, at the doors to the players' lounge where we raised the curtain on the VANE and ZORA show, on the gold nameplate outside a private viewing box that bears Brian Juno's name.

The camera's focus would catch the moment I settle into place behind the door at the top of the left-side stairs, the same one Cass failed to close quietly on the first day of the academy. Five weeks ago could have been five minutes. Time, like everything I've done this summer, is just something people make up to give structure to our stories. My eyes, shaded dark in the already dark hall, would glance to the other theater door, the one that leads down to the right-side aisle, and catch the slightest glimpse of a brown-haired someone over the shoulders of my entourage. Push focus, fade my face into the foreground, bring him into the light. Make sure his face gets nice and clear, along with the unsubtle roll of his shoulders. He does not look at me, so I stop looking at him. This is how the story is supposed to go.

Through the metal doors we hear, off-screen: Brian Juno. I cannot see him, but I know what he looks like. I know how he grips the mic with both hands and rumbles through his boxing-announcer voice to get his show on the road. Brian's tailored suit, rectangular face, and tall hair are exactly as they look in every promo in which he's ever starred, every faux-candid fan interaction, every con panel for decades. Everyone knows what propaganda is; they just don't know what they know.

*"Please welcome to the stage, mad as heck and ready to kick some butt, the one, the only—Zora Lyon!"*

The first time I walked through this door, the theater felt light and airy, with house lights on and barely a tenth full of just the academy students milling around, and my grand entrance was met with unknowing stares until Ivan broke the silence to greet me. Today it's immersed in an artificial midnight, with only the blue-and-purple LED strip lighting on the floor to guide me as I glide down through the aisle step by step. The spotlight is so tight it only illuminates a precise circle around wherever I step, making me feel like the steps don't exist until I put my foot out to meet them.

And then there's the noise. All summer I've thought of Wizzard's fans as nothing more than numbers on a screen, points to earn and calculate as I level up with each interaction. Now that I hear them in person and feel their breath moving real air around the arena, it strikes me that the academy students weren't the only people Brian lied to this summer. Everyone who participated in the competition on the other side of the screen got scammed as well. They thought they were voting with their attention and having any impact on what happens behind the scenes at their favorite game company. Except the whole time, their attention stayed exactly where Brian wanted it, boosting and demoting everyone's WiTch accounts at his will.

When the small pool of my spotlight touches the stage, my feet deposit me at the ground level, where my second mark awaits. The stage itself seems somehow undressed with only two stations set up for play instead of fifty. The distance to my seat feels the same, though, and when I spin around and raise my arms to acknowledge the real people behind my rise this summer, their bellowing cheers push me back into my seat. I can't see a single one of their faces from here and feel a pang of guilt, but I know I'm doing the right thing.

Highlight, copy, paste the section again. Replace Zora with Ivan, maybe swap the color scheme in his sequence to really push the me vs. him narrative. He comes to the stage, he walks to his seat, and for the first time in a week he and Zora are alone again. Her, the warrior who planned on brute-forcing her way toward a finish line barely worth crossing, and him, the ruthless bard who dipped and swerved his way around the truth to achieve the exact same worthless goal.

And of course we aren't alone. We are two people onstage in front of hundreds who boo for him as loudly as they cheer for me. I wonder if Brian is watching from up in his suite by now, waiting for his two prizefighters to start tearing each other apart live on the streaming service he created. It's fine for him to wait. It will all be over soon.

I'm proud of Ivan for coming back, for standing across the stage from me and looking me in the eye. I'm proud that he'd take this reputational bullet for me just to make sure I came out of the academy on top. I'm glad he found a way to start making his mistakes up to Emilia, and I'm even gladder that he found the strength to turn this whole stupid deal with Brian down. Eventually. No credit awarded for getting into that mess to begin with, but I didn't ride here on a mile-high horse either. A mini horse at best. Or not a horse at all. More of a skateboard.

Are we awful people? I don't know. Being with Ivan didn't feel awful, even when I thought he was faking everything. Those little bursts of pleasure I felt when one of his compliments slipped under my radar and made me believe he was serious were real. It was my confusion, my anxiety that made those nice things sound discordant. Ivan took me seriously the whole time. If I had taken him seriously too, maybe this summer would have gone a little differently.

Who am I kidding? This is where we're meant to be. Across the stage I lock eyes with my . . . fake real ex-boyfriend. No, my ex-real fake boyfriend. My—Ivan. The boy's name is Ivan, and he knows what I'm thinking because he always does, somehow. We finish each other's sentences, for Pete's sake. So let's finish each other's stories.

Every round of *Guardians League Royale* starts the same way, but *1v1* mode is different. Instead of crowding just two players on the enormous starting barge, we have our own little mini barges that soar in from the opposite sides of the map. Mine is green and more heavily branded than a racing car. I don't bother to look at the logos; I didn't have any say in what they would be. I do look through my character's spyglass to see where Ivan's barge is coming from, and if he's jumped out yet.

His barge is purple, for what it's worth. Figures he'd get my favorite color and I'd get the color of his eyes. Our headphones block the sound of the crowd, but since I'm just cruising at in-game altitude, I chance a peek up to see if my eyes have adjusted enough to spot anyone in the audience. I don't, this shit is *way* too bright, but in the movie I'd see Clive in the front row, sharing a bucket of popcorn with Cass. Emilia and Jake would be there, Kavi and Trieu, of course. Chaz, for sure. But he'd have spilled a big red slushie on himself or something so he looks ridiculous for a comedic beat. Poor Chaz. I cast him as a total sideshow without ever getting to know him. Will I try to get to know him after today? Absolutely not.

By now the crowd must be getting suspicious. I'm still sitting pretty in my barge, and as far as I can tell, Ivan is too. I just think it would make for a better ending if we both did it at the same time, you know? Ivan seems to think so too. A nice, clean landing. Right below the spot the barges cross . . . in the center of the *Guardians League Royale* map.

VANE jumps; then ZORA jumps too. We pull our parachutes together and land right where it all started. Where it started twice, now that I think about it. It really does look like the one in Central Park—or is that just how I see it in my memory? For the sake of the story, let's say that it does. Let's say they're identical, so when ~~Ivan and I~~ VANE and ZORA land on its tower and the battle horn finally rings, it makes a good image for the cover.

The clock starts ticking, there's a loot chest right there, but neither of us take it. Both VANE and ZORA begin to idle on-screen, their digital puppet-selves bounding on heels that don't exist and swinging arms made of nothing but refracted light.

Pause. Back to the script. Let the cursor blink here once, twice, as long as it takes to get the next part right. Because this isn't a movie moment. It's a video game. And that means I'm in control of what happens next. There are so many people, with all of their eyes trained on me, on Ivan—on us. I wonder for a moment which pair they're watching more, the two fake avatars on screen or the two real people on stage. I wonder how many of them care about the difference.

Because, as I'm realizing now . . . I don't. Not anymore. Brian Juno's game can go to hell. He can go with it, and after I start telling people what he pulled this summer, he just might.

Okay, Ivan. Let's beat this level and end the game for good.

VANE and ZORA are still motionless on screen, but Ivan and I are on the move. We take off our headsets, stand up from our desks, and walk center stage together to cue up our finishing move.

Ivan's hand feels strong and warm when we clasp hands, bring our arms up, and swing them low to bend our backs in a theatrical bow. The hands stay clasped as we walk offstage, ignoring the chaos as people around us scream and stomp, pointing madly as they wonder why we're throwing everything away. Great question, by the way, and the answer comes to me when Ivan pulls me through the stage door and out onto the sidewalk. The afternoon sun temporarily sears the sight from our eyes, but it's okay, because Ivan and I could find each other blindfolded and spun around in the dark or too-bright light. We can sense each other because I know what Ivan's done and Ivan knows who I am. We're the only ones who know why we are like this.

There are plenty of people passing by us on the street, but no one blinks an eye when I kiss Ivan. They don't care when he kisses me too, and they don't hear our earnestly murmured "I'm sorry"s and the few whispered variations on "me too, it's fine, shut up." Everyone who would want to see or hear this is still inside the theater, and Ivan and I are finally offstage.

Game over. Roll credits. But before we go, I have the answer to that question: Why throw everything away?

Because sometimes, the only way to win the game is not to play at all.

# ACKNOWLEDGMENTS

We survived and that's what matters. Of course, we didn't do it alone.

First thanks go to my family—Mom, Dad, and Ashley. You are all very stubborn when it comes to your belief in me, but I need that stubborn, so thank you. Your love is my anchor as well as my sail and none of this happens without you. Bruno and Marlowe, you're family too. Thank you for being the best boys.

Thank you to Sarah Shumway at Bloomsbury, for your patience, understanding, and insight into Zora—I learned so much about myself through your care for the character.

Thank you to my agent, Steven Salpeter, for fielding my chaos; and to the team at Assemble Media for propping me up and advocating for me in all the ways I couldn't.

To The Group Chat and all subsidiaries thereof, including but not limited to Enchanted Requisitions Inc. and Book Hell. Thank you, Alanna, Anna, Hayes, Krutika, and Matt, for listening, for loving me, and for all the good advice.

Thank you to David Sugarman, who answered the call in my hour of need and then just didn't leave, so here we are, I guess. Love you, Daisy.

Thank you to Adam Rosenberg, for having my back and always reminding me of what's important.

Thank you, Proma and Belen, for being sickos with me.

Thank you to Susan O'Connor, The Narrative Department, and all the wonderful friends I've made for your lessons and encouragement; video games have always been important to me and thanks to all of you I have the words to explain why.

And a final thanks to the real human beings who make video games all over the world. Your imaginations and hard work are appreciated, valuable, and irreplaceable.